BYE, BYE BIRDIE

Pots spilling over with pretty flowers surrounded the double-roof octagonal structure. It was the perfect centerpiece to the lush sanctuary Birdie had created. Hope drew closer and looked for Her Crankiness. But she was nowhere in sight.

Hope approached the gazebo's entry, flanked by two potted hydrangea bushes, and glimpsed a muffin on the floor deck. It looked like one of her apple streusel muffins; crumbs of the streusel topping littered the red cedar flooring. Her gaze continued along the gazebo, and she spotted her basket on the floor. Her breath caught again as she saw Birdie on the ground, next to a chair, tipped on its side.

As her brain registered what she was looking at, her breath whooshed out, propelling her forward. She raced across the deck to Birdie.

Had she had a heart attack? She always seemed to work herself up over the silliest things. Hope crouched down beside her neighbor and checked her pulse.

None . . .

Books by Debra Sennefelder

Food Blogger Mysteries

THE UNINVITED CORPSE

THE HIDDEN CORPSE

THREE WIDOWS AND A CORPSE

THE CORPSE WHO KNEW TOO MUCH

THE CORPSE IN THE GAZEBO

Resale Boutique Mysteries

MURDER WEARS A LITTLE BLACK DRESS

SILENCED IN SEQUINS

WHAT NOT TO WEAR TO A GRAVEYARD

HOW TO FRAME A FASHIONISTA

Published by Kensington Publishing Corp.

The Corpse in the Gazebo

Debra Sennefelder

www.kensingtonbooks.com

KENSINGTON BOOKS are published by

Kensington Publishing Corp.
119 West 40th Street
New York, NY 10018

First Printing: October 2021
ISBN: 978-1-4967-2893-7

ISBN: 978-1-4967-2894-4 (ebook)

10 9 8 7 6 5 4 3 2 1

Printed in the United States of America

Chapter One

Hope Early had her Explorer's windows rolled down and the sunroof open so she could inhale the sweetness of spring blooms and feel the gentle breezes that rolled through swaying trees on her drive to Cleo Sloane's house.

Clusters of daffodils stretched along the side of the road as far as she could see. The bright orange flowers were a definite sign that spring had arrived, and summer wasn't too far off. Everywhere she looked, Hope saw the stirrings of homeowners as they emerged from winter hibernation. Winter wreaths were traded out for spring florals, hanging planters were added to porches, and lawns had their first cuttings.

Spring has always been a season of transformation, and for Hope it was more so than ever before. Life had taken some unexpected turns over the past year. Some were welcomed, while others had been interlopers in her life. But she chose not to dwell on the past. No, she embraced the season of optimism.

At an intersection, she eased to a stop. To her left was a fenced field of Jersey cows, and to her right was a rambling ranch-style house with a flower stand set up on the property line. There she spotted Cleo loading potted plants into a cart. The president of the Jefferson Garden Club had been selling her cuttings to help offset her daughter's college tuition.

Hope flicked her blinker on and eased her vehicle onto the edge of the Sloane property. After shutting off the ignition, she got out and walked toward Cleo.

She surveyed the flower stand, a simple wood table with a price list for the gallon-sized containers.

"Hey there, Hope. Good to see you." Cleo dropped a pot onto the cart and then removed her work gloves. She was a thick-set middle-aged woman who always had dirt under her nails and a random fact about insect control on the tip of her tongue. "Beauty of a day, isn't it?"

"Speaking of beauty . . . this hosta is stunning." Hope moved to the cart for a closer inspection. The plant's green leaves were highlighted by a creamy central pattern that made for a striking two-tone design.

"Angel Falls. She prefers light shade. Did you know grasshoppers enjoy dining on hostas? It's important to inspect their leaves for holes, gaps, and tears at the edges. Early detection is crucial."

"I have so much to learn about gardening." Hope could bake a soufflé blindfolded, but garden? It was a talent and skill she didn't possess. Not like Cleo. She was an expert. "Are you closing for the day?"

"Actually, I'm closing down for good." Cleo trudged to the table and grabbed the sign. "I can't even have a going out of business sale."

"Why? What happened?"

"Birdie Donovan. That's what happened. She reported me to the town, and since I don't have any permits, I can't sell my plants. Turns out, my little nursery is illegal. Go figure." Cleo set the sign on the cart.

"Why did Birdie report you?" The moment Hope asked, she realized how silly it sounded. Everyone knew Birdie liked to stir the pot and was the perpetual squeaky wheel.

"Got me! All I can figure out is that she is still angry with me for the disagreement over last year's Mother's Day Flower Sale. Remember, we sold bouquets of flowers and gallon pots of perennials?"

Hope nodded. What she remembered was dropping a lot of money that weekend. When she bought her farmhouse, not only had the home been neglected, but so had the gardens. Her garden beds had desperately needed perennials.

"There was a disagreement? About what?" Hope browsed the pots remaining on the flower stand, awed by the healthy and flowering plants.

"She wanted us to buy the plants from a greenhouse she'd dealt with but we'd already agreed to get our plants from Timmy's Garden Supply out on Old Saw Mill Road like we'd done for years. A big brush-up ensued, and she left the club. Well, I said, good riddance. She's been nothing but trouble. And now this." Cleo gestured to her almost empty flower stand.

"Have you explored getting a permit?" Hope knew little about business permits and what restrictions there were to running a retail business from home. Her blog didn't require any such things.

"Even if I could get one, it would be expensive. The whole point of selling my cuttings was to earn some extra cash to help pay for the expenses not covered by Julia's scholarship. But it turns out, according to zoning, I'm not supposed to be operating a retail business in this area."

"I'm so sorry this happened."

"Thanks . . . I'm sure I'll figure something out. Maybe I can scrape enough money to get a booth at a flea market." Cleo put her gloves back on and then lifted the Angel Falls Hosta off the cart. "Take this. It'll look real nice in your garden."

Hope raised her hands to protest. "That's so nice of you. Let me pay you."

"Nope. I can't take any money because I need to keep this all legal. It's a gift. Take good care of her." Cleo thrust the pot into Hope's hands. "Consider it my thank you for that delicious monkey bread recipe you shared last week on your blog."

"You're welcome. And thank you for this plant. I promise to take care of her."

"You do that. And I'm going to get these back to my greenhouse." Cleo grabbed the handle of the cart. "Let me tell you, I'm doing my best not to hold on to my anger against Birdie, but it's hard to do. One day, she will come face to face with karma, and it won't be pretty. Mark my words. She'll get what's coming to her." She turned and pulled the cart behind her as she crossed the lawn toward her backyard.

Cleo's warning concerned Hope, yet she understood the sentiment. She carried her new plant back to her Explorer. She pointed her key fob at the back cargo door, and when it opened, she set the plant inside. After the door closed, she took a final look at the dismantled flower stand. She wished she understood Birdie's motivation for causing trouble for people. But more so, she hoped Cleo did nothing in retaliation that she'd be sorry for.

* * *

The SUV jolted as it hit a pothole as Hope turned onto Main Street. Her grip tightened on the steering wheel. The remnants of a harsh winter had finally vanished, but it left behind a minefield of potholes. She spied a parking space in front of her sister's shop, Staged with Style, and pulled in to check her tire and rim. Both looked good. But how long would her luck hold out? The last thing she and her tight budget needed was a bill for a new tire.

Remembering her choice to embrace optimism, she straightened up and glanced around Jefferson's primary hub. Customers came and went from the many shops that lined the charming street. Jefferson, known throughout the northeast as an antique mecca, drew tourists all year long. Collectors descended upon the town looking for their next *find*, from the most expensive and refined antiques to diamonds-in-the-rough.

Hope spotted a cluster of seniors leaving Ellie's Cafe with to-go cups and heading toward the library. Next, she saw Mrs. Teager outside the Jefferson Historical Society.

The spry octogenarian was fussing with a planter of flowers but waved when she noticed Hope. Hope returned the wave and continued around her vehicle to the sidewalk.

Nate Batchelor was sweeping outside his antique shop as Jeffrey, the postal carrier, passed. She waved to both men and then turned her attention to her sister's shop.

The quaint red clapboard house was a town landmark. Downstairs had been the first general store, and upstairs the town's first mayor had lived. In recent years, antique businesses had come and gone, and now it was Claire's home accessory shop.

She had made the risky decision to open a retail store

after walking away from a successful career as a real estate agent.

Claire Dixon stood in front of the large window with her arms crossed and her lips pursed. A lace headband pulled her blonde hair off her face. The ankle-length turquoise pants she wore had a delicate lace edging and her eyelet top completed the fresh and springy look. Hope frowned as she glanced to her dark jeans and dark green tank. Claire looked like a flower in a spring garden, while Hope definitely looked more like a weed.

"What are you doing out here?" Hope's gaze drifted from her sister to the window back to her sister.

Claire's head turned at her sister's voice; her face pinched with annoyance.

"Lola and I have been trying to figure out this display all morning." Claire threw her arms up in the air. "Nothing looks right."

Hope inched closer and studied the display.

Claire and her sales associate, Lola Granger, had set a vintage three-drawer chest in the window. They topped the cream-colored dresser with a vase and propped up a silver-tone picture frame.

"Maybe some texture? Like a throw or pillow?"

"You think? I guess we can add a chair." Claire clapped her hands together. "Ooh, I can bring up the tufted chair we got in last week. And then drape a throw over it. I can use the lavender throw. You're a genius!"

Hope tucked a lock of her shoulder-length brunette hair behind her ear. Maybe she should try a headband. "I'm glad I could help."

When Claire had first shared that she'd be starting a second career, Hope had had serious concerns. Retail was a fickle business that demanded a lot of time and energy.

Now, a few months later, she realized she had been right and wrong. Claire had a lot to juggle because of being tethered to a brick-and-mortar store. But she also realized Claire was right because she had followed her heart and was happy being her own boss.

"How was the workshop at Emily's House?" Claire propped her hands on her slender hips and looked at her sister. She made it a point to go to Jefferson's only gym, The Fix, at least four mornings a week before the shop opened. The other mornings she favored yoga at a studio down the street.

"Good. The gals are great, and they're so excited to learn about online businesses." Hope adjusted the handle of her overstuffed brown leather tote on her shoulder.

She had been recruited by her friend Erin Thomson to teach a workshop at the nonprofit. Emily's House aided women coming out of troublesome situations. Over the winter, she brainstormed ideas and came up with one about starting an online business. Her experience with creating her food blog, *Hope at Home*, made her a natural to teach the curriculum. She'd taken her hobby, started in her two-bedroom New York City condo, to a full-time career.

"On my way back, I stopped by Cleo's house. She was taking down her flower stand. Did you hear Birdie Donovan reported her?"

Claire tilted her head. She had a funny look on her face that couldn't be read. Before Hope could ask what was going on, the shop door swung open, and Lola bounded out. She hurried to Claire's side and studied the window.

"So what do you think?" Hired before Christmas, which made her Claire's longest employee to date, Lola had become indispensable thanks to her solid work ethic.

The other hires had survived a max of two weeks because of Claire's lofty standards. She wasn't the most easy-going person to work for. Hope was forever grateful to their parents for making sure their daughters always had separate bedrooms.

"Hope suggested we add some texture." Claire's expression returned to normal.

"Splendid idea, Hope." Lola's expression then mirrored the one that had been on Claire's face only a moment ago.

What was going on? Self-consciously, Hope touched her cheek. Did she have something on her face? Had her new mascara given her raccoon eyes?

"Thanks." Hope glanced at her watch and was glad to see the time. It was getting weird with her sister and Lola, and she still had a bunch of work to finish up before she could clock out. "I should get going."

Lola leaned into Claire. "Did you tell her?"

Claire shook her head, and her expression faltered for a split second.

Hope clutched her tote's strap. "Tell me what?"

"There's something you should know." Claire lowered her eyelids, and Hope's belly quivered. She recognized the mannerism and combined with the funny look Claire had on her face moments ago, Hope knew her sister had something to confess. Like when Claire took her favorite pair of jeans—back then, they wore the same size—and wore them to paint signs for the cheer team's car wash event. A rainbow of paint colors smudged the jeans, and no amount of stain remover helped remove the paint. Hope still didn't know why Claire took her jeans while she had a drawer full of them. The only explanation that made sense was Claire hadn't wanted to ruin a pair of her own.

"One of your neighbors came in earlier and mentioned something that's happening on your street," Claire said.

Hope searched her memory. She couldn't recall anything special going on in her neighborhood. *Shoot*. She'd left her planner in her car. If anything was happening, she jotted it down in there. She did remember that the Gilberts were planning on their annual barbecue in a few weeks. Other than that, she couldn't come up with any other event.

"It has to do with Birdie Donovan," Lola said.

Hope groaned.

Whenever Birdie's name was mentioned, what followed was seldom positive. The woman was persnickety, blunt, and of the mindset that she was always right. Thankfully, Hope had few interactions with her. Fingers crossed, it would stay that way.

"What happened now?" Hope asked, though the question should have been who had the unpleasant experience of being Birdie's next victim?

Claire and Lola exchanged a look, and then Lola's gaze quickly diverted toward a passing pickup truck.

Claire's lips twisted. Clearly, she realized she'd been stuck with telling Hope whatever the news was.

"Birdie is circulating a petition among your neighbors to encourage . . . you to move." Claire rushed her words as if she were pulling off a bandage. Then her face scrunched up, waiting for her sister's reply.

Hope opened her mouth and then closed it. She couldn't believe she heard Claire correctly. "What . . . Are you serious? A petition to get me to move. Why on earth? My neighbors love me!"

On her first day in her new residence, Hope baked muffins and delivered them to her neighbors. She introduced herself to the ones she hadn't known and reconnected with old acquaintances. That's when she met Ted Donovan for the first time, but his wife hadn't joined him at the door. He told Hope about his work at Emily's House and about Birdie's passion for gardening. He even mentioned she was writing a book on the subject. As she continued passing out her muffins, she collected names, phone numbers, and recommendations for workers to help get her old house into shape.

None of them would have signed such a ridiculous petition.

"They do love you!" Lola jumped back into the conversation after her boss delivered the unpleasant news. "And Caroline Reynolds told us she refused to sign the petition. But Birdie is determined. She intends to present it to you and to Maretta. She's hoping the town can do something."

"What?" Hope's voice raised an octave, and she quickly checked herself when a passerby did a double take. "What does she think Maretta could do?"

Maretta Kingston had become the town's mayor after a special election last summer, beating Claire. A shiver worked its way through Hope's body at the memory because the aftermath wasn't pretty. Claire had resorted to sloppy clothes, Crocs, and eating carbs. Scary times indeed.

Hope knew the win was because Maretta's connections and roots ran deep in town. Plus, her husband owned the real estate agency. Those two things made it easy for Maretta to get votes. She was also best friends with Birdie. They were like two peas in a pod.

Claire shrugged. "I don't know. There's probably nothing Maretta or the Town Council can do."

"Town Council? Oh, my goodness. This is getting out of hand. What's the reason why Birdie wants me to move? Is it about the chickens?"

One of the first things Hope did after settling into her home was to buy chicks. She'd converted a stall of her barn into a chicken coop for the flock. Growing up, she'd always wanted chickens, but her parents always found a reason to say no. So when she was house hunting, she made sure there would be enough property to have chickens. There were also a few other must-haves on her list: a large kitchen for recipe testing and a generously sized family room. She also wanted space for a vegetable garden. Now, as the homeowner, she could have all the chickens she wanted, but Birdie thought otherwise. She had complained to Hope and then to the Zoning Department about the birds, even though having them was well within the zoning laws.

"Birdie said that since you moved into the neighborhood, there has been too much chaos." Claire fingered her necklace, a sign Hope recognized that she was feeling uncomfortable.

Hope opened her mouth to protest, but she couldn't in all fairness. There had been a few situations involving the police at her home over the past year. Then there was the fire at a neighbor's house, though that wasn't her fault.

"It's no longer the quiet enclave it used to be . . ." Claire continued.

"Enclave? She really said that?" Hope's head was spinning. How could this be happening?

Claire nodded. "And she's concerned about her property value."

Hope sighed. "This is crazy. Absolutely crazy. I have

no intention of moving. I love my house. I've done a lot of work on it."

"And it's beautiful." Lola patted Hope on the shoulder as she walked to the shop's door. "Don't let her bully you."

"Oh, believe me, I have no intention of allowing her to do that or run me out of my home." Hope glanced at her watch again. Her to-do list needed to be tackled, but there was something more important to take care of.

"Good for you." Lola gave a firm nod and then broke away to return inside the shop.

"Well, don't do anything rash. Remember what mom used to say, kindness starts with one person." Claire pressed her forefinger on her sister's chest, over her heart. It was a gesture their mom did when she reminded them that kindness was essential to give in the most difficult situations.

Hope covered Claire's hand with hers and squeezed. "I'll do my best."

"Do better." Claire took back her hand. "I have to get back to work."

Hope considered her sister's suggestion and wanted to take their mother's advice. But it hadn't done a lick of good in previous dealings with Birdie. Kindness seemed to roll off her like rain off a duck.

Hope pushed off after Claire entered the shop and headed for the library. Her steps quickened as her nostrils flared, and her blood boiled the more she thought about the petition. Each step closer to the library, her anger ratcheted up a notch.

The gall of that woman.

What possessed Birdie to believe for one moment she could force Hope to move? Why didn't she move if she was so miserable living on their road? Pack up her gardening tools and her life to move somewhere she wouldn't have neighbors like Hope.

Hope dashed across the street, ignoring the crosswalk, and stomped up onto the curb. She continued along the sidewalk, and the sturdy two-story brick building came into view. The library had come a long way since Frieda Bishop started it over a century ago. She lent books to her friends and neighbors from her house on Main Street until the money was raised by the town to build a permanent library.

Hope slowed her pace and willed herself to calm down. The last thing she needed was to barge into the beloved sanctuary all hot under the collar.

Her calm down lasted only seconds, and she huffed out an aggravated breath as she stared at the library's main door. Two women emerged and descended the front steps to the walkway. Hope recognized them both.

Jane Merrifield was talking and gesturing with one hand as she held onto the railing with the other. The seventy-something-year-old always seemed in good spirits. And as a retired mystery author, she always seemed to be looking for a mystery to solve. On that warm afternoon, she wore a navy floral dress and low-heeled blue pumps. Her white hair was styled with wispy bangs, and she wore her trademark pink lipstick.

Walking beside her was the person Hope was looking for. Birdie Donovan. She descended the steps as if she hadn't a care in the world, with a canvas tote bag slung over her shoulder. It appeared to be weighed down by books. Like she wasn't worried one iota about the wreckage she left behind as she targeted neighbors and acquaintances. When she reached the bottom of the steps, Hope noticed she cradled three thick books in her arms.

Hope made a scant distance of the space between them.

"Good afternoon, dear." Jane smiled, her blue eyes twinkling as she came to a stop. "I was just telling Birdie about the new nursery I visited last week in Litchfield." She loved her day trips because they provided her with tourism information she could share with the guests at her family's inn.

Birdie halted but said nothing. Her heart-shaped face was expressionless as if she couldn't be bothered with greeting Hope.

Couldn't the woman at least say hello? Hope's fingers itched to ball into fists, but she resisted. They'd have a civil conversation.

"Actually, Jane, I'd like to speak to Birdie." Hope's body tensed, and her belly bubbled with irritation and frustration.

"I don't have time," Birdie said briskly as she passed Hope without a goodbye to Jane.

"Make time!" Hope swung around to face Birdie's back.

"Hope!" Jane admonished as she shuffled next to her. "What's the matter?"

Birdie slowly turned back around. "So you've heard?"

"Heard what?" Jane looked puzzled as her gaze bounced between both women.

"She started a petition to force me to move from my home. How dare you!" Hope pointed her finger at Birdie.

"Is that true?" Jane looked at Birdie. "Why would you do that?"

Birdie rolled her eyes. "It's been a circus since you've moved onto the street. Police cars, ambulances, graffiti, arson, murder! You've ruined our lovely neighborhood, and you have to go!"

"You can't force her to leave her home, Birdie." Jane tsked.

"Well, she thinks she can since she got Cleo to close up her flower stand. How could you do that to her? She wasn't hurting anyone. She just needed a little extra money."

"She was breaking the law. Someone has to enforce them," Birdie said.

"And that someone is you? Well, you can take your petition and shove it! I'm not going anywhere."

Hope's fists balled up, and her lips formed a thin line. So much for a civil discussion. She knew she was acting poorly, but she couldn't help herself. And that infuriated her more than Birdie.

"We'll just see about that. By the time I finish with you, you will be moving. I'm getting my street back." Birdie smirked.

"Oh . . . you keep it up, and . . . you'll be the one moving!" Hope stumbled over her response, her anger getting the better of her as she struggled to come up with a stinging reply.

"Over my dead body." Birdie swung around and stormed off toward the parking lot.

"I'm guessing that didn't go as you'd planned, did it dear?" Jane looked up at Hope.

Hope shook her head as remorse filled her. "No. Not at all."

Hope pushed open the mudroom door and entered her house. Once over the threshold, she let out a deep sigh of relief. It felt good to be home.

She dropped her keys on the countertop of her charging station.

One of the first projects she had tackled when she moved into the old farmhouse was the mudroom. It had been added on decades ago and needed an update.

The uninspired space led to the kitchen, the laundry room, and her office. Which meant it had been a catch-all space that was disorganized and cluttered. Hope had whipped the room into shape by adding a custom hall tree bench made with beadboard paneling for a charming country vibe and discreet shoe storage. Next, she had a tile floor laid for easy cleanup and a fresh coat of paint to brighten the room. While function was of the utmost importance in the mudroom, she couldn't help but add decorations to cozy up the space.

On a trip to a consignment shop over the winter, she had found an old wooden sign with the word "Bakery" painted in a deep blue against a white background. Despite some fading and chipped edges, the sign was in good condition. She propped it up next to the kitchen's entry.

One more project she had in the works was changing out the old wooden door into the laundry room and office with a sliding barn door. All the material was waiting in the garage for her boyfriend, Ethan Cahill, to have a spare weekend to tackle the DIY project. She'd already planned out the blog post. It would have step-by-step photographs of the installation and a recipe for her quick and easy skillet mac and cheese.

She opened the door to her kitchen and was greeted by a happy bark. Her rescue dog, Bigelow, ran toward her.

She never tired of the warm welcome home from the medium-sized pup, whose coat was tricolor—white, brown, and black. He looked up at her with what she swore was a smile on his face.

She patted his head and then scooped up the tennis ball on the floor and threw it.

He swung around and chased after it into the family room. A moment later, she heard a screech, and she grimaced. It sounded like her cat, Princess, had been interrupted by either the ball or Bigelow. Probably both, Hope thought.

Either way, Princess wasn't pleased.

A woof followed. They'd been working out their boundaries since Hope rescued the cat after her owner had unexpectedly died.

Hope offered an apology to Princess as she continued to the granite-topped island. There she found a note from her assistant, Josie Beck. Josie worked primarily from her apartment but came to Hope's house a few hours each week.

Shrugging the tote bag off her shoulder, Hope snatched up the paper on her way to the table. The pumpkin pine floorboards creaked beneath her in spots. She'd found the flooring, salvaged from an old barn, up in Vermont. To some, the sound was a nuisance and something to be fixed, but to her it was comforting. Besides, quirks gave character to homes.

She skimmed the note as she set her bag on a chair. It was a checklist of what Josie accomplished before she left.

Confetti video – edited

Newsletter – scheduled

Thumbnail image for video – created

Hope approvingly tapped the paper. Having such an efficient assistant was a godsend. Otherwise, she'd be up to her eyeballs in work. She considered herself lucky that Josie moved from Florida to Connecticut.

She then scanned the family room for her pets. When she purchased the house, the kitchen and family room were closed off, resulting in small, dark rooms. She had the wall taken down. The rooms combined for a sizeable space bathed in sunlight, thanks to the bank of windows that ran along the exterior family room wall. The view of her three wooded acres never failed to astonish her. Nor did seeing her pup tucked on his bed beside the fireplace with his tennis ball. Princess, on the other hand, was nowhere to be found.

Certain the white fluff ball would show herself soon enough, Hope walked to the coffee maker and prepared a cup. Because of her job, a functional and well-organized kitchen was a must-have. She'd wasted no time in gutting the room. She had replaced cabinets, installed high-end appliances, and modernized all the lighting. The plan had been a cook's dream but a new homeowner's nightmare.

Between tight budgets, demolition, and the months it took to complete, there were days when Hope wasn't sure she'd survive. Thanks to her general contractor and pep talks from her sister and her best friend, Drew Adams, she'd not only survived the remodel but was now thriving as a full-time blogger.

Hope busied herself while the coffee brewed by grabbing apples from the bowl on the island. During her drive home, the scene in front of the library replayed in her mind. And one thought knotted her stomach: what if Ethan's daughters had witnessed the unpleasant exchange with Birdie? Molly and Becca had been spending a lot of time with her since Hope and Ethan's relationship had become serious over the winter. She wasn't exactly setting a positive example for the girls to follow. She didn't have a choice; Hope had to resolve the issue between her and her cranky neighbor.

Despite Birdie's animosity, Hope wanted to make amends. She also wanted to open a dialogue between them. Surely they could reach an agreement, or at least agree to be civil toward one another.

Hope pulled a carving board out of a lower cabinet and retrieved a knife from the butcher block.

While she disagreed with Birdie about where she should live, she acknowledged that her neighbor had one valid point. Her home had been a crime scene one too many times.

But it really wasn't her fault.

She was good at sleuthing, and that led to a few risky encounters with murderers.

What was important to remember was that she helped bring murderers to justice.

Maybe she shouldn't point out those facts when she offered Birdie a basket of freshly homemade apple streusel muffins and an apology.

She gathered the ingredients for the muffins. Her movements were practiced and precise, like a well-choreographed dance of baking. In less than an hour, she would have a peace offering.

No one could resist Hope's hot-out-of-the-oven muffins.

Not even a curmudgeon like Birdie Donovan.

Chapter Two

Before heading out of her house, Hope harnessed Bigelow and grabbed the muffin-filled basket lined with a blue and white checked tea towel. Together they walked down the driveway to the road and then turned toward the Donovan house.

The immaculate two-story Colonial with pristine landscaping came into view, and Hope's resolve wavered.

Maybe a surprise visit wasn't the best idea.

Bigelow woofed, as if to say, keep moving. Hope glanced at her dog and admired his don't-give-a-care attitude as he pranced along the road. She'd love to share in his carefree feeling, but the doubts rattling around in her head wouldn't let her.

She walked along the brick path that stretched from the Donovan's driveway to the slate-gray house's front door. She passed by the meticulous garden bed. Hope recognized the boxwoods, the dwarf rhododendrons, and most of the perennials, but many were a mystery to her.

Two colorful floral containers welcomed her at the front steps.

For a nanosecond, she considered turning and going home. But she'd come this far, so she might as well follow through. She pressed the doorbell and waited while Bigelow sniffed a container.

"Pleasant smells?" She liked the fact that he was curious, but sometimes his curiosity got him into trouble. Last week he had a run-in with a skunk. The aftermath wasn't pleasant for either of them.

The front door swung open, startling Hope.

"Get out of there!" Birdie wagged a finger at Bigelow. "What on earth is that mutt doing here?"

Hope's surprise quickly morphed into irritation at Birdie's criticizing tone.

"He's not a mutt." Hope tugged on Bigelow's leash to get his attention. His head swung up, and he gave her a what-the-heck look. "The flowers smell nice."

"Of course they do." Birdie dropped her hand to her side. "What do you want?"

Hope swallowed. Birdie would not make this easy for her. "I came to apologize for my behavior earlier. I shouldn't have raised my voice."

"Or accosted me on the street." Birdie propped her hands on her thick waist. She'd changed clothes since coming home from the library. Now she wore a pair of dark green gauze pants and a beige tunic. Though she still had the same uninterested look on her face.

Hope wanted to challenge Birdie's description of their encounter but realized it would do neither of them any good. It wouldn't change Birdie's mind.

"I baked a batch of apple streusel muffins." Hope offered her neighbor the basket.

Birdie took the basket as if it was a ticking bomb. She eyed the muffins suspiciously.

"It's one of the most popular recipes on my blog." And for a good reason. Buttery and moist, they were loaded with chopped apples and topped with streusel. There was a depth of sweetness from the brown sugar that mingled with the freshly grated nutmeg.

Birdie didn't look convinced.

"They were also the best seller at the Community Center's bake sale." Hope gave herself a mental shake. Why was she explaining her muffins to Birdie? If the woman didn't want the muffins, Hope would gladly take them back. There were a dozen other neighbors who would be happy to receive them.

"Are there any peanuts in them? I am allergic to peanuts," Birdie said.

"I assure you there aren't. No nuts. Not even in the streusel."

Birdie blinked.

"Good afternoon!" a cheerful voice called out from the road.

Relieved for the interruption, Hope looked over her shoulder. Casey Armstrong, a newcomer to Jefferson, stood at the curb, dressed for her daily run, waving. Hope returned the wave and then turned back to Birdie.

Birdie's gaze was fixed on Casey. Her face twisted and her lips puckered.

"What is *she* doing jogging here? She doesn't even live on this street."

Hope gave a quick glance back to Casey and then looked back at Birdie. "This isn't a private road. . . . Anyway, I'm hoping we can discuss our differences . . ."

"I'm busy." Birdie stepped back and then closed the door.

Hope gaped. She couldn't believe Birdie took the muffins without a thank you and then shut the door in her face. It was beyond rude. And it was also a good thing she used a basket she'd found at a tag sale because it looked like she wouldn't be getting it back.

Bigelow hadn't seemed as offended and was ready to move on. He tugged on his leash, signaling he wanted to visit with Casey. Since Hope wouldn't get any further with Birdie, she might as well chat with Casey for a few minutes. They'd met soon after Casey had moved to town. An avid runner, Casey used her daily runs to explore her new town.

Casey continued jogging in place until Hope and Bigelow reached her. A thin layer of perspiration covered her forehead, and her face was flushed.

"Visiting with Birdie?" Her eyebrows raised. She may have been Jefferson's newest resident, but she knew all about Birdie and the fuss she made around town. She grounded her feet and did a brief side stretch.

"I dropped off a basket of apple streusel muffins." Hope opted not share why she delivered them. Though she didn't doubt news of her argument with Birdie would soon spread throughout Jefferson.

"Boy, I wish I lived closer to you." Casey's voice was wistful. "None of my neighbors drop off treats."

Bigelow let out a yawp and wiggled in his harness. Clearly, he wasn't getting enough attention.

Hope rubbed him on the head and received a grateful grin from her pup.

"We'd better get going so you can continue with your run." Hope also had administrative work to do and dinner to make. She was on her own since Ethan had to attend a Town Council meeting. But she probably could convince her best friend, Drew Adams, to join her for a pasta dish featuring the fresh asparagus and shiitake mushrooms she had in her refrigerator.

Casey's head bobbed up and down. "Okay." She pushed off but slowed and looked over her shoulder. "See you at the library's cookbook meeting."

Hope wave and smiled as Casey jogged away, but inwardly she groaned. She'd forgotten about the research she needed to complete by the next meeting. "Come on, little guy, let's head home."

Bigelow picked up his pace, and together they walked back home. She used the stroll to give herself a brief pep talk about the library's fundraiser.

Somehow, she had been volunteered to lead the project. She was the only person on the committee with experience in publishing cookbooks. The other volunteers were enthusiastic, which meant she wouldn't endure all the workload. But she would still be responsible for tracking the assignments, which could be a ton of work itself. It was for a good cause, she reminded herself.

"I'm starving," Drew Adams declared as he entered Hope's kitchen right on time for dinner. He dropped his messenger bag on a chair at the table and Bigelow trotted over to greet him. "What's on the menu?"

"Penne with mushrooms and asparagus. All the salad ingredients are out so you can start putting it together." Hope drained the pasta and then dumped it back into the pot.

Drew feigned an outraged look. "I have to work for my supper?"

"No such thing as a free meal." Hope laughed. They'd been best friends since elementary school. Together, they'd been through all kinds of ups and downs that life had to dish out. They loved and squabbled like siblings.

Hope added the sautéed sliced mushrooms and asparagus to the penne. She grabbed a smaller pot from a stovetop burner. She gave the cream sauce a quick whisk before pouring it over the pasta and vegetables and gave a toss.

"You're mean." He winked as he tossed the greens with a simple balsamic dressing.

Hope laughed at the lighthearted jab and then transferred the pasta and vegetables to a serving bowl. She sprinkled chopped herbs on top of the dish. After a quick tidy-up, she lifted the bowl and carried it to the table.

While they ate their meal, Drew talked about his day at the *Gazette*, the newspaper that covered their corner of Connecticut. After graduating from college, he had offers to work in larger newspapers in the region. They were tempting, but he returned to Jefferson and worked at the paper he grew up reading. That night he was excited about the story he was working on regarding Emily's House. Their anniversary was on the horizon, and a big celebration was being planned. He'd been interviewing former clients of the nonprofit and shared that the article was shaping up to be one of his favorites.

When they finished eating, Hope cleared the table while Drew fed Bigelow and Princess their dinners. After adding the dish detergent, Hope closed the dishwasher door and set the controls to begin the cleaning cycle.

"I hope you saved room for dessert. There are cupcakes I have left from yesterday's recipe testing."

Drew patted his firm midsection, which was the result

of a strict workout schedule, and grinned. "There's always room for cupcakes. Chocolate?"

Hope returned the dish detergent to the cupboard and then walked to the refrigerator.

"Orange creamsicle."

A perk of being a food blogger was that she always had food left over. The cupcakes were from a baking session the day before. She'd been thinking about her favorite frozen treats from childhood. She got the idea to whip up a cupcake reminiscent of those bright orange and creamy vanilla bars.

Drew sulked. "You know, chocolate cupcakes are my favorite. But I guess I can eat an orange creamsicle cupcake, whatever that is. If I must."

"I appreciate your sacrifice." Hope removed the lid from the container. "Tea or coffee?"

"Tea." Drew turned on the electric kettle and then pulled out two mugs from an upper cabinet. "So I shared with you about my day. Now I'd love to hear all about yours."

Hope pressed her eyes shut and worked her lower lip. It was only a matter of time before she'd have to tell him the whole gory truth about her run-in with Birdie at the library and then getting snubbed when she delivered the muffins. Maybe now wasn't the time.

"Not too much happened." The prize for understatement of the year goes to Hope Early.

"Don't skirt around the truth, sistah. Claire filled me in on what Birdie is doing. I can't believe she's circulating a petition." Drew dropped a tea bag into each mug.

"Neither can I." Hope set three cupcakes on a plate and then returned the lid to the container. She glanced up and saw the smug look on Drew's face. He already knew about what happened outside the library.

"You lost your cool. Little Miss I'm-Always-in-Control lost her cool." He folded his arms in front of him, and his eyes were lit with glee.

"How? . . . Oh, Jane."

"Oh, honey, she couldn't wait to text me. You caused a scene!" Drew snatched a cupcake off the plate and dashed to the table. "Don't forget, you're a celebrity. You need to be careful about your public image. Yelling at a neighbor isn't good PR."

"Hey, I wasn't the only one involved. Birdie yelled, too."

"Of course. Everyone expects that of Birdie."

Hope sighed. "I know. I know. Believe me, I'm not proud of my behavior. I got so worked up that I could barely think straight." She'd been so flustered that the best she could come up with was, "you'll be the one moving." Not much of a comeback in response to Birdie's proclamation that she'd get her street back.

Hope carried the plate with the remaining two cupcakes to the table. While she knew she should concentrate on what Drew was saying because he was right about her public image, all she could do was stare at those cupcakes. Simple looking, actually. Vanilla cake topped with a swirl of whipped cream frosting. But inside packed a punch with the moist vanilla cake infused with citrus flavor and a crème-filled center. It was so hard to focus on anything else.

"Like it or not, you need to set an example. Especially now for Molly and Becca."

"It's just that woman can be so frustrating. Like when I took muffins to her earlier."

Drew stopped in midbite of his cupcake. "Wait. What? You need to explain why on earth you'd bring her muffins. And where are the rest of them? You always bake way too many."

"What, you want a muffin now?" Hope dropped onto a chair.

"Not now, but I'd like them for breakfast tomorrow."

"Of course you would. And yes, I have some extra I can send you home with. Anyway, I went to apologize for my behavior."

"And you took muffins."

"Yes, we've already established that."

"It's just you're the only person I know who would bring baked goods to apologize for standing up for herself."

Hope heaved a sigh. "Do you want to hear what happened or not?"

Drew nodded. "I do. Please continue."

Hope lifted a cupcake off the plate and pulled back its wrapper. "I offered an apology; she took the muffins and then closed the door in my face." She bit into the cupcake; the orange flavor shined through, and the crème filling was smooth.

Drew chuckled and quickly clamped a hand over his mouth.

"It's not funny!"

Drew nodded as he lowered his hand. "It is, actually." He took another bite of his cupcake and then declared, "This is superb!"

Hope wanted to be annoyed with Drew for finding humor in her embarrassing incident. Still, she couldn't because he loved her cupcake. "Thank you."

The house phone rang, and Hope set her cupcake down. She stood and went to grab the handset off the counter. She did a double take at the caller ID. Ted Donovan. She wondered if there was anything wrong with her workshop or whether he was calling because of what happened with his wife.

Hope pressed the phone's ON button. "Hello."

"Good evening, Hope. It's Birdie."

Hope's eyes widened in disbelief, prompting Drew to give her a curious look.

"Hi, Birdie," Hope said as she walked back to the table. She needed to sit for their conversation.

Drew mouthed, "Birdie?"

Hope nodded as she dropped into the chair. "I wasn't expecting to hear from you."

"No more surprised than I am. Listen, I've been thinking. We should talk. Why don't you come over tomorrow, and perhaps we could come to some compromise?"

Hope blinked, and then she pressed her lips together. There would be no compromise that entailed her moving. None. But she would accept the olive branch.

"Sounds good. See you then."

"Come over at ten-thirty before I go to the library for my research." Before Hope could say goodbye, the line went silent. It seemed Birdie had a habit of abruptly cutting things off.

Drew leaned forward with an expectant look on his face. "Well? Don't keep me in suspense. What did she say?"

"We're meeting tomorrow morning to talk and come to a compromise."

"Boy, if I wasn't sitting here, I wouldn't believe it. Compromise? Her? She'll probably agree to you moving only two towns away instead of out of state. You know she reported Cleo Sloane to the town, right? I don't think you'll be getting the better end of whatever compromise she has in mind."

Hope reached for her cupcake and took another bite. She wanted to disagree with Drew, but her gut told her he was right. Then again, it would be far better to go into the visit being optimistic. Otherwise, who knew what could happen. Well, at least there wouldn't be any witnesses.

The next morning, Hope's day started early with barn chores and a quick baking session before she left for Emily's House to teach her workshop. All the while, her belly buzzed with anticipation of her sit-down with Birdie after the class. She arrived at Emily's House and climbed the sweeping veranda's steps, carrying a container of her favorite new indulgence—brownie chips. They were thinner and crunchier than traditional brownies. In her blog post, she called them little chocolatey bites of heaven.

Hope adjusted the strap of her hefty leather tote bag on her shoulder. Inside was her laptop, the handouts for her workshop, and all of life's necessities. Always the Girl Scout, Hope was prepared for anything from smudged mascara to small wound care to stain removal.

She crossed the expansive porch to the primary entrance, passing containers overflowing with colorful flowers. Pops of pink and yellow zinnias brought a smile to her face. At the same time, the peek of blue calibrachoas reminded her of the flats back at her farmhouse waiting to be planted. Once again, she was juggling too much and stretching herself thin. A spring breeze flitted through, jostling a musical wind chime.

The front door opened, and out came Ted Donovan, the director of the nonprofit. And Birdie's significant other.

His intensity and focus offset his short stature in a way that made Hope feel like he was towering over her. He ran the twenty-year-old organization like a well-oiled machine, pinching pennies expertly and fundraising like a boss to keep the doors open to help clients carve out new lives. How someone as kind and compassionate could be married to someone like Birdie astonished Hope.

"Good morning." He stopped short of bumping into her. His gaze had been fixed on his cell phone. "I'm hearing rave reviews on your workshop."

Hope's cheeks warmed at the compliment, though she wondered if he'd heard about what happened between her and Birdie. She also wondered if Birdie told him about her petition.

"The gals are great and are so excited about starting their own businesses."

"With your guidance, they'll be successful. And you know how I feel about Emily's House alumni." His thin lips slipped into an amiable smile. "They're good for the bottom line. Always willing to give back and support our mission."

Hope raised a brow at the comment. She had heard it a few times before from Erin, an alumna of the center. While all the services at Emily's House were free to those who needed them, Ted had an expectation of reciprocation from each person who benefited from those services. There were ample opportunities, such as selling raffle tickets, donating door prizes, and volunteering to mentor. Erin had assured Hope she never felt pressured and wanted to contribute as much as possible.

And Hope believed her because she knew Ted personally. He'd been nothing but respectful and considerate of his neighbors, unlike his wife.

"Well, I'm off." Ted sidestepped Hope as he slipped his phone into his blazer's breast pocket.

"Oh, sorry to keep you. Off to an important meeting?" Hope shifted closer to the front door.

"Ah . . . well. Yes, you could say that. Have a good class." Ted jogged down the steps and disappeared around the side of the beautiful Victorian house the nonprofit had taken over fifteen years ago.

Hope entered the house and closed the door behind her. Voices drifted from the kitchen. She guessed the center's small staff were chatting over morning coffee before their workday began. She checked her watch. Class didn't start for another fifteen minutes. There was enough time for another cup of coffee and a brownie chip. Even though she shouldn't indulge, she knew once she lifted the lid off the container, she would.

Which meant her jeans were getting a little snug despite her morning runs.

Avery Marshall, Ted's assistant, popped her head out of the kitchen doorway and waved Hope forward. "Oh, hey, Hope! Come on back here."

Hope walked along the polished hardwood floor toward the kitchen. The original parquet flooring was long gone, and Hope couldn't help but think it was a pity to lose something beautiful. But considering the home's new purpose for the twenty-first century, it made sense to go with sensible oak flooring. She passed by the two front parlors, which were turned into a community room and a meeting room. While their doorways were trimmed with intricate, dark woodwork, the rooms had a light and airy vibe.

In the kitchen, Hope found two other staffers along with Avery, who was filling a coffee mug. She looked polished, as always, in a navy sheath dress and nude pumps. Her glossy auburn hair was smooth and cropped at chin length. Her makeup was subdued except for the swipe of dark berry gloss on her lips. Her co-workers said good morning to Hope as they shuffled out of the room.

"You should have heard Ted going on and on about your first class earlier." Avery stirred creamer into her coffee.

"I just ran into him on his way out." Hope set her container on the counter and then dropped her tote on a chair at the table. The efficient kitchen was set up to service staff as well as clients. A large round table, big enough to seat eight, was placed in front of the double doors that led to the back porch.

"He left?" Avery tensed as she glanced over her shoulder toward the hall.

"Everything okay?" Hope asked.

"Yeah, I didn't know he was going out. It must be a last-minute appointment." Avery's voice was wary. When she turned back to Hope, a cloud of concern flitted through her eyes.

"He doesn't stop, does he?"

Avery chuckled. "Look who's talking. I saw your live video chat last night. And I admit, I have pantry envy. Who knew that even existed?"

Every now and again, Hope liked to do a live video to connect with her followers. Last night she did a pantry tour and gave tips on what should always be on hand.

"Then I advise you not to go onto Instagram." Hope returned to the counter and removed the lid from the brownie container.

"Oh, I can just imagine those photos. Enough about pantries, what have you there?" Avery didn't wait for a reply; she reached into the container and pulled out a brownie. "What are these? Brownies? Cake?"

"Brownie chips. They're leftovers from my recipe testing. Take a taste."

"You don't have to tell me twice." Avery bit into the brownie and chewed. Her face lit up as her eyes did a these-are-freaking-delicious eye roll. That was the kind of eye roll Hope loved seeing.

"You like?" Hope asked as she debated whether to take a brownie for herself. No. She'd be good. But boy, did it hurt to be good. She covered the container. "I thought a little treat for the class would be nice."

Today was her second class, and she wanted to do something special for her eight students. Each had a crisis or tragedy that prompted them to reach out to Emily's House for help. One student lost everything she owned in a fire, resulting in also losing her job because she was consumed with trying to figure out how to replace her home and belongings. Another student escaped a bad domestic situation. Another had her home foreclosed and lost her life savings due to overwhelming medical and legal bills from her late husband's car accident.

Hope knew a thing or two about having life turned upside down. Though her losses weren't as terrible as some of the stories she'd heard from the center's clients, she'd gone from successful magazine editor to losing competitor on a reality baking show to divorced in the blink of an eye. Yet nothing compared to the situations of the women she was helping.

"That's so nice of you. They will enjoy this treat." Avery finished her brownie and then reached for a napkin. "So everything is going okay with the workshop?"

Hope removed her cardigan and draped it over her tote. The sweater was just the right weight to fend off the chill that morning. Spring in New England was a constant ping-pong of temperatures. Cold, hot, warm, and then back to cold. Layering was the best defense against the unpredictable weather, as was having an umbrella handy, like the one in her tote.

"It is. I was a little nervous about teaching the class, but I was worried for nothing. The gals are great, and they're all eager to take control of their lives." Hope hoisted the tote onto her shoulder, and with the container in hand, she headed for the back staircase. When the house was first built, mainly the servants used that passage. Now it was a convenience not to have to walk through to the house to the foyer.

"Good to hear. Have a great class." Avery walked to the table and sat to finish her coffee. Her mood shifted, and she looked pensive as she stared at her mug.

Hope paused at the first step. "How about you? Is everything okay?"

Avery looked up and offered an unsteady smile. "Sure. Just a lot of things going on."

"Well, if you need to talk anything through, let me know."

Avery nodded. "Thanks, I'll keep that in mind."

Hope's gaze lingered on Avery for a moment longer. She didn't know the woman very well but sensed something was off. She couldn't help but wonder if it had to do with Ted's unexpected trip. She shrugged. Whatever it was, it was none of her concern. She was there to teach a class, not stick her nose into Emily's House business.

Chapter Three

When class was over, Hope stayed longer to help a student purchase a domain name, which left her twenty minutes to get back to Jefferson. Confident she would make it on time, she relaxed on the drive back. She wouldn't be late, and her perpetually irritated neighbor would have nothing to complain about.

Hope's Explorer coasted along the back roads that connected several towns together in her northwestern corner of the state. Her mind even drifted off to a new recipe inspired by the lovely day. She was in a deep daydream of creamy butter and sugar oh-so-delicately whipped with a dash of homemade vanilla when a figure in the road caught her eye.

She slammed on the brakes, and the vehicle came to a hard stop just feet from someone standing in the middle of the road.

The man wearing an orange vest yelled something, but she couldn't hear him over the noise of the truck's chugging engine. But she saw him gesture to the stop sign he held in his hand and then to the two other town workers filling a pothole.

Next, she noticed the long line of cars in the opposite direction.

How had she not seen the work crew? She gave herself a mental shake. All her focus should have been on driving.

The worker with the sign turned his attention to the other cars and waved them forward.

Hope waited as patiently as she could until each one of those cars passed by. She tapped her fingers on her steering wheel.

The dashboard clock indicated she had less than ten minutes to make it to Birdie's house. She estimated that if there wasn't any other road work, she'd make it right on time. For most people that would be okay, but for her, it was akin to being late. Why? Hope had no clue. It was just the way she was wired.

Finally, the road worker flipped the sign around and waved her forward. Careful with her speed, Hope shifted the vehicle into gear and drove past the town employee. She lowered her window and called out "Sorry" as she drove by the road worker. He hadn't acknowledged her, so she wasn't sure if he heard or just didn't care.

Hope arrived at her destination with mere minutes to spare. She tamped down her nerves as she walked along the path to the front door, pressed the doorbell, and waited. The day before, Birdie had appeared at the door in a blink of an eye, as if she'd seen Hope and Bigelow approaching the house. Spying from her living room window seemed like something she'd do. How else would she know was going on and be able to report her neighbors so efficiently?

A few seconds passed before Hope pressed the button again.

Where was Birdie? She peeked into the entry hall through the door's sidelight but the only movement within was an orange cat darting by. She pulled back and considered her options. There were only two—leave or stay.

There was plenty of work to do at home. Or she could look in the backyard for the lady of the house. Birdie might have been puttering back there and lost track of time. She opted for choice number two because, eventually, they needed to sit down and talk.

Hope backtracked along the path and made her way to the gate leading to the backyard. It was solid wood with an inlay of metal scrollwork and arched by an arbor. Striking, yet simple enough not to take away from the beautiful landscaping. Hope pushed open the gate, and her breath caught.

Sprawled out in front of her was a hidden gem of a garden worthy of a magazine spread. She stepped forward, the gate closing behind her, into a soothing sanctuary of lushness.

She traveled along the meandering garden beds. Her pace was slow as she absorbed all the beauty, peace, and quiet within the confines of this suburban oasis. Bright, welcoming primroses nestled among smatterings of crocuses and forget-me-nots. There was nothing low maintenance about Birdie's property. Now she understood why Birdie hadn't been eager to socialize with her neighbors—she'd spent all her time maintaining her garden.

Hope's gaze lifted from the friendly flowers, and she

surveyed the open acre. There were varying elevations, sunny areas, shaded spots, towering trees, and mature shrubs with woods in the far back. Envy and awe consumed Hope. It was the kick in the pants she needed to get back on track with her own outdoor chores. She was weeks behind on her spring cleanup. Between the workshop, coaching, and her part-time helper, Iva Johnson, out of work for the foreseeable future, she was barely keeping up with the necessities. Iva had taken care of the chickens and did odd jobs around the house. Those jobs were small but having someone else do them gave Hope time to work on other projects. Now a new to-do list formed as her gaze drifted around the yard and landed on the gazebo.

Pots spilling over with pretty flowers surrounded the double roof-octagonal structure. It was the perfect centerpiece to the lush sanctuary Birdie had created. She drew closer and looked for Her Crankiness. But she was nowhere in sight.

Hope approached the gazebo's entry, which was flanked by two potted hydrangea bushes, and glimpsed a muffin on the floor deck. It looked like one of her apple streusel muffins; crumbs of the streusel topping littered the red cedar flooring. Her gaze continued along the gazebo, and she spotted her basket on the floor. Her breath caught again as she saw Birdie on the ground, next to a chair, tipped on its side.

As her brain registered what she was looking at, her breath whooshed out, propelling her forward. She raced across the deck to Birdie.

Had she had a heart attack? She always seemed to work herself up over the silliest things. Hope crouched down beside her neighbor and checked her pulse. None.

"No, no, no. Birdie, come on. You can't be dead." Hope pressed her lips together as she forced herself to focus and think calmly. She had to call 9-1-1 and get help.

She pulled out her phone from her back pocket.

"No, no, no. Ugh." She huffed as she rocked back on her heels. The cell phone's battery was at zero. Why hadn't she charged it on the drive back?

She leaned over Birdie's body, looking for her cell phone. None. Then she lifted herself up. She looked on the table, set with a tea service and cloth napkins for their meeting. Hope gave herself a mental shake. The tablescape wasn't relevant any longer. She needed a phone, and there wasn't one on the table. She'd have to go inside the house.

Hope stood and hurried down the steps. Her mind swirled from finding Birdie dead, and her pace was quick as she darted across the immaculate lawn to the patio off the back of the house. She crossed over the paver stones and reached the sliding door.

She grabbed the handle and slid the door open and then entered the eat-in kitchen.

"Is anyone here? Ted?" She'd seen him leave Emily's House earlier for a meeting, he said, but he could have stopped home before going back to work. She really hoped he'd stopped home.

When there was no answer, she walked across the oak floor, past the oval table in the breakfast nook covered with journals and textbooks. There was a stack she recognized. They were the hefty books she'd seen Birdie carrying when she left the library yesterday.

"Ted? Are you here?"

She waited for a reply, and there was none.

Convinced she was alone in the house, she set out to find a phone. There was one on the peninsula, lying next to its charging cube.

"Thank goodness," Hope muttered as she hurried to the phone. She picked up the handset and pressed the talk button. No dial tone. "You gotta be kidding me." She glared at the phone—of course it was dead. She stuck the phone into the charger and set off in search of a charged one.

She looked back at the slider. Maybe she should have stayed and started CPR. Then she wouldn't be able to call for help. The property lots on her road were generous and offered seclusion. A neighbor passing by wouldn't have seen her struggling to revive Birdie. The best thing she could do was to call for help.

She rushed out of the kitchen, passing through the two-story rear foyer into the great room. An impressive brick fireplace flanked by floor-to-ceiling bookshelves anchored the room. The furnishings were casual and inviting guests to sit, relax, and stay. But Hope's thumping heart wasn't about to rest anytime soon.

She needed a phone.

Her gaze swept over the room, and she didn't see one.

Hope continued with her search. She passed through the wide doorway into the hall. Directly ahead was the front door. To the left was the dining room. She resisted taking a closer look because she wasn't there for a house tour. She was looking for a working telephone.

To the right was a closed door. She knocked before turning the knob and pushing the door open. It looked like she'd found Ted's study. Eureka! There was a landline on his desk. Those didn't need charging.

Hope entered the room, making a beeline for the desk. She slid the chair back and reached for the phone's receiver. She punched the buttons for 9-1-1.

A dispatcher answered. Hope summarized what she'd found and declined the offer of staying on the line with him until officers responded.

She returned the receiver to the telephone and allowed her breathing to return to normal. As her body settled from the unexpected discovery, she took in Ted's tidy home office for the first time. He was a kindred spirit. An organized paper tray sat on one corner of the desk, and opposite it was a color-coded file holder. The desk blotter didn't have any markings or stray papers.

She stepped back and went to arrange the ergonomic chair that probably cost a small fortune back into place when she noticed something on the floor beneath the desk.

Hope bent down and, on closer inspection, discovered it was a passport, and it reminded her that hers needed to be renewed soon. She straightened up and set the passport on the paper tray.

She was about to leave the study and wait outdoors for the responding officers when she realized she should call Ted and have him come home. Of course, she wouldn't break the news of his wife's death over the telephone.

She picked up the phone and dialed again. On the third ring, Avery answered. "Good morning. Emily's House, Ted Donovan's office."

"Avery, it's Hope. Is Ted back yet?"

"No, I'm not sure when he'll be returning. Why don't you call his cell, or can I take a message?"

"No, there's no message. I'll try his cell." Or the police

will, since that number was in her dead cell phone's contacts list.

"Is everything okay? You sound funny." Avery's voice had shifted, and now it was laced with concern.

Hope was about to answer when she heard a thump from above. She looked up to the ceiling. Was someone in the house?

Another thump.

There's someone in the house.

Was it Ted?

"Thanks. But I really should speak to him." She ended the call and walked out of the study. In the hall, all was silent. Maybe it was her nerves playing a trick on her. Just in case, she moved toward the staircase and rested her hand on the newel post. Looking upward to the small landing, she called out, "Is anyone up there?"

Another thump. Her grip on the newel post tightened.

"Ted?" The front door was only a few feet away, giving her an easy way out, yet she climbed the stairs. Halfway up, a yowling sound erupted from a ball of fur that flew past her legs.

It was the cat.

She stopped and rested her hand over her racing heart. Inhaling a deep breath, she turned to face the bottom of the stairs. There the cat stood, squinting at Hope.

"You nearly gave me a heart attack."

The cat blinked with disinterest and then turned, flicking his tail as he strolled off.

"And you couldn't care less." Hope trod down the steps, and when she reached the foyer, she heard sirens outside.

She exited through the front door and approached the police vehicle.

Officer Roberts exited the vehicle and greeted her.

It wasn't the first time she'd seen him at a crime scene. Not too long ago, he'd intercepted her from entering a burning house on a fool's errand to save a neighbor. In her panic, Hope hadn't been thinking clearly and had been on her way into direct harm until Officer Roberts stopped her.

Now they met again.

He instructed Hope to wait on the patio after she pointed to where Birdie's body was. She plopped down on a chair at the table, suddenly exhausted. Her body's adrenaline surge was catching up with her. Before the officer went to check on Birdie, he'd mentioned the responding detective would want to speak with her. When asked, he'd confirmed the detective on duty was Sam Reid.

Of course he was on duty. It seemed every time she called 9-1-1, he showed up. Weren't there other detectives on the JPD?

He arrived minutes after Officer Roberts and joined her at the table after he inspected the gazebo and the deceased. Now his eagle eye was trained on her.

"Why were you meeting with Mrs. Donovan?" The detective looked up from his notebook. Over a crisp white shirt he wore a tailored navy blazer. An avid runner, he was tall and lean with a buzz cut.

His scrutiny no longer fazed Hope.

They'd been seated across from each other at too many crime scenes for her to be nervous, especially now since Birdie's death appeared to be from natural causes. Even to her untrained eye, it didn't seem to be murder. Though Birdie's face had looked flushed, there were no apparent wounds, no sign of strangulation when Hope checked Birdie's carotid pulse, and no weapons nearby.

Hope fixated on the glazed ceramic jug filled with purple hydrangea cuttings on the table.

"We had a few things to discuss."

"So this morning when you had plans to meet Mrs. Donovan, you found her dead."

Here we go.

"This is not how I expected it to turn out." Hope had a way of being at the wrong place at the wrong time and finding dead bodies. It was a wonder anyone invited her anywhere, given her track record.

"Then tell me how you expected it to turn out."

"We hoped that we could reach an agreement." While she was hopeful, she had been sure Birdie would have used the time to air more grievances.

"Agreement about what?"

A breeze swept by, and wisps of Hope's shoulder-length hair flitted into her face. She tucked the strands behind her ears.

"She was circulating a petition around the neighborhood to get me to move."

"Mrs. Donovan started a petition against you? Why?" He appeared to be struggling not to smile. She couldn't say she was surprised. Why wouldn't he find amusement in the situation? If he could, he probably would have started a petition to ban her from sticking her nose into his cases.

"Yes, she did." Hope lowered her eyelids. "I found out about it yesterday from Claire. One of her customers told her." Hope leaned back and told him the whole humiliating story. It wasn't as if it were a secret. Half her neighbors had been approached to sign the stupid petition.

"You and the deceased argued yesterday?"

"Well, I wouldn't say argue."

Reid arched a brow at her statement.

"We had differing views, and we may have raised our voices. But it wasn't as bad as it sounds. She called last night and invited me to come over this morning to talk about the petition."

Reid jotted something down. "Please continue."

"When I arrived, I rang the doorbell, but there was no answer. I checked to see if she was puttering in the garden. I lose track of time when I'm working outside. Anyway, I came around here and found her in the gazebo." Hope pointed toward the structure. "Do you think she had a heart attack?"

"I can't speculate on the cause of death at this time." He set his pen down. His eagle eye softened, and his facial expression relaxed. They'd come a long way since their first meeting when he suspected her sister of murder. Since then, he'd complimented Hope's ability to observe things that others hadn't seen and her ability to get people to talk to her. It had been a turning point in their relationship.

As was his use of her first name during the last murder to have rocked Jefferson.

But no matter how far they progressed, he still never wavered from his commitment to arrest her if she overstepped.

She guessed it was all about baby steps.

"Of course I understand. I guess she could have had a medical condition besides her peanut allergy."

"Allergy?" Reid cocked his head sideways.

"I had no idea until I dropped off a batch of apple

streusel muffins yesterday. She asked if they had peanuts in them and told me about her allergy.

The glint of amusement in Reid's eyes that flashed earlier reappeared. "You baked her muffins after she started a petition to get you to move?"

"Wait . . ." A question popped into her head. "Isn't redness a sign of an allergic reaction? Birdie's face was flushed. You saw that, right?"

"Several things could cause that reaction. Let us do our job."

Hope leaned forward and rested her arms on the table. "Is there anything else you need? I'd really need like to go home."

Reid closed his notepad. "Thank you for your cooperation, Hope. I'll be in touch if I have any further questions."

And he would, Hope was sure. She said her goodbyes and tried not to look back as she approached the gate, but she couldn't resist. All the beauty that had taken her breath away now seemed to have faded. In its place was a stillness, and somberness settled over the landscape.

When Hope returned home, she found Josie sitting on the patio enjoying the company of Poppy, Hope's Rhode Island Red chicken, and reading a book. Poppy was a gentle soul of a bird and liked to hang out close to the house.

Guilt twisted in Hope's stomach for not calling Josie when she was delayed at the Donovan house. After she apologized, Josie told her not to worry about it. She was curious about what happened and wanted to hear all the details. Hope gave her a recap and then went into the living room while Josie made coffee for them.

"Here you go." Josie entered the living room, carrying two coffee cups. She handed one to Hope.

Hope shifted from her spot in front of the window and took the cup. She inhaled the fragrance. Hazelnut. Her favorite. "Bless you."

"Is he home yet?" Josie gestured to the window.

"No, I haven't seen his car."

Hope planted herself in front of her living room window after greeting Bigelow and left a message for Ethan. The spot gave her a view of the road so she'd see the comings and goings. Keeping track of her neighbors wasn't typical behavior she indulged in, but she wanted to see when Ted arrived home.

"Avery had no idea where he was going earlier?" Josie asked.

"No. It's strange because since I started volunteering, I got the impression she controlled his calendar." She took a long drink of the coffee and stared back out the window. "I can't believe I'm doing this. Birdie's dead and now I'm stalking her husband."

Once the police left, Hope planned to go back to the Donovan house to offer her condolences and bring over something for Ted to reheat. She had a few servings of baked ziti left over from recipe testing that she could pack up with a side salad and rolls. But maybe going over there that day would be too intrusive. Surely, Ted had to make calls to family and close friends. Like Maretta Kingston, who was the only friend Hope knew Birdie had. So maybe the list of calls wouldn't be that long.

"You're not stalking. You're concerned for your neighbor. Come on, let's sit." Josie drifted over to the sofa and relaxed down on the deep cushion.

Over the winter, Hope had finally finished remodeling the room. There were still a few minor jobs left, like decorating the bookshelves and hanging artwork.

Other than that, she was pleased with the results, though she and Ethan were at an impasse on where to hang the flat-screen television she ordered. He wanted it over the fireplace, but she wanted to hang a painting she'd found at an estate sale. She didn't pay much attention at the time, but there was a television in Ted's study, and she wondered if it was there because his wife forbade one in their great room. The thought she was anything like Birdie had Hope reconsidering her decision about a television in the living room.

"I don't like how I left things off with Birdie yesterday." Hope joined Josie on the sofa. She kicked off her sneakers and then tucked her feet under her legs. If it weren't for the fact they were discussing her newly departed neighbor, she would have felt cozy and relaxed with her coffee cup in hand.

"Don't beat yourself up. You went over there to work out a truce. You even baked her muffins!"

Hope sipped her coffee. She was hearing what her assistant was saying, but she wasn't feeling any better. Why did she have to lose her temper yesterday?

"I know we shouldn't talk ill about the dead, but we all know Birdie was a mean person. She liked to pick on everyone and didn't need much provocation to do so. You're not at fault here." Josie dipped her head and sipped her coffee.

A slight smile slid over Hope's lips. She appreciated

Josie's support, but she couldn't join in with her employee on bashing a very dead Birdie. Even though they worked in an unconventional workplace, they were working, and she was the boss.

"Okay, enough talk about Birdie." Josie lowered her cup. "I checked out Annette's site. She's making progress."

"I agree." When Hope started coaching, she had opted to keep the number of clients small. The last thing she wanted was to be a boilerplate coaching program. Instead, she recognized that each blogger had her own set of issues, strengths, and weaknesses. The only way to help was to dedicate enough personalized time to each client.

"It's nice to see she's listening to you."

"It's hard to tell if someone is really ready to take advice." Annette was what Hope called a baby blogger. Her site was less than three years old, and it was clear all the work that was required overwhelmed Annette. It showed in a haphazard design, inconsistent posts, and barely any social sharing. It was a shame because the Massachusetts blogger was a talented cook and took fabulous photographs.

"Her baked manicotti she posted last week looked to die for. Do you think I could get her to cook for me?" Josie laughed.

"Well, she's not too far away up in Cambridge. You can drive up there."

A smile twitched on Josie's lips. "Hmm . . . how much do I want that manicotti?"

"Make a weekend of it. There's a lot to see."

"You're right. And since it's spring, there's no real chance of snow." Josie sipped her coffee. "One winter there was one brutal blizzard that dumped over two feet of snow, and everyone was stuck inside for days. Being confined with your family . . . let's just say it can get a little crazy. Well, I'd better get going. Are you going to be okay?"

"Yes, I'm good. Enjoy the rest of the day." Hope leaned forward to the coffee table. She set her cup on a coaster.

Josie gave a carefree shrug and then stood. "I will. See you tomorrow." She walked out of the room.

Hope's cell phone buzzed. She'd given the phone a quick charge after she arrived home while telling Josie what happened.

The caller ID told her it was Ethan.

She grabbed the phone and accepted the call.

"Hi, babe, how are you holding up?"

Hearing his voice settled the uneasiness that had riddled her body since finding Birdie dead.

"Better now." And with those two paltry words, she stood and went back to the window. Ted wouldn't be feeling good anytime soon. Her heart ached for him.

"Do you know if they have reached Ted? Told him about what happened to his wife?"

"Hope." Usually, when Ethan said her name, her heart melted a little. Sure it was silly for a thirty-something to feel that way, but it was true. However, the tone he just used hadn't left her all warm and fuzzy. Quite the opposite since it clearly was a warning tone to mind her business. And stay out of police matters.

"Fine. Forget I asked." Time to change the subject. "Are you coming over for dinner?"

"Yes, ma'am." He chuckled because he knew she hated being called ma'am. But considering what had just happened, she let it slide. *This time.*

"Good. I'll grill a couple of burgers." She glanced over her shoulder at the fireplace. "Oh, I'm rethinking my stance on having a television in the living room."

"Really? I'll bring my best persuasive argument with me when I come over."

Okay, there was the warm and fuzzies. "See you later. Love you."

"Love you."

Hope ended the call just in time to see Gilbert Madison's Jeep drive past her house. She spotted his wife, Mitzi, in the passenger seat. She drew back so they wouldn't see her staring out her window. Though given that her house was set back from the road and it had a covered porch, she doubted they'd seen her. Gosh, how she hated snooping on her neighbors. How had Birdie done it? Why had she been so persnickety?

And where was Ted?

Chapter Four

Hope shooed Bigelow back from the oven as she set down her second cup of morning coffee. He gave her an "I'm starving" look with his big brown eyes when she approached with potholders.

He'd watched her slide the casserole dish she prepared after finishing her breakfast into the oven an hour ago and had remained vigilant during the cooking process.

As a food blogger, she was used to making all sorts of dishes at odd hours. Having the mouthwatering aroma of homemade sauce, fresh herbs, and cheese wafting through the morning's air was nothing new for the Early household.

"You can't be hungry. Your belly is full from breakfast." When Hope rescued him, she'd had a steep learning curve because she'd never owned a dog before. She quickly learned that no matter how many meals she fed him, Bigelow was always hungry.

So she didn't feel guilty about shooing him away

when the timer finally dinged. Before she could turn back and close the oven door, Ethan swooped into the kitchen and closed it on his way to the coffee maker.

She leaned forward and inhaled the delicious aroma of her latest success. Spinach lasagna with cheese. Lots and lots of cheese with a creamy ricotta sauce. It gave her hope for a better day than yesterday, which had been dampened by Birdie's passing and the unexpected news Ethan shared over dinner last night.

As they ate, he filled her in on the latest turn of events with his ex-wife, Heather, and none of it was pretty. The once popular cheerleader had become addicted to opioids after a car accident two years ago. Her struggle weighed heavily on Ethan, who refused to turn his back on his ex. He wasn't the type of guy who abandoned someone, even if she had shredded his heart. Though he had his limits. Hope saw he'd reached it after Heather confessed she had gotten into a perilous situation two nights ago. Ethan had been hesitant to share all the details but what Hope was able to find out was that Heather left the girls in her car while she met with an unsavory individual. She was a little upset by his reluctance to fill her in but understood he was processing all the what-ifs and needed some time for mental clarity. He immediately took swift action by consulting his attorney and taking custody of his daughters, Molly and Becca.

She sighed. On the one hand, it relieved her knowing Heather was finally getting help for her addiction. Still, on the other hand, she was angry with the woman for endangering the girls.

"Too bad you have to be at Heather's house in an hour. You could use a few more hours of sleep." Hope dropped her potholders on the granite countertop and joined Ethan at the coffee maker. Her nose wriggled. He was dressed in a denim shirt and khaki cargo pants and he smelled warm and spicy with a note of citrus.

"Wish I could, babe. Though I don't think I'd get any more sleep."

"Monkey-chatter brain?"

Ethan looked up. "Monkey what?"

She propped a hand on her hip. "You know when your brain is unsettled. Thoughts keep going through your head; you can't shut them off."

"I guess it was something like that last night. I have to check in at the PD before heading to Heather's house." Being the police chief, he was rarely off-duty. "I want to be there when she leaves with her sister. I'll take the girls back to my place."

Hope reached out and squeezed his arm. She wished she could do more to help his situation than an offer to babysit. "You can bring them by today."

"I'll keep that in mind. The girls love the chickens and Bigelow." He filled a travel mug and secured its lid.

Bigelow's ears perked at his name, and his attention diverted from the casserole for a moment.

"He loves them too." Hope returned to the island, and she picked up her camera.

The lasagna was for Ted so he'd have something to eat, and it would be easy to serve when family members came to the house. She snapped a flurry of photographs of the dish. Somehow, she resisted the urge to grab a fork and dive into the dish of deliciousness. After it cooled, she'd deliver the casserole to Ted with a salad and a loaf of bread.

"I'm really sorry it was all about me, the girls, and Heather last night." Ethan moved to Hope and wrapped an arm around her. "I know you had a rough day yesterday."

Hope set her camera down and maneuvered to face Ethan. She frowned. His eyes were hooded, and his brows drooped from the weight of all the worry caused by Heather. Even those sexy little lines at the corners of his dark eyes looked deeper that morning.

No matter how exhausted he was, he would be there for his family. And that's why she loved the man so much. And why she kept her opinion of Heather to herself. Her focus was on the girls. Where it belonged.

"Don't be silly. It's not like I haven't found a dead body before." She knew she sounded cavalier about the incident and wondered if it was to make him feel better or herself. "I'm just curious about the cause of death. I wondered after I found her if she had a heart problem. Though she was red, and I think that's a sign of an allergic reaction."

A slow smile crept on Ethan's lips, and he pulled her closer to his chest.

Her brows furrowed. "Why are you smiling?"

"Because I know what you're thinking, and I advise you not to get involved with Reid's case."

"I'm not getting involved. I'm merely curious."

He shook his head before he lowered his lips over hers and kissed her. She responded by wrapping her arms around his midsection and prolonging the kiss until Bigelow wedged his snout between their bodies.

She gave him the stink eye for his bad timing, though the interruption probably was a good thing. Ethan had to get going, and she had to change out of her barn chore clothes before dashing out to visit Ted.

"I'll call you later." Ethan broke away from her and headed out of the kitchen.

A few moments later, she heard the mudroom door open and close. She looked down at Bigelow, who stared at her with interest because she was still close to the lasagna.

"He's worried about me for no reason. If there's no murder, then there's no reason to get involved, right?"

The lasagna cooled enough for Hope to cover the dish. She wrapped an extra baguette she had and set it on top of the casserole dish. She gave herself a final check in the mirror before heading out to deliver the food to Ted.

Stepping onto her front porch, she was greeted by the birdsong carried by a soft breeze. For a moment she forgot she was paying a condolence call as she descended her porch steps. Then reality hit when she saw her neighbor Zara Myers walking away from the Donovan house.

"Hope!" Zara waved as she stepped off the curb. Her coppery black hair fell to her shoulders, and her round face was makeup free. Zara and her family lived on the other side of the Donovans in a quaint Dutch Colonial home.

"Good morning." Hope came to a stop. She rarely got the chance to visit with Zara, who was always on the go between her long commute to her job as a college professor and three kids under the age of ten. "Did you see Ted?"

"I did. I wanted to pay my condolences." Her expression was neutral, as was her tone.

"How's he doing?" Hope glanced at the house. There

weren't any other vehicles in the driveway, as she expected to see. Where were his family and close friends like Maretta Kingston?

Zara shrugged. "Guess he's doing the best he can. Honestly, it was very awkward. I only came over out of respect for him. Birdie wasn't the friendliness neighbor, as you found out with that ridiculous petition."

"She asked you to sign it?"

"She did! Talk about the nerve. After what she did last summer, she wanted a favor from me. Unbelievable."

Hope searched her memory and came up with an incident about Zara's property line. "She had a problem with a shrub of yours, didn't she?"

Zara rolled her eyes. "It was ludicrous. She nearly had a cow over the shrub. She didn't like how it looked. Sure, it was overgrown. I assured her I'd cut it back when I had time, but it wasn't top of my list between work and my kids. Not having either, Birdie didn't understand that, so she took it upon herself. One day I came home and found that she had pruned the shrub and cut it down to the nub. I couldn't believe it."

Hope's mouth dropped open. "She didn't?"

"Oh, yes, she did. And to hack away at my shrub, she had to trespass on my property. Anyway, it doesn't matter now, does it?" Her gaze landed on the covered casserole dish in Hope's hand. "You're so considerate to bring food to Ted. I'm sure he'll appreciate it. I've got to get going. I have a class starting soon. Good to see you!" Zara turned and hurried toward her home.

On any other day, Hope would have found comfort in knowing she wasn't the only neighbor that Birdie had a problem with, but as Zara said, all that didn't matter now. She inhaled a breath and continued on with her mission.

Halfway up the driveway, Ted appeared. He'd come out of the garage side door with his hands in his pants pockets.

"Good morning, Hope." His salt and pepper hair was mussed, and redness rimmed his deep-set eyes.

"I'm so sorry for your loss."

Ted heaved a weary breath, and his shoulders slumped in his gray collared shirt. "Thank you."

Silence fell between them in the space where Hope would have usually said something nice about the deceased. She struggled to find a kind word about Birdie and felt terrible about that.

"I made a lasagna." It was the only thing she could think of saying. She offered the dish to Ted.

"This is very thoughtful of you considering what you went through yesterday, discovering . . . Birdie." Emotion cut off his words. He worked his lips and nodded his head slightly.

Hope could only imagine what was going through his mind. The would-haves, the should-haves, and the could-haves. Every marriage had them. "I wish I could have done more." Maybe if she'd gotten there earlier, Birdie might still have been alive.

"Don't beat yourself up. What happened wasn't your fault."

Then why did she feel so responsible? But he was right. She wasn't the cause of Birdie's death. Whatever happened occurred before her arrival.

"Logically, that makes sense. Who would have thought when we ran into each other yesterday morning at Emily's House, we'd be here today?" Hope folded her arms.

A shadow crossed Ted's face as his lips twitched. His cell phone rang, and he juggled the lasagna dish to retrieve his phone from his pocket. He glanced at the caller ID and looked relieved. "I'm sorry, I have to take this."

"I understand. Let me know if you need anything."

Ted nodded. "I appreciate the offer. Thank you again." Ted turned and lumbered back to the garage door and closed it behind him after he entered.

Seated alone at the table, Hope rubbed her temples and then dropped her chin into her hands. So much for being productive. She had arrived at Emily's House intending to work on a handout for class but found herself unmotivated with barely a word written.

Her unusual lack of drive could have resulted from finding Birdie dead. Or it could have been due to learning that Ethan's ex was causing turmoil yet again. Or that Ted had had a funny reaction to her bringing up their run-in the morning his wife died.

"Knock, knock."

The interruption pulled Hope from her thoughts. She looked toward the doorway and found Erin Thomson standing there with a grim look on her face. It appeared she'd heard about Birdie.

"Hey, there." They'd met through a friend of Hope's who'd hired Erin to control the chaos in her home. Hope and the enterprising organizer quickly bonded over label makers and clear storage containers. They were soulmates.

"I can't believe Ted's wife is dead. And you found her?" Erin entered and sat at the round table where Hope's students gathered for their lessons. "What happened?"

Hope shook her head. Even though she'd lived through it, the entire scene was surreal. One minute she expected to be face to face with the person who disliked her enough to want to force her to move, and the next minute she was staring at a dead body.

"I'm not sure. I found her on her gazebo. Did you know her?"

"Not really." Erin leaned back. She was a petite brunette who favored barrettes to keep her hair off her face and twinsets worn with tailored slacks. "I met her once at a fundraising event, and all she talked about were her dahlias. Our conversation was brief since I know nothing about gardening."

"But you know a lot about organizing spices." Hope smiled.

"I do." Erin pointed a finger and smiled. "You know, the thing I noticed about her was that she didn't ask me about what I did. All she talked about was herself and her plants."

Hope wasn't surprised. A part of her felt sorry for Birdie because she had missed out on Erin's inspiring story.

Eight years ago, she escaped an ugly domestic situation after a late-night emergency room visit that was the final straw. When she was discharged, she drove to her sister's home and never looked back. With help from family and Emily's House, she launched her professional organizing business. She was now dating a terrific guy who treated her like a queen.

"Oh, and about the book she was writing on plants."

"I heard about it." And from the looks of Birdie's garden, she understood gardening hadn't been only a hobby but a passion. "She had been working on it for years. I wonder how far she'd gotten with it . . ." *Before she died*, was the last part of her sentence, but she left it unsaid.

Erin's brows drew together. She probably had the same thought as Hope.

"Poor Ted," Erin said, breaking the quiet. "You know, in all the time I've known him, he rarely spoke about Birdie. Don't you think that's odd?"

Hope shrugged. "He seems like he has a clear separation between work and his personal life. Though he always seemed to talk about this place."

Erin leaned forward and whispered, "Maybe he loved Emily's House more than his own wife."

Hope gasped. "Erin! That's how rumors start."

"Just sharing an observation." Erin winked.

A buzz of chatter approached, signaling to Hope that her students were on their way into the room. She opened her portfolio and pulled out her lesson plan. "Just be sure to be careful sharing your observations. We'd hate to ruin Ted's or this center's reputation."

"Duly noted, Miss Early. You sound like a very proper teacher." Erin laughed as she stood. "Let's do lunch soon." She exited the room as three women entered.

While Hope liked Erin, the one thing she didn't appreciate was Erin's propensity for gossip. After being on the receiving end of half-truths and blatant exaggerations about her personal life, gossiping rubbed her the wrong way. But she hated to admit that there always seemed to be a kernel of truth to rumors.

Was that the case with Erin's observation about Ted and Birdie's marriage?

Hope checked her emails on her phone as she walked to her Explorer after class. Shading the phone with her hand to eliminate the glare, she scanned her inbox. There was a reply from a website she'd pitched to a week ago. They wanted tips and advice for 9-to-5ers transitioning to a digital nomad lifestyle. She didn't consider herself a nomad, though her new career offered her the flexibility to work from anywhere there was a kitchen. Besides sharing her advice, she'd be getting exposure for her blog.

She made a mental note of when the tips were due and moved on to the next email from her agent, Laurel. The update was positive. Graham Flour had made a sponsorship offer. It took all her self-control not to squeal with excitement because Graham Flour was a staple in her pantry. If they worked together, Hope would promote their different flours in upcoming fall recipes.

"Hope! Hold up."

Hope stopped and turned around. She lowered the phone as Avery hurried down the veranda steps and sprinted toward her. Gone was her polished persona from the day before. Wayward strands of auburn hair gave her a bedhead vibe but worked well with her pullover cotton dress and navy sneakers.

"I looked for you earlier, but you weren't in your office." Hope adjusted her tote's straps on her shoulder. She really should reconsider carrying around everything but the kitchen sink. Or up her Pilates workouts to improve her posture.

"It's been hectic today. We are all in shock about Birdie." Avery set her hands on her hips and chewed on her lower lip.

"I can imagine. I'm sorry I didn't tell you what happened when I called yesterday looking for Ted."

"I understand. Don't worry about it. I didn't know you and Birdie were friends. I'm sorry for your loss." Avery gave a half-smile, the kind that expressed sympathy and kindness.

Hope fidgeted with the tote bag straps and cleared her throat. "We weren't exactly friends."

"But you were at her home."

"We were meeting to discuss neighborhood business." Yes, that sounded good. Much better than saying they were meeting to work out a truce and find a way to coexist peacefully on the same street.

"I see. Have you seen Ted? Do you know if he's okay?"

"I saw him this morning when I went over with some food. You haven't talked to him?"

"No. He left a message about Birdie and said he'd call later. I haven't seen him since yesterday morning when he left out of the blue."

"He never returned here?"

Avery shook her head. "Which isn't like him, but I just thought he had back-to-back meetings. He does a lot of his fundraising with private donors on the golf course, and the weather was beautiful yesterday."

"It was a lovely day." Up until Hope found a dead body. "I hope you don't mind me asking, but did Ted talk often about Birdie?"

She had no idea why she was asking. Maybe it was because of what Erin said, and her own observations about the married couple. Ted and Birdie seemed to be such opposites and not in an oh-that's-so-cute way where one loves spicy food and the other prefers not even to salt their meal. No, from what Hope had seen since moving onto her road, Ted was a people person while Birdie repelled them. Well, except for Maretta. Now there was another relationship she couldn't wrap her head around.

"Sure, he did. Well, not as much as Woody talks about his wife, Loretta. I swear the man thinks she walks on water. Ted is just more private about his personal life. Why do you ask? Do you think Ted . . ."

"No, no. I'm just curious."

Avery's face closed off immediately, and her tone changed. "I think you're suspicious, and that gets you into trouble." Hope opened her mouth to defend herself, but Avery wouldn't be interrupted. "From what Ted said when he left his message, it sounds like Birdie died from natural causes. I'd hate for baseless suspicions to derail all the outstanding work that's being done here."

"I couldn't agree more."

"Good. Because Ted is a wonderful person. He's very committed to this organization. So much so, he's cut back on traveling. He's having our program director attend events and conferences on his behalf." Avery looked at her watch. "I need to get back. See you at your next class." She swung around and marched back to the house. Gone was the spring in her step when she approached Hope.

"Avery, one more thing." The comments about Ted no longer traveling reminded her of the passport she saw under his home office desk. "Do you know if Ted has any personal travel coming up?"

Avery halted and turned, looking annoyed. "No. I'm not aware of any travel plans. I really do need to get back to work."

"Thanks!" Hope waved, though she didn't receive one back from Avery. She lowered her hand and continued to her vehicle.

Inside, seated behind the steering wheel, she started the ignition.

She wondered why seeing the passport sparked her curiosity.

Maybe it was because hers was safely tucked away after a heart-stopping incident of not finding it after her move back to Jefferson. She finally located it in a box of miscellaneous papers a week later. Since then, she'd made sure it was in the fireproof document box in her office. Since Ted was as meticulous as she was, it seemed out of character to have his passport carelessly lying around. Unless he'd been preparing for a trip and had to get it out from its secure spot.

She shook her head. Now her curiosity was getting out of control. As Avery said, Ted was a wonderful person who was doing good work. She backed out of her space and one lingering question from the day before still rattled around her brain.

Where had Ted been between the time he left the center and the time Birdie died?

Chapter Five

Hope closed her Explorer's door, locked it, and then dropped the fob into her cavernous tote. Immediately, she regretted not placing the fob in the bag's side pocket. Now she'd have to fish it out when she was ready to head home. Why wasn't she using the purse organizer Claire had given her at Christmas? She had no clue. Maybe she would when she figured out why everything was organized in her life but not her tote.

An answer wasn't coming anytime soon to that lifelong quirk, so Hope shoved the thought away and continued her walk to the entry of Jefferson's Town Hall.

On her drive back from Emily's House, she decided to visit Maretta Kingston and pay her condolences.

Like Jane, she'd known Maretta since childhood, but her relationship with both women was very different. Jane was warm and kind while Maretta had a sharpness to her, from her tone to her nod to her bony figure. She always seemed old to Hope even though she was about the same age as her mother. Maybe even a few years younger.

"Good afternoon, Hope. It's nice to see you." Denise Moody looked up from her computer and smiled. The full-figured woman had been a long-time town employee, and now she worked as Maretta's secretary.

"Hi, Denise. How's Benny doing?" Hope stopped at the desk and marveled at how neat and organized it was. Even the bowl of hard candies was tidy. She helped herself to a butterscotch candy.

Denise's eyes widened and lit up. "He's graduated top of his class, and now he's off to medical school. I can't believe my little boy is going to be a doctor. But he goes by Ben now. I guess it sounds more mature."

"That's so exciting. You must be so proud of him."

"I am. But it costs a fortune." Denise raised a hand. "I'm not complaining."

"It's not easy. Cleo is also going through something similar."

Denise lowered her hand and pushed back wisps of hair off her face. Her brown hair was still growing out from her round of chemo treatments. Her prognosis had been grim, but she fought, determined to see her son graduate medical school. "I heard Birdie complained, and we had no choice but to close her down. Policies and regulations are in place for a reason, but she wasn't hurting anybody. But boy oh boy, was Cleo steaming after she received her notice."

"She came here? What happened?"

Denise leaned forward. "I did my best to calm her down, but she was so angry with Birdie and Maretta. She accused Maretta of being influenced by her personal relationship with Birdie. I tried to tell Cleo that it wasn't Maretta's decision. She didn't want to hear any of that."

"Did she talk to Maretta?" Just as Hope finished asking the question, the interior office door opened, and the mayor appeared with a scowl. She wondered how much of the conversation Maretta had overheard.

"What brings you by, Hope?" Maretta opened the door wider and stepped out of her office. Her lips puckered, and her thin brows drooped.

"I was hoping you could spare a few minutes for me." Hope nodded to Denise and then walked toward the mayor, expecting Maretta wouldn't turn her away.

"Well, since you're here, I suppose I can spare a few minutes. But keep in mind I do have a full schedule like always because there's a town to run."

Hope lowered her gaze and held back an amused smile. Maretta acted as if she was running a nation rather than a sleepy Connecticut town known for its abundance of antique shops.

"I appreciate you squeezing me in." Hope flashed a satisfied smile and then followed Maretta into the office.

Maretta's drab black skirt flitted as she crossed the room to her desk. The coordinating blouse did nothing for her pale complexion, and her mousy brown hair was styled in a chin-length bob. But not the bouncy kind that was fun and youthful. No, her hair was thin with no bounce, much like Maretta. She'd never been a high-maintenance kind of woman regarding her appearance, but she was over the top in other ways. She constantly yapped orders and went through life like a bull in a china shop. Yet she had many friends and supporters in town.

Hope declined the offer to sit in one of the visitor's

seats facing Maretta's desk. She doubted she'd be there long enough to get comfortable.

"I wanted to pay my condolences to you on the passing of your friend Birdie."

Seated behind her desk, Maretta blinked, and her hand rested on her chest, just below her clavicle. The perturbed look on her face slipped away, revealing a hint of another emotion. Hope guessed it was sadness.

"It's very thoughtful of you. Thank you." Maretta's eyes watered. "I can't believe she's dead."

"How long were you friends?" Hope stepped farther inside the office, which was functional and neutral in décor. Two tall windows looked out onto Main Street, and a bookcase ran the length of one wall. Hope's gaze skimmed the shelves and then an oil painting depicting Main Street that hung over a credenza. Painted by a local artist, it was donated to the town a century ago. Hung beside it was a map of Jefferson. Up close, Hope could pinpoint her road and the horseback riding trails that wove through the wooded sections of Jefferson.

"Let me think." Maretta snatched a tissue from its box, dabbed at her eyes, and regained her composure. She then sat and clasped her hands together on top of the blotter. "Birdie came to Jefferson after marrying Ted . . . twelve years ago."

Hope eased forward as if she were approaching her dough for sticky buns to knead—prepared for the unruly and unpredictable, much like Maretta could be.

"Where did she move from?"

"Somewhere up in Massachusetts."

"Birdie must have been a nickname?"

"Her Christian name was Berta. Berta Oliff. She said that her grandmother nicknamed her Birdie because she loved watching birds at feeders when she was a toddler." Maretta smiled. Reminiscing about her friend seemed to relax her.

Hope tried not to wrinkle her nose at Birdie's given name. Berta was a good name, she reminded herself. Though it would be hard for her to call a baby Berta. Maybe Bertie. Little baby Bertie. She tried to imagine Birdie as an infant, swaddled in a cozy blanket with tiny rolls of baby fat and ten cute little toes. But the image never came; all she saw was the mean woman telling her to move out of her beloved home.

"You two were close?" Hope said after she decided to stop struggling to imagine Birdie as an infant.

Maretta shrugged. "You could say. Birdie didn't make friends easily."

Now there was an understatement if Hope ever heard one, but she wasn't about to interrupt Maretta.

"She didn't like talking about herself very much. I'd say she was very much a closed book."

In some respects, Hope envied the boundaries Birdie had around her life. There were some days when she wished she had them, but thanks to her time on a reality show and her blog, her life was pretty much an open book.

"We met when she came to a book club meeting at the library. Sally was still the head librarian and suggested that she join the Garden Club."

Sally Merrifield had nurtured the library and the Garden Club for nearly her whole adult life. Both were passions, and she always found a way to combine them. One of her most significant accomplishments was the Jane Austen Garden at the library. Inspired by the author's classic books and her love of English gardens, Sally spent years planning the outdoor space. Eventually, she got a grant and volunteers. The garden became a place where you could sit, read, or daydream.

"She enjoyed being a part of the Garden Club, so it surprised us when she abruptly resigned." Maretta unclasped her hands and lowered her gaze to the file folder off to the side of her.

"Why? What happened?" Hope asked.

Maretta lifted her chin, and her critical gaze landed on Hope. "You're full of questions, aren't you? Don't tell me you're snooping around Birdie's death trying to make it into some scandalous murder?"

"I'm doing no such thing. I was just asking a question." And she'd probably overstayed her welcome.

"I have no intention of taking part in idle gossip. I suggest that you stay out of Detective Reid's way because we'll all be watching Chief Cahill during the investigation."

"What are you talking about?"

"Thank you for your condolences. I'm sure you can show yourself out." Maretta broke eye contact, turning her attention to the folder.

Hope huffed and then turned to leave the office. She'd overstayed her welcome. Like with her sticky bun dough, timing was everything.

As she passed through the outer office, Denise was on the telephone but waved as Hope passed through. Hope exited the building through a side door. Once out on Main Street, she checked her watch. She had a few minutes to spare before heading home and decided to stop by Claire's shop. There was something she wanted to run by Claire.

She decided to walk to the shop because the beautiful spring day had brought people out, and there wasn't a parking space along Main Street. She also didn't want to be bothered with the hassle of finding a space in the lot behind the shop.

A leisurely walk would do her some good and help clear her mind. In the past twenty-four hours, she was dealt two significant events. Deep down, she knew she should be concentrating on the upheaval in Ethan's life and not be worried about Birdie. She'd done all she could when she came upon Birdie's body, made food for Ted, and paid her condolences. There wasn't any more she could do. So why did Maretta's comment about Birdie not liking to talk about herself or her past keep turning over in her mind?

Hope sidestepped a flustered mom pushing a stroller and struggling to hold onto a toddler. She flashed the mom a sympathetic smile and then spotted Sally Merrifield exiting the Historical Society. Walking beside Sally was Jeffrey, the postal carrier. They were laughing as they approached the curb. Hope caught Sally's attention, and the older woman's laughter ended. She said something to Jeffrey and then dashed across the street. He waved to Hope and then went on with his route. Hope was confused by Sally's reaction to seeing her. Then again, sometimes Sally got moody, especially when she was juggling too many volunteer projects. Maybe that was it. Hope shook off her friend's weird behavior and continued to Staged with Style.

A bell jingled, announcing Hope's arrival at the shop as she opened the door. She was welcomed by a refreshing citrus scent and another note her nose couldn't identify. Lola was arranging Em Bailey Candles on a three-drawer chest. The luxe candles had intoxicating fragrances Hope would binge-buy if it weren't for their three-digit price tag.

Lola looked up from the display of sleek glass containers, all with minimal branding, after she adjusted three travel-sized candles. She offered a hesitant smile.

"They smell amazing." At the dresser, Hope lifted a jar and inhaled deeply. *Got it!* It was a peppery basil scent that mingled with the citrus aroma.

"They should for what they cost." Lola lifted a shipping box stuffed with packing paper. "I heard what happened yesterday. It must have been awful finding Birdie dead. Did she have a heart attack or something?"

Hope wished she had an answer to Birdie's cause of death, but she was in the dark like everyone else. "I'm sorry, but I don't know what caused her death."

Lola pursed her lips. "Well, I guess it really doesn't matter, does it? Heart attack, allergic reaction, bursting aneurysm . . ."

"Hope! What in the world happened?" Claire emerged from the back office with her arms open, heading for her sister. She pulled Hope into a tight hug. "Why do you keep finding dead bodies?"

Hope shrugged. It wasn't as if she went looking for them. "It just happened. You're squeezing me too tight." She wriggled free of her sister's hold. Finally able to breathe, she wanted to argue but couldn't because it did seem she found more than her fair share of the recently departed.

"Don't be surprised if people stop inviting you over," Claire warned.

"The police really didn't give you any indication of what caused her death?" Lola asked as she walked from the dresser to the sales counter, where she deposited the box.

"I'm sure it will be released shortly," Claire said. "I feel so bad for Ted. He's such a nice man."

"He is. Until I started volunteering at the center, I really didn't know how much work he does. It's amazing. So many lives have been changed because of his dedication." Hope returned the lid to the candle.

"Yeah, a real saint," Lola said before moving away from the sales floor and into the back office.

Hope and Claire shared a glance. "What's that supposed to mean?" Hope asked.

Claire looked over her shoulder and then back at her sister. "She's been a little cranky. Come to think of it, she's been cranky since Birdie came in here the other day." She walked to the table where she had her consultation with staging clients and tidied up.

"When was Birdie here?" At the table, Hope pulled out a chair and sat. Paint chips, fabric swatches, and Claire's journal were scattered on the tabletop.

"A day or so before you had your run-in with her at the library. I was busy with a client, so Lola attempted to help her." Claire sat opposite of her sister and closed her journal. But not before Hope got a look at a drawing of a floorplan. Claire kept all her notes on projects in there and always had it handy for when inspiration struck.

"Attempted? What happened?"

"Birdie bought nothing. Guess she didn't see anything she liked, and I didn't think much of it because we all know what she's like. She probably was put off by the prices. But I'm not a box store. I sell fine home accessories."

Like Em Bailey Candles. Hope's gaze drifted back to

the candle display. It tested her resistance, and she was failing.

"Though her home is nicely decorated," Hope said.

"When were you in her house?" Claire asked.

"The day I found her in the gazebo."

"Why? You found her outside."

"True. I had to call the police, and I discovered my cell phone wasn't charged, and she didn't have a phone with her, so I had to use the landline." Hope fell silent at the memory. The one and only time she'd been in the Donovan house was to call the police. That was disconcerting. They were neighbors; they shouldn't have been strangers.

Claire leaned forward and reached for Hope's hand and squeezed. "You can't blame yourself for what happened. You're not responsible for her death."

"I know." Hearing Ted's sentiments echoed again forced her to accept the fact. It was time to let go of the guilt and put her disagreement with Birdie where it belonged—in the past. "Anyway, I didn't come to talk about Birdie. I came to see if you'd like to join me on an antiquing outing this weekend. I want to decorate the girls' bedroom since they'll be staying over more."

Over the winter, she'd purchased twin beds and bedding sets for Molly and Becca to set up a spare bedroom as theirs. A coat of paint and curtains freshened the room. Now she wanted to add more touches to it to make the room feel more like theirs rather than only a guest room.

"How are they doing?" Claire pulled back her hand and picked up her journal. She stood.

"I'm not sure. Ethan said they were agitated when Heather left for rehab. I'm hoping they'll come over tonight, but I think he'll keep them at his house. They need to know they're safe, and we have to make sure they have stability."

"And routine. That's very important. And, yes, I'd love to go shopping with you." Claire walked to the sales counter and set down the book.

"Great. I'll text you later after I know what Ethan's plans are for the weekend." Hope stood and walked to the chest of drawers and lifted one candle. The splurge wasn't in her budget, but she justified the impulse purchase by telling herself she needed a little pick-me-up.

"Hope . . ." Claire channeled their mother's tone when she recognized her daughters were about to do something foolish, unwise, or reckless.

Hope grinned. "What? I get a family discount, don't I?"

Chapter Six

Shoot. Josie's Mini Cooper was parked in the driveway when Hope arrived home. Her assistant was leaning against the vehicle, scrolling on her phone. This was the second time in two days she'd had to wait for Hope to get back home. Hope glanced at her watch and was relieved to find she wasn't late. But the fact that Josie arrived early and had to wait outside made her feel bad.

"Hey, there!" Josie pushed off her vehicle and lifted her backpack to her shoulder.

"I'm so sorry. I should have been home earlier." Hope shuffled toward the mudroom door.

"No worries. I'm early. Besides, I'm all caught up on Instagram." She shook her phone. "Love the photo of the lasagna. Any chance there are leftovers?"

With the door unlocked, Hope entered the mudroom. "Sorry. I took it over to Ted this morning."

"Bummer!" Josie closed the door behind them, and together they walked through to the kitchen, and Bigelow finally appeared. His sleepy eyes revealed he'd been in a deep sleep only moments before. "Hey, little guy."

"I stopped at Town Hall and then Claire's shop on my way back from the center. I really should take him for a walk." Hope dropped her tote bag on the island and pulled out her new candle to admire. It was a luxury she should have resisted, but she was weak.

"Oh, no, you didn't." Josie's sight was set on the generously sized jar.

"I know, I know. But I couldn't help myself."

"You work hard, you deserve a little splurge."

"It's not like I have one for every room." Finding a rationale for the extravagant purchase was easy. She dashed back into the mudroom to get Bigelow's leash with him right on her heels. He definitely needed to go for a walk.

"Go on. I'll start editing the video." Josie pulled out a chair at the table and set her backpack down. She unzipped the main compartment and pulled out her laptop. "We do need to go over the affiliate links and update the spreadsheet. Have you heard anything about Graham Flour?"

Back in the kitchen, Hope slipped the leash on Bigelow's collar.

"Nothing yet from Laurel. Hey, have you seen the charging cube? I went to charge my tablet this morning, and it was missing."

Josie glanced at the outlet at the counter where they charged their tech equipment. "That's strange. It was there yesterday. At least I think it was."

"It is strange. When I get back, I'll look in my office."

"No need. I have an extra one right here." Josie jumped up and dug through her backpack. She pulled out a black cube with a victorious smile. "Here you go."

"Thank you. You were a Girl Scout, weren't you?" Hope took the charger and inserted it into the outlet. Then she returned to the counter. She stared at her key ring for a moment and an idea occurred to her. "You should have a key to my house."

Josie looked up from her computer. "What? I was only outside for a few minutes. Besides, I was early. You were on time." She tapped on the keyboard.

"We have a lot of work to do, and you don't need to be wasting time waiting for me to arrive home. My mind is made up. When I get back from our walk, I'll give you a key."

"Well, if you insist."

"I insist." Hope trusted her assistant not to abuse the access to her home. Since the beginning of the year, they'd been working together, and not once had Josie done anything to warrant any concern about her professionalism.

"We do have a lot of stuff to do. And with you having to do the morning and evening chores for the chickens, it probably would be a good thing for me to set up and start working when you're either out in the barn or at EH."

"Then it's settled." And now Hope had to do the gardening by herself, and she had Ethan's girls to look after when he needed help.

"Do you have any idea when Iva will be back?"

"Not yet. Her mom is in bad shape." Bigelow nudged Hope with his snout. "We'll be back in a few minutes."

Outside, Hope and Bigelow strolled along their road. She usually was lulled into a sense of tranquility as she passed by each neighbor's house. Some she knew very well, while others she knew by sight only.

Like Gilbert and Mitzi's neighbors, the Benedicts,

who were always away, either traveling in their motor home or on a cruise.

Unlike the Benedicts, Gilbert and Mitzi hosted a barbecue each spring for everyone on Fieldstone Road.

Then there was Leila Manchester and Dorie Baxter. Best friends for decades, they power-walked in the morning and often stopped to shoot the breeze with neighbors. At times, Hope found them to be a bit too curious, but it was what endeared them to her.

Besides, she'd rather deal with a nosy neighbor who was friendly than deal with another Birdie. Or another petition.

Bigelow kept a steady pace beside Hope, who eyed the homes dotted along the street. At first glance, they all had well-maintained lawns and welcoming facades. And she guessed behind the front doors there were plenty of secrets. Like the secrets Birdie must have had since she barely spoke about her past. Okay, now Hope was being nosy and suspicious. Just because someone remained private about her past didn't mean she had deep, dark secrets.

But too often, that was the case.

She gave herself a mental shake.

Even if Birdie had a shady past or a skeleton in her closet, it hadn't appeared that it killed her.

It seemed Hope's previous sleuthing adventures were prompting her to look at every death as a murder. It just wasn't the case this time.

A minivan drove by, and the driver gave a quick wave at Hope. She returned the wave to Amelia Carlson and watched the vehicle pull into the driveway of a dark red Colonial. The home's garage door opened, and the car drove inside and disappeared.

Hope slowed her stride as a memory wiggled to the forefront of her brain. Four months ago, there was a dispute between Amelia and Birdie over the use of a chainsaw on a Sunday afternoon. A little-known ordinance in Jefferson said that power tools weren't allowed to be used. Clearly, the cutting up of a tree that had fallen after a storm disturbed Birdie's day. She called the police and forced Amelia's husband to stop chopping up the tree.

Hope shook her head. It amazed her how many enemies Birdie made on the street where she lived. Not being liked by her neighbors hadn't seemed to faze her at all.

A bark interrupted Hope's thought and reminded her that she was out for a walk, not out stalking her neighbors' homes.

"Okay, okay, let's go." She propelled forward, forcing Bigelow to do a little gallop to catch up, and they were off to finish their walk without any more morbid thoughts.

In the days following Birdie's death, Hope dodged interview requests from media outlets throughout the state and even gossip websites, though she had no idea how her name was associated with those sites. She then had a not-so-great conversation with her agent. Laurel wasn't pleased with Hope's knack for finding dead bodies. By the end of the call, she believed Hope's claim that it didn't look like foul play, and within a few more days, a death certificate would be issued, and Birdie would be buried. On her few outings to walk Bigelow and get the mail, she fielded questions from curious neighbors and her mail carrier. She always escaped by simply saying she had no idea what happened to Birdie. And that was the truth.

She filled in the rest of her time writing blog posts,

photographing food, and baking cookies with Ethan's daughters.

Yet, as she stood outside the Bishop Room in the library, her stomach quaked with a feeling that Birdie was going to be as difficult in death as she was in life. Was it a sixth sense? A premonition? Whatever it was, she would have loved for it to go away.

She drew in a deep breath as she looked into the room. The cookbook fundraiser committee was waiting.

"I really appreciate you coming with me," she said to Drew, who stood behind her. "I don't know why I'm nervous."

"Hope! We've been waiting for you. Any update on what happened to Birdie?" Cleo asked between bites of a muffin she enjoyed at her seat at the table.

"Cleo! Let her come in and get settled before barraging her with questions." Sally gave a stern look as she walked from the refreshment cart to the table with her coffee. Even though she was in her seventies, she remained very active in the community. When she wasn't managing her family's inn with her sister-in-law, Jane, she volunteered at the library daily. She looked relaxed in a pair of navy slacks and a white pullover. Her gray hair was cropped short, and the only jewelry she wore was her gold cross necklace.

"Like you weren't thinking the same thing." Cleo looked unapologetic as she wiped her fingers on a napkin.

"Well, just to be safe, I'm going to keep my distance. People have a way of dropping dead when Hope is present." Meg Griffin dramatically took a gigantic step away from the door. She and Hope had been frenemies from elementary school. Their rocky relationship dated back to a school play when they were up for the same role. Hope got the part, and Meg got mean. Though somehow they remained civil toward one another. Well, most of the time.

Drew leaned over Hope's shoulder and whispered, "Gotta go."

Hope's head swung around. "Wait. What?"

"Not my circus, not my monkeys. It's all yours." Drew shoved Hope into the Bishop Room and wiggled his fingers in a wave before dashing from the doorway.

Hope steamed as her eyes widened at her best friend's abandonment. He had told her he could hang out for a bit while she got the cookbook meeting started. A little moral support would have been appreciated. Then he dropped her like a hot potato to face the curious committee members alone.

Oh, he would pay dearly.

She chased him down the hall. Even though his pace picked up, she caught up with him and grabbed him by the shoulder.

He turned around. "Shoot. How'd you get so fast?"

"Remember, I run three to four miles most mornings? You're going in there with me." She pointed to the meeting room.

He shook his head in protest.

"Come on, you promised."

"You can handle them on your own. Just tell them something they don't know. Like how Birdie was lying on the gazebo's floor when you found her. Face up? Facedown?"

"That's gruesome."

"Yes, it is. And they'll lap it up."

Hope huffed. "You said you'd write a story about the fundraiser for the *Gazette*. So I'm guessing your editor is expecting that."

Drew pouted like a petulant child.

Ah-ha! She had him now. "Come on." She yanked him and dragged him into the meeting with her.

They entered the quiet room, and Hope pointed to an empty seat at the table to settle on. He pulled out a notepad from his messenger bag and opened it to a fresh sheet.

"Great, Hope's here." Angela Green, the head librarian, broke the awkward silence. "Let's get started."

"What about Casey?" Jane asked as she pulled out a chair and sat at the round table. In front of her were a steno pad and a pen. She'd volunteered to be the committee's secretary.

"She called to let me know she's running a little late, but she'll be here." Angela took a seat at the table and opened her sleek portfolio. She was organized and efficient. Those skills allowed her to oversee many programs, increase the library's patronage, and engage with fellow book lovers.

"Perhaps we should wait a few minutes before starting." Jane clasped her hands together and fixed her curious gaze on Hope. "I think we should take a few minutes to reflect on our recent loss."

"What are you talking about?" Sally stirred her coffee and then walked from the refreshment cart. "You mean Birdie? It's not as if she was a town elder. Actually, there's another word I'd use to describe her."

"That won't be necessary, Sally." Jane's tone toward her sister-in-law was firm.

"She was a supporter of the library, wasn't she?" Meg asked from her spot by the glass cabinet that contained several town historical documents and journals.

"Well, she was a regular here at the library. Practically five days a week, she came to research and write," Angela said.

"Hope, dear, come sit here." Jane patted the chair next to her.

Hope nodded and obeyed. It felt like she was back in Jane's Mystery Book Club. In high school, she attended the monthly meeting. She always kept a composition notebook to jot notes, clues, suspects, and motives. Often, she figured out the murderer before anyone else in the group. But the usual twinkle in Jane's blue eyes was missing that morning.

Hope gulped. *Oh, boy*. Regardless of how busy she'd been, she ought to have called Jane to fill her in on every detail of finding Birdie's body.

"It'll allow us to chat." Jane reached for her coffee cup. "Catch up on what's been going on in your life. Like finding Birdie dead." She slid Hope a sideways look to go along with the admonishment and made her feel about as small as she could feel.

"I can explain." Hope knew Jane loved a good mystery, but there wasn't a mystery to solve with Birdie's death. Before she could begin giving her explanation, Angela clapped her hands together, and everyone's attention drew toward her.

"Thank you all for volunteering to work on this project. We haven't published a cookbook in years. Our patrons and fellow Jeffersonians have been asking for one." Angela glanced toward Hope. She gave a grateful smile.

"With Hope's guidance, I'm sure we'll be able to produce a fresh, modern cookbook that will raise the funds we need for the renovation of the children's activity room."

"What type of cookbook will it be?" Cleo had her coffee cup close to her lips and then took a drink.

Angela nodded to Hope and gestured for her to answer. Hope was caught off guard.

She thought they'd be reviewing all the jobs and tasks associated with publishing a cookbook. She'd created a list for them to review, from recipe selection to formatting to printing to advertising. All the jobs were detailed, so volunteers could find one that matched their skill set.

"Maybe we should publish our favorite recipes. You know the ones our family and friends always ask us to make. We could call the cookbook *Family and Friends' Favorite Recipes*." Meg smiled, apparently pleased with her suggestion. Content and a title. Wasn't she creative? Hope reigned in her snarky thoughts. They were supposed to be trying to get along. Or, at least, coexist peacefully.

"Perhaps we should use this meeting to discuss options and then vote." Hope pulled out her notepad and pen from her tote.

"Excellent idea," Sally said.

Meg scowled. "Well, my vote is for *Family and Friends' Favorite Recipes*."

"Should we focus on one type of meal, like breakfast and brunch recipes?" Cleo finished her muffin and then wiped her mouth with a paper napkin.

The woman next to Cleo seconded the idea and suggested they focus on potluck recipes because she always needed them.

The woman across from Hope suggested featuring their mother's best recipes. The older woman next to her raised her hand to second the idea.

The discussion began, and Hope did her best to keep track of all the ideas, jotting them down as fast as she could, but stopped midsentence when Jane leaned into her.

"Why didn't you call me right after you found Birdie?" Jane asked.

Hope kept her gaze fixated on her notepad. She adored Jane and knew she had risked her ire by not filling her in ASAP after the incident. But with work, the class at Emily's House, and Ethan's daughters, her cup was overflowing, so she felt like she was drowning at some moments. Before she could answer Jane's question, Casey rushed into the room, muttering apologies. She found an empty seat at the table.

"Casey, we're tossing around ideas for the cookbook. We have a few suggestions. Mine is a family and friends' favorite recipe collection." Meg stood to refill her coffee cup.

"I like it." Casey dug into her hobo bag for her electronic tablet. "It sounds very inviting, something I'd love to cook with."

"So far, we have Meg's suggestion." Hope resisted the urge to give her the stink eye. "We also have a cookbook theme of potluck recipes, a breakfast and brunch collection, and an everything chocolate recipe book."

"Ooh, I like all those too." Casey typed the suggestions.

"Why don't we take a vote?" Meg suggested.

"Hope, do you want to have a vote now, or should we discuss a few more ideas?" Angela must have picked up on the same thing Hope had. Meg was trying to take over the meeting and the fundraiser.

"Let's vote now. Then I will go through what goes into the production of a cookbook. From there, we'll assign some jobs so we can get started and raise some money." Hope looked around the table and saw all heads nod affirmatively.

They voted and the potluck idea was the overwhelming winner, much to Meg's dismay. For the next forty-five minutes, the committee reviewed all the tasks Hope laid out. For each one, she gave a brief overview. There was quite a bit of technical information, and she did her best to keep it from all sounding too complicated. A few times, she noticed a few glazed-over eyes, but mostly everyone seemed enthusiastic about the project. Even Meg. She volunteered to create promotional and sales materials.

"Excellent job," Drew said as he passed Hope on his way out of the meeting room.

"Thanks for staying." Hope packed her tote.

"Like I had a choice?"

"Ha-ha." Hope lifted her tote and slung it over her shoulder.

"Hope, dear, why don't you come by the inn for tea?" Jane suggested as she gathered up her coffee cup and napkins.

"Sounds like she wants to grill you," Drew said.

Jane squinted and shook her head. "No, just a little conversation."

"Well, to be honest, as much as I haven't wanted to talk about what happened, I can't shake a nagging feeling," Hope said.

"What are you saying?" Drew asked.

"It looked like Birdie died from natural causes. But . . . it turns out that Ted left Emily's House and Avery didn't know where he went. And then Erin mentioned something that didn't seem important, and now I'm wondering . . ."

"If he killed his wife," Jane finished the sentence.

A chill swept through Hope. Jane had just said what she'd been thinking but had been hesitant to voice.

"Wait, back up. Ted was missing during the time of his wife's death?" Drew asked. "Are you sure?"

Hope nodded. "I saw him leave the center. And when I called to tell him to come home after finding Birdie, he still wasn't back at the office. Then Avery told me he never returned to the center."

"Interesting." Drew pulled out his phone and typed a note. "I'm going to talk with Avery. You know I've been trying to talk with Maretta since she was, like, besties with Birdie. But she hasn't been available for an interview."

"She seemed upset the other day when I spoke with her," Hope said.

"You spoke with her?" Drew asked.

"I paid my condolences for losing her friend. She told me Birdie's name had been Berta Oliff. I had no idea," Hope said.

Drew grimaced. "No surprise she stuck with a childhood nickname."

"Drew! It's a perfectly suitable name. I had an aunt named Berta, and we called her Bertie. Let's get back to what's important." Jane patted Hope's hand. "Your intuition is telling you that Birdie's death is suspicious. You know, Barbara relied heavily on her instinct."

Hope lowered her eyelids. Jane had a habit of comparing her to Barbara Neal, the co-ed crime solver featured in the five mystery novels Jane had written. After they published the fifth book, Jane retired to raise her family. She still had a knack for rooting out mysteries and enjoyed nothing more than solving a whodunnit with Hope.

"Maybe I'm trying to make sense out of her death." Hope smoothed back a lock of hair that had fallen from her loose ponytail.

"Or you feel guilty for yelling at her the day before," Drew said.

Jane looked sharply at Drew. "Not helping."

"Well, he could be right. Anyway, I'm going to pass on tea this afternoon, Jane. I have a coaching call, and then Ethan is bringing the girls over for dinner." Hope walked toward the door.

"I'm sorry for your troubles. How are the girls doing?" Jane followed, with Drew next to her.

"Okay. It's hard for them to understand what's going on." She and Ethan were trying to figure out how much to tell them about what was happening with their mother. Because they were four and six years old, Ethan didn't think they would understand addiction, and he didn't want them to think their mom was sick, so he told them Heather was at a spa to get some rest.

"What's important is that they feel loved and safe. I have books to return. You may be busy today for tea, but I insist you come by soon." Jane shuffled off to the elevator, joining Cleo and Sally before the door slid shut.

Hope looked around the hall and saw Angela talking with Meg, who no doubt was trying to hijack the committee. She hated not being in charge and hated it even more when Hope was.

"I want to do a little research before I head out. Talk

later?" Drew asked as he broke away, heading for the staircase.

"Sure." Hope glanced at Angela and Meg, who were now on the move and following Drew down the stairs. Footsteps behind her prompted her to look over her shoulder. "Hey, Casey. I love your suggestion about creating recipe cards to promote the cookbook."

Casey blushed. "Thank you. The idea just popped into my head. Sorry if I spoke out of turn, but these days if I don't write it down or say it out loud to someone, I'll forget it. Between the new house and the kids' schedules, it's crazy. Pregnancy brain lasts pretty much until the kids are out of college." She laughed.

"No need to apologize." Hope walked beside Casey toward the staircase.

"I know I'm new, so if this is out of line, forgive me, but I can't help but notice that's there's something between you and Meg. Am I right?"

"Yes. It goes way back to elementary school." Hope had a hard time believing their rivalry continued into adulthood. After all, they were in their thirties; shouldn't they have been long past what happened when they were kids?

"Wow. She holds grudges."

"Meg has a hard time letting go of things. As for me, I'd rather focus on the present." Hope descended the staircase.

"Your present," Casey hooked her fingers into air quotes around the word *present,* "has been a little morbid."

Hope pressed her lips together. Because Casey was new in town, she wasn't fully in the know about Hope's involvement in some previous police investigations. Now wasn't the time to shine a light on that part of her life.

"It was a shock finding Birdie dead."

"Do you think she was murdered?" Casey asked quietly.

"Why would you ask that?"

"I hate gossip, but I've heard she wasn't well liked by many people. I always take that stuff with a grain of salt. Two days before you found her dead, she and Angela had a heated discussion right here on this staircase." Casey pointed to the step.

Hope had a hard time believing what Casey said because Angela always maintained her calm, even with the most challenging patrons. "Do you know what they were talking about?"

"No, I wasn't close enough to hear what they were saying. Their voices were low, but their body language said that they disagreed passionately about something." Casey's cell phone buzzed, and she fished it out of her purse and read the text message. "Geez. My oldest forgot her collage for art class. I have to go home, get it, and then drop it off to her."

"You're such a good mom," Hope said.

Casey's cheeks reddened. "Thanks. I guess I'm trying to be the mom I didn't have."

"I'm so sorry."

"My mom died when I was ten years old. She'd been sad for a while. To this day, I still don't know why." Casey glanced at her phone. "Anyway, I better get going. I'll do a mockup of the recipe card and email it to you."

"Great. Thank you," Hope said.

Casey trotted down the stairs, and Hope's lips twitched.

A part of her wanted to march up to the circulation desk and ask Angela about the incident Casey described. Had she and Birdie really argued library-style? The thought almost made her giggle. Library style. Hushed with dramatic hand gestures. But a woman was dead, so it really wasn't a laughing matter. Even if the two of them had argued, what difference did it make? Most likely, Birdie went too far with her complaints, and Angela had had enough. After all, she was human.

No, what happened between them wasn't any of her business.

Chapter Seven

Hope flicked off the light switch on her way out of the bathroom, and when she reached the bedroom's doorway, her heart squeezed at the sight of Ethan reading in bed.

He looked relaxed propped up against the headboard, lost in an autobiography of a favorite football player. He had come over for dinner with the girls. Molly and Becca had played with Bigelow, and then tagged along with Hope out to the barn. They helped with the evening chores and got to say night-night to Poppy. They loved putting the chickens to bed and giggled when they said it. Now they were tucked into their own beds for the night, and Hope was about to do the same.

Ethan looked up from his book with a wicked grin on his face and waggled his brows. With her hair pulled up in a messy bun and bunny print pajamas the girls loved, she felt far from attractive.

"How are you not exhausted?" Barefoot, Hope padded across the sparsely decorated room. She'd been focusing on the first floor. The plan was to start remodeling the upstairs by summer. What wasn't included in her plan was building a garage and then repairing her house after a fire. Those two things had set her projects back for a while. She lifted a tube of hand cream off the nightstand and squeezed out a dollop. She rubbed the lavender-scented cream into her hands.

"I am exhausted." Ethan closed his book. "A good night's sleep would sure be great."

She understood why he was fatigued. He'd spent a chunk of his day in a hearing for his daughters' temporary full custody while Heather was in rehab. Even though they'd agreed to it, they needed it to be official. In a rare moment of vulnerability, he expressed to Hope that he was worried because you never knew what to expect when dealing with the court system.

"Then that's what we'll do. Sleep." She pulled back the luxurious white comforter and six-hundred-count top sheet. Despite the room being far from finished, she created a cozy sleep haven. From the fluffy down pillows that made her feel like her head was resting on a cloud to the feather bed that molded to her body to the cashmere throw draped at the bottom of the bed, everything gave her the feeling of being pampered while she slept. Indeed, all the bedding was an indulgence. Still, she justified the lofty investment expense because she spent the majority of her day on her feet—recipe testing, photographing food, DIY projects, and gardening.

Plus, she kept a tight rein on her spending in other areas.

Well, except for the Em Bailey candle.

Her gaze drifted from the tub of hand cream to the jar candle on her nightstand. She lit it when she and Ethan retired to the bedroom. The citrus scent wafted through the room, and her guilt for buying it also floated away.

She climbed into bed, and her body sank into the feather bed. When she had first seen the price tag, her eyes had nearly popped out of their sockets. But on nights like tonight, she was glad she had bought it. Ethan wasn't the only one who was bone tired. She arranged her pillows and leaned back. She raised her hand and touched Ethan's chin with the tips of her fingers. He had stubble. It was an unusual look since he prided himself on good grooming, but she kind of liked a more rugged side of him. It was a little sexy.

He covered her hand with his and squeezed. "Thanks for being here for me and the girls."

"There's no place I'd rather be." She pulled her hand back and shimmied against the pillows, finding a comfy spot. Her gaze wandered to the walk-in closet. After purchasing the house, she learned the closet had been a nursery and, at some point, was converted to a basic walk-in closet. While it was big enough for two, it was totally disorganized, and it grated on her every morning she went in there to dress. "I'm thinking about having Erin come over for a consultation on the closet."

"Good idea. It's a nice space but not very functional." Ethan closed his book and set it on the nightstand. He stretched his arm over Hope's shoulder in a familiar and smooth move. Even the tug closer to him was effortless.

She snuggled against him, resting her head on his chest. "This is nice. It's been a heck of a week, hasn't it?"

Ethan made a noise, and she interpreted it as agreement.

"Do you know if Reid has an official cause of death for Birdie?"

She felt his body move slightly, but she remained steady. She was too comfortable to move.

"Hope."

She cringed at his tone. It was the one where he was subtly cautioning her not to get involved. But she wasn't. She was only making conversation.

"What? I'm not the only one who's curious about what caused her death."

"Really? Who else is curious?"

"Well, Erin. Cleo. Lola. Jane. To name a few."

"Jane? Everything is a mystery to her. Some deaths are caused by undetected underlying medical conditions. I've gone on my share of unattended death calls when I was on the force in Hartford. It happens."

"I suppose you're right." She snuggled deeper and inhaled Ethan's clean scent from his body wash. "Do you know where Ted was when he was notified about Birdie's death? He wasn't at his office."

Ethan removed his arm from around Hope, leaving her feeling suddenly chilled. He propped his elbow on the pillows. "How do you know he wasn't at Emily's House?"

"I saw him leave the center when I arrived for the workshop that morning. And remember, I called him after I called 9-1-1? Avery said he wasn't there. It seemed like he took a long time to return home." She'd seen him pull into his driveway thirty minutes after returning home from finding Birdie's body.

"Hope, you're doing it again. You need to let it go."

"I'm only asking a few questions."

"Stay out of it." Ethan pulled back his arms and tugged the sheet up, shifting his body under the covers, resting his head on the pillows.

"What's going on? I'm allowed to be interested. And as I said, I'm not the only one." *So there.* She yanked her covers up to her chin.

"You are the only one who had an argument with her the day before she died, and you found her body." He gave her a sideways glance, and regret flashed in his dark eyes. "I'm sorry, I shouldn't have said that."

"No. Don't be sorry. I'm glad you said it because it's what you've been thinking. I would be a suspect if she didn't die from natural causes?" Heat flushed through her body, and her cheeks burned as her heart rate spiked. "How . . . how can you even . . . ugh." She tossed off her covers and jumped out of bed.

He reached for her, but she was too fast. "Come on, don't be like this."

"Like what? Shocked that my boyfriend would think I was involved in a murder?"

"Hope, you know I'm the chief of police."

"So who was I about to fall asleep with? Jefferson's top cop or my boyfriend? Who? Tell me?"

"Both."

"Actually, neither. I'm going to the guest room tonight."

She spun around and stormed out of the room.

Because the girls were asleep in the next room, she resisted slamming the door. But boy, did she want to.

She crossed the hall to the spare bedroom that wasn't much of a guest room with only a double bed and a nightstand.

Princess appeared in the hall as Hope pushed open the bedroom door. The sleepy white feline meowed as she slinked her body against Hope's leg. She bent down and scooped up the cat. Princess gave an unexpected bump of her nose and a purr. Hope swallowed the lump in her throat, and tears seeped from her eyes. She was becoming undone by a cat.

Hope looked over her shoulder at her bedroom door.

Why hadn't Ethan followed her and said he'd never believe she could hurt anyone no matter how angry she got?

The next morning Hope and Ethan did their best to keep a happy face and enjoy a waffle breakfast with the girls, though the meal was far from enjoyable for Hope. She silently seethed as she ate her waffle. Ethan made no attempt to apologize. Not a whisper in her ear or a gentle brush of her arm accompanied by an apologetic smile. Instead, there was barely any eye contact at all between them.

Pouring her second cup of coffee, she believed it was for the best that they were quiet. Sleeping separately under the same roof felt weird, and she didn't like it. But the time for a conversation about what happened last night wasn't there at the table with Molly and Becca.

The girls were eager to go to their aunt's house for the day. She saw the girls off with hugs and one double chocolate chip cookie each. She even gave a hug and a cookie to Ethan. Her small act of kindness did earn a grateful smile from him, though he still wasn't out of the doghouse. He promised to call later. She let him wait a few seconds before saying she'd answer his call.

After a quick cleanup of the kitchen, she went upstairs to shower. Dressing in shorts and shirt, she called Claire to tell her what happened last night. Like a good sister, Claire was outraged by Ethan's statement and gave Hope kudos for making him sleep alone.

Next on her to-do list was to get some planting done

before Claire arrived for their antiquing day trip. The hour of digging and planting helped work off some steam from last night. Bigelow curled up on the patio for a mid-morning nap while Poppy preened on the lounge chair's back. Neither of them had a care in the world.

The Angel Falls Hosta Cleo gave her was finally set in the flower bed when Claire's Mercedes pulled into the driveway. Hope checked her watch. Her sister was early.

Claire exited her vehicle and closed the door behind her. Dressed in a pair of cropped denim pants, a cardigan twin set, and ballet flats, she looked ready to shop.

"I'm almost done." Hope sprinkled plant food around the hosta's base. "Then I just need to freshen up and change."

"No problem. I finished up with my staging job early, so I thought I'd just come over." Claire stepped closer and inspected the hosta. "Nice. You got this one from Cleo?"

Hope nodded as she backfilled the plant with soil. "She has beautiful plants. It's a shame she had to shut down because of Birdie."

"How did Birdie sleep at night? Picking on someone like Cleo? Her husband died last year, for goodness sake, and she's been trying to pay medical bills and college expenses for her daughter." Claire shook her head and tsked.

Hope looked up. "Beats me. Zara told me yesterday that Birdie cut down her shrub because Zara hadn't gotten to it soon enough."

"What?" Claire shook her head. "It's sad, but I don't think many people will miss her. Maybe only Ted."

"And Maretta. I don't know who her other friends were."

"Well, I can see her and Maretta being BFFs." Claire sat on the portable step stool that Hope had hauled out to the garden. "How was the cookbook meeting?"

Hope leaned back on her heels and pulled off her gloves. "It would have been a lot more pleasant without Meg."

Claire made a face like she'd been offered a plate of white bread and pasta. "She tried to take over? You know she can't help herself. Never could."

"She wastes a lot of energy trying to compete with me. I don't get it. She has a nice life. Why isn't she happy?"

"Who knows? People are complicated. Like relationships."

"Tell me about it. I know Ethan and I have to talk tonight. He's under a lot of pressure right now, so I should cut him some slack." Hope wiped her forehead with the sleeve of her shirt.

"Don't let him off the hook too easily. Remember, he's not dealing with the whole Heather thing all on his own. You're shouldering some burden too."

Hope hoisted the bag of potting soil and set it in the garden cart along with her shovel. She slipped her gloves back on and reached for the cart's handle. Her sister's point was valid, but in the light of a new day, she was thinking she might have overreacted last night. He hadn't come right out and said she was a murder suspect. Or that Birdie had been murdered.

A dark SUV pulled into the driveway, and from where Hope stood, she saw Detective Reid behind the wheel.

"What is he doing here?" Hope let go of the cart and stepped out in front of it.

"What did you do?" Claire asked.

"Nothing! He probably has a few questions to wrap up

the case." She walked around the cart, prompting Bigelow to jump up. He trotted to Hope's side.

Reid exited his vehicle and removed his sunglasses.

His dark eyes were trained on Hope and revealed nothing to her as he approached until Bigelow let out a couple of deep woofs. The pup wasn't a fan of Reid's. The detective grinned. He didn't seem fazed by the fact that the dog wasn't welcoming.

"Good morning, Hope, Mrs. Dixon." Reid pocketed his sunglasses. "I'm sorry to interrupt your planting."

"Is there something I can do for you?" Hope signaled to Bigelow to sit, and she patted his head when he obeyed.

"There is. I have a few more questions about Mrs. Donovan's death," Reid said.

"What more questions could you have? You interviewed my sister the other day." Claire glared at the detective. Claire still held a grudge against him for arresting her for murder months ago.

"Often, more information comes to light, and it requires a follow-up." Reid's voice was flat, and his expression was neutral. Hope imagined he could clean up in a poker game.

"What's the new information?" Claire asked.

"The way it works is that I ask the questions, Mrs. Dixon," Reid said.

Claire bristled. "Then perhaps my sister should have an attorney present."

"No, I don't think it's necessary. I'm happy to help any way I can." Hope appreciated her sister's concern, but she wanted to understand what happened to Birdie. If answering a few more questions would do that, then she was all for it.

"I appreciate your cooperation, Hope," Reid said. "Do you cook with peanut oil?"

Talk about a question coming out of the left field. Why was he interested in which cooking oil she used? "Not really. I think the last time I used it was last summer. I fried chicken for a Fourth of July picnic. Why?"

"We've received lab results, and it appears Mrs. Donovan died from an allergic reaction to peanuts. We found traces of peanut oil in the muffin she'd been eating right before she died. The muffins you baked for her," Reid said.

Hope's mouth fell open as her skin tingled. "No, it's not possible. I baked them with canola oil. Like I always do. Well, unless I bake an olive oil cake."

Claire rushed to her sister's side. "Stop talking."

"This is crazy. I don't bake with peanut oil," Hope said.

"You and the victim had a contentious relationship. You argued with her the day before she was murdered," Reid said.

"Murdered?" Hope's head spun as the word repeated in her head. "I . . . you have to believe . . . ouch!" Hope looked at her arm. Claire had it in a vise grip, and she wasn't letting up.

"Stop talking now!" Claire turned her head and set her sights on Reid. "Are you going to arrest my sister?"

"No," Reid said.

"Then you need to leave, because she's done talking." Claire pulled on Hope's arm and dragged her away from the detective. "Looks like we're not going antiquing today. Come on, Bigelow."

Walking around the side of the house, Hope looked back at Reid in utter disbelief. How could he seriously think she would murder someone?

"I'm innocent, Claire. I can straighten this out," Hope said.

"No. You can't. I'll call Matt Roydon and get him over here."

"Is he in town?" The last time Hope saw the criminal defense attorney was a month ago. He had his law practice in the city and a weekend house in Jefferson. He'd represented Claire when she had been arrested for murder, and now it looked like Hope needed his services.

"Yes. We were planning to get together for brunch tomorrow. Look, from now on, you don't speak to Reid without Matt," Claire said. Her pace was quick, and in her stupor, Hope was having a hard time keeping up.

"I have to call Ethan and tell him what's going on." Hope glanced at Bigelow. He was walking beside her with his tail high and his eyes alert. Meanwhile, Poppy chattered as they passed by to enter the house. Hope recognized the contented sound and wished she shared the same sentiment at the moment.

"What is wrong with that chicken? Shouldn't she be foraging or something?" Claire opened the French door and entered the house. She slipped her phone from her back pocket and tapped on the screen. "Go change your clothes. I'm calling Matt now."

"But . . ."

"But nothing! I will not let Barney Fife railroad you like he tried to do with me when Peaches was murdered."

Hope hugged her sister and then hurried upstairs. She washed up before changing into a denim dress and slipping on tennis sneakers. She did a quick up-do with her hair and returned downstairs. Claire informed her that Matt was on his way over. She also made it a point to tell Hope that he agreed with her decision to end the conversation with Reid. She wouldn't come out and say she was right considering the circumstances, but she wanted to make sure Hope knew.

"Thank you." Normally it grated on Hope when her sibling was right. It didn't matter what the topic or situation was, though this time she was very appreciative of Claire's butting in.

"What are you doing?" Claire sipped her iced tea.

"Baking." Hope gathered the ingredients to bake a batch of chocolate chip scones.

Baking centered her far better than yoga ever had. After paying for pricey lessons, she learned that creating in her kitchen did a far better job at soothing her when she was stressed or overwhelmed by life.

By the time the scones were divided into eight wedges and set in the oven to bake, Matt had arrived, and Claire ushered him into the kitchen and settled him at the table.

Her nerves were on edge, so she kept busy during the meeting by cleaning up the baking area. "I couldn't believe what I was hearing. I would never have put peanut oil in Birdie's muffins."

"But you did know about her allergy?" Matt asked. The ex-cop turned attorney looked like he'd been enjoying a leisurely Saturday before Claire's phone call. Dressed in a pair of jeans and short-sleeved shirt, he was probably puttering around his cottage doing one of the many DIY projects he'd shared with Hope after purchasing the home.

"Only after I delivered the muffins to her."

"You had no prior knowledge of the allergy before then?" Matt took a drink of his coffee.

Hope yanked open an upper cabinet door. "Look, my cooking oils. No peanut oil. Olive oil, canola oil, grapeseed oil, avocado oil. No peanut oil. This is ludicrous."

Matt looked at Claire. "Tell me she didn't let Reid see the cabinet?"

"No, she didn't. I told him if he wasn't here to arrest her, then he needed to leave." Claire dropped a pod into the coffee maker and pressed a button to start the brew cycle.

"With Birdie's death ruled a murder, the police will want to make an arrest." Matt spoke from experience. His last few years on the police force were spent in the homicide division. He knew how the system worked.

"Well, they can't arrest me. I didn't do it." Hope came out from behind the island.

"I think you've been hit on the head too many times because you're suffering from memory loss. Reid arrested me for murder, and I didn't do it." Claire took her cup to the table and sat across from Matt. "Mark my word, he's not your friend."

"Reid knows me. He can't really think I murdered someone. He's probably just ruling me out." Hope was grasping at explanations for Reid's visit, but deep down she knew her sister was right. Sam Reid wasn't her friend. They'd just become friendlier since the first murder case Hope got caught up in, though she'd like to believe he knew she wasn't a murderer.

"When is Ethan going to get here?" Claire asked before she sipped her coffee.

"Soon. He had to pack an overnight bag for the girls. Their aunt is keeping them tonight."

"You spoke to him since Reid left?" Matt leaned back. His caramel-colored eyes looked concerned. "Did he know already?"

Hope chewed on her lower lip. "That Birdie's death was ruled a homicide? Oh . . ." Her words trailed off as their conversation last night came to mind.

"Oh, what?" Matt asked.

"He cautioned me."

"Wait." Matt raised his palm to signal Hope to stop talking. "I'm sorry, Claire, you can't be here for this."

"I'm her sister," Claire protested.

"If you're present, Hope won't have attorney-client privilege."

"I don't need it. I didn't kill Birdie!" Hope threw her hands up in the air.

"Innocent people are entitled to privilege too," Matt said.

"He's right. I'll go into the living room until you two are finished." Claire walked out of the kitchen.

"Now, continue what you were saying about Ethan cautioning you," Matt said.

"Last night, he warned me about being too curious about Birdie's death. He didn't say it was a homicide. Why didn't he tell me that Reid suspected me?"

"He's in a tough spot, Hope." Matt leaned forward, resting his elbows on the table and lacing his fingers together. He steepled his forefingers and stared intently at Hope. "What can you tell me about Birdie?"

Hope shrugged. "Not much. I barely knew her. It wasn't until I visited Maretta to offer my condolences that I learned Birdie's real name was Berta Oliff Donovan. She was from Massachusetts."

Her mind flashed back to the conversation with Maretta,

and she remembered the vague comment about Ethan's position as police chief. If Hope was actually a suspect, of course, there was a chance he could be compromised, and he could be put on leave or worse . . . fired. She gave herself a mental shake. Neither would happen because she would prove her innocence.

"I know she spent hours every day at the library researching a book she was writing and spent more hours in her garden. She also liked to make everyone's life miserable."

Matt lowered his hands. "Tell me more about that."

The oven timer dinged, and Hope dashed to the double wall ovens and removed the baking sheet. She set it on a cooling rack. For a moment, all her worries disappeared as she inhaled the fragrance of the scones. Warm chocolate chips mingled with brown sugar and sweet butter in a moist, crumbly edged wedge of heaven. She called on all her resolve not to pluck one off the cooling rack. In a few minutes, the one in the top right corner was all hers.

Two cups of coffee and a scone later, Matt was all caught up on Hope's relationship with Birdie, the petition, and the havoc Birdie wreaked on a whole slew of people. On his way out, he instructed Hope not to talk to the police, including Ethan, about the case.

Hope felt like she'd been sucker-punched. How could she not talk to Ethan? "I've already told him everything. What difference would it make to continue confiding in him?"

"Ethan is a good man, but he's now in an exceedingly difficult position, and I wouldn't be surprised if the State Police came in to take over the case. I know it's hard, but you have to avoid talking to him about this matter." Matt gave her a hug and then left.

Hope watched him descend the porch steps and then felt her sister's presence behind her.

"I heard what he advised. He's right. Maybe it's best if he doesn't stay here until the investigation is closed. With the girls, it may be would be easier for them not to be jostled back and forth. It's probably confusing for them anyway." She gave Hope a hug before she left.

Hope stood at the front door with Bigelow by her side, mindlessly stroking his head. Her life had been turned upside down in a matter of hours. Suspected of murder, warned to stay away from the man she loved, and alone. A coldness swept through her despite the warm temperature.

Bigelow looked up at her and nudged her with his snout.

She choked back a sob. She hated feeling helpless, vulnerable, and scared. It was a wicked combination, and nothing good ever came out of it. There was no way she'd sit around and wait for Reid to complete his investigation. Nor would she give the State Police time to swoop in and take over the case.

She rubbed Bigelow's chin, and he lapped up the attention. "Reid and Ethan have said in the past, I'm a pretty good sleuth."

Bigelow's head tilted.

"Okay, not in those exact words, but I'm paraphrasing. Since I'm good, there's only one thing for me to do. Find out who killed Birdie."

Chapter Eight

"Eat," Ethan said as he pierced a quartered roasted potato. He'd shown up after Claire left and wasted no time in pulling Hope into a big, comforting hug. When she apologized for their fight last night, he shushed her with a kiss and assured her they were good. He also assured her there was no way he was staying away from her.

"I don't have much of an appetite." She pushed around the serving of potatoes on her plate and considered the slices of steak Ethan had grilled. He had a limited repertoire when it came to cooking—steaks, burgers, ribs.

Ethan reached out with his hand and covered hers. "It's going to be okay."

"I want to believe you." She propped her elbow on the table and rested her chin in her palm. "Is Reid earnest about investigating me?"

Ethan squeezed her hand. "I can't talk about the investigation, babe." He lowered his eyelids, shielding his emotion from Hope. But his dense, luxurious lashes distracted her momentarily. He was born with model-quality lashes, while she had to shell out money for ridiculously priced mascara to get the same look. How fair was that?

"Right." She pulled her hand back and straightened, removing her elbow from the table. "Matt said I shouldn't talk to you about the case either." She picked up her fork and pierced a potato and chewed.

"You need to listen to him." Ethan returned to eating his dinner.

"Since we can't talk about the fact they might arrest me for murder, what do you want to talk about?" She drizzled the horseradish pan sauce she'd prepared over her meat and then sliced off a piece.

"I think you're getting ahead of yourself." Ethan took a drink of his beer.

"I don't agree. But we can't talk about it." She heard the bitterness in her voice and regretted it. Ethan hadn't deserved it. They were both doing their best given the situation.

"There's plenty of other things we can talk about." Ethan's lips turned upward and his eyes warmed. "How's the workshop going at Emily's House? And your friend Erin?"

"Safe topics." Hope chewed her piece of steak and swallowed. "Erin is good. She's busy with work. And the gals in my class are eager to take back control of their lives, and it's inspiring."

"What about your coaching program?" Ethan added a few more slices of steak onto his plate from the platter.

Hope reached for her water. She usually liked a glass of wine with steak but because she had a headache right behind her eyes, she opted for a nonalcoholic beverage. The pain sprouted just after Reid left and bloomed to almost crushing by the time Ethan arrived home. Two aspirins and a warm compress had helped ease the worst of the discomfort.

"It's going well. Annette is really taking my advice." She set her glass down.

"Why wouldn't she? You've built a successful food blog."

"I have. I also had imposter syndrome when I launched the coaching program, but now I see how much I have to offer." She cut off another piece of steak.

"I've seen it all along. Never, ever sell yourself short. You can do anything you set your mind to." Ethan lifted his bottle of beer to his lips.

"Really?"

"Really, babe." He nodded and winked.

"Good. Because I'm going to find out who killed Birdie." She popped the piece of steak in her mouth and chewed while Ethan sat speechless.

The next morning, Hope woke up in an empty bed, and her heart slammed against her chest. Where was Ethan? Had he left without so much as a kiss goodbye? Had her declaration to find Birdie's killer driven him away? Permanently? The thought sucked the air out of her lungs. Then her nose wriggled at a familiar aroma, and the panic subsided. She collapsed onto her pillow and breathed an enormous sigh of relief. Ethan hadn't given up on them; he was down in the kitchen making breakfast. Bacon and eggs. Though she couldn't dawdle too long. Bigelow was a big-time bacon fiend, and there was only half a package left over from earlier in the week, so she had to hustle.

Downstairs, dressed in a pair of torn jeans and a tank top, Hope sidled up to Ethan and wrapped her arms around him. He greeted her with a kiss. Yes, it was the best way to start the day.

A woof interrupted the moment. Hope pulled back and saw Bigelow seated by the stovetop. He was concerned she was hindering the cooking of the bacon.

"Oh, hush, you'll get some," Hope said lightheartedly. It felt good to have a moment of levity.

"I hope you're hungry." Ethan plated the eggs. "The toast will be ready any minute."

Her appetite hadn't fully returned, and her headache still lingered from yesterday. "I think I can eat something."

"Good. Take this to the table and eat." He handed her the plate and then patted her bottom as she walked away with Bigelow trailing her. The multigrain bread slices popped up in the toaster. "I can't stay because I have to pick up the girls before my sister-in-law leaves for work."

Hope had a mouthful of eggs, so she nodded.

"Are you going to be okay?" Ethan buttered the toast and then set it along with the bacon slices on a plate he carried to the table.

"Yes. I have to feed the chickens—"

"Already taken care of." Ethan swiped a piece of bacon and bit into it.

"Thank you." She surveyed the plate, and then glanced up at Ethan and thanked her lucky stars that he'd come back into her life. What other man would have done all this without being asked to?

"You need to eat something."

"I will."

"I'm going to take the girls to the diner for breakfast." He glanced at his watch. "Gotta go. I'll call you later." He patted Bigelow on the head, gave Hope a quick kiss, and then hurried out of the kitchen.

Bigelow quickly turned his attention back to Hope. His disappointment at not getting a piece of bacon from Ethan was obvious in his sad brown eyes.

"I shouldn't, but only this one time." She broke off a piece of bacon and fed it to Bigelow. He acted like he'd won the lottery. His eyes widened, his tail perked up, and he gobbled the piece so fast Hope barely had time to wipe her fingers before he was looking for another piece.

"Sorry, little guy. That's all you get." It was hard to ignore her pouting pup, but Hope powered through and finished her breakfast. After she set her dishes in the dishwasher, she headed outside with Bigelow to finish planting her flowers.

Reid's visit yesterday had interrupted her gardening, and afterward she'd had little energy to finish the chore. She hoped being outside in the fresh air and sunshine would reap her some sort of holistic benefit. So far, it had. Her mood brightened as she removed the annuals out of their flats and positioned them in the holes she had dug. Digging in New England soil was always a challenge. There were rocks—big, small, flat, heavy—everywhere.

A playful bark broke her concentration, and her gaze traveled to the patio. There Bigelow was busy batting around a toy. Earlier, he'd tried to dig his own hole in the garden bed, and Hope had to distract him. Luckily, she found the squeak toy. In some ways, it was a bribe, but since it kept the dog out of her garden, she was okay with it.

Poppy was perched on the lounge chair again while the rest of the chickens grazed along the property line. Their loud chatter was comforting to her. Given what happened yesterday, she'd take all the comfort she could get.

Satisfied with the location of the flowers, she backfilled the holes. Two more flats of annuals were waiting to be planted before she could call it a wrap. She looked at Bigelow again.

Would the toy keep him occupied long enough for her to finish the job?

She hoped so and continued digging holes, sprinkling in plant food, and working until all the annuals were firmly planted and doused with water.

Tugging on the hose to move along the curved garden bed beneath a maple tree, she heard her name called from the road. She looked over her shoulder. Mitzi Madison was approaching.

Dressed in yellow capris and a white T-shirt, the energetic senior citizen looked refreshed and ready for a walk.

Bigelow discarded his toy to visit with Mitzi. He trotted toward her, meeting her halfway.

"You're becoming quite the gardener, Hope. This area is looking good." Mitzi stopped to pet Bigelow and then continued walking to the shade garden with him beside her. When she reached the border, she placed her hands on her hips and scrutinized the area. Hope braced herself for a constructive critique. "Nice hosta. Superb choice with these annuals. They'll do great in the shade."

Hope wiped her brow with the back of her hand. "I'm finding gardening to be very therapeutic."

Bigelow dropped down to the ground and rested his head on his front paws. He looked tuckered out She'd read that pets could pick up on their owner's energy. She wondered if he sensed her distress over Reid's visit yesterday.

"Ahh, I know the feeling. How do you think I survived our daughter's teen years?"

Hope laughed. "Really?"

"It was also about the same time Gilbert took up woodworking." Mitzi dropped her hands and knelt in the garden bed. She picked up a begonia and gingerly removed it from the container. "You'll need a good, thick layer of mulch."

"On my list to buy." Even though Mitzi had shifted her gaze to the flower, Hope had noticed the worried look in the older woman's eyes. Unlike some other neighbors, she wasn't one to pry. Mitzi had known Hope since she was a baby. Any curiosity on her part came from a place of concern. "You saw Detective Reid here yesterday, didn't you?"

"I did. Is everything okay?" Mitzi picked up a spade and plunged it into the soil. She scooped out a few inches of dirt.

Hope heaved a sigh. "He had a few questions about Birdie."

"I'm guessing the questions weren't pleasant."

"You'd be right. It turns out Birdie was poisoned."

Mitzi looked puzzled. "They're certain? How?"

"She was eating one of the muffins I baked when she died." Hope sprinkled plant food into the hole Mitzi finished digging. If they weren't talking about Birdie's death, gardening with her neighbor would have been enjoyable.

"He can't think you poisoned Birdie? That's ridiculous." Mitzi set the begonia into the ground. Despite having arthritis, she worked with ease, backfilling the dirt and firmly placing the plant. She said once she wouldn't let the condition rob her of what she loved most, besides her family, in the world. "Birdie was a difficult person to warm up to. We chatted a few times about flowers and shared tips, though she seemed hesitant to share. Which is kind of odd for a gardener. We love sharing what we know."

"I'm not surprised to hear she was stingy with information. I can't figure out why she went out of her way to make people's lives difficult. Have you heard what she did to Cleo Sloane?" Hope knocked another begonia out of its container and loosened its roots.

"I did, and I heard yesterday Timmy's Garden Supply will be selling her plants on consignment. It looks like everything has turned around for Cleo, and she'll get the extra cash she needs."

Hope's head lifted at the comment. Mitzi was right. Cleo's fortunes seemed to have turned around now that Birdie was dead.

"Though the same can't be said for all Birdie's other unsuspecting targets," Mitzi continued. "Like Zara. She's still seething after her shrub was cut down, and the poor thing doesn't look like it's bouncing back."

Hope cut off her train of thought about Cleo and Birdie to focus on Zara. "She told me about what happened. I can't imagine coming home and finding any of my shrubs cut down to the nub."

Hope patted down the soil around the seedling. She was almost done and expected to be finished by lunch.

By the rumble in her stomach, it appeared her appetite was returning.

"She was furious. I was out tending to my rhododendrons when I saw Zara's reaction. Boy, oh, boy, it was a doozy. She marched next door and banged on the front door. When Birdie came out, they got into a shouting match. It escalated into a shoving match. Zara almost knocked Birdie to the ground."

Hope lowered her spade. Zara had omitted that part of the story when she told Hope about Birdie's trespassing and cutting down the shrub. She couldn't help but wonder how angry Zara really was with her neighbor.

Angry enough to kill her?

Monday morning rolled around, finding Hope with pent-up energy to track down Birdie's killer. But first, there was a list of domestic duties she needed to tend to before she could don her Super Sleuth cape.

Task number one was feeding the chickens and collecting their eggs. Even though she was in a hurry to head out for the day, she forced herself to slow down in the barn. It was important not to rush through the morning routine.

As she tipped the feed bucket over the feeder, her girls, as she liked to call the hens, scrambled to get their spot for breakfast. Feathery bodies brushed her legs, and loud clucks filled the barn. She giggled. She'd been grateful for Iva's help over the past few months, but she missed this morning ritual.

She returned the bucket to the table and removed her gloves. Leaning back against the workstation Ethan had built from scraps of wood, she looked at each hen. This was the perfect time to check to see if any ailments were starting to form. They all had bright eyes, smooth feathers, and no physical issues. Satisfied the hens were in good shape, she pushed off the table and completed the rest of the chores. Starting with cleaning up droppings, she moved onto freshening the nest boxes and finally opening the door to the outer enclosed pen. Then she opened the exterior enclosure to allow the chickens to free-range for the day.

She entered her house with a basket of eggs and an eager Bigelow, who needed his morning walk. Once he was taken care of, up next was a quick run and even faster shower. A check of her watch told her she was barely staying on schedule. If she didn't hurry, she would keep Jane waiting.

When Hope arrived at the Merrifield Inn, Jane swept her into the parlor off the impressive Victorian home's entry hall. Unlike their last encounter at the library, Jane was all smiles. She had on her pink lipstick and pearl stud earrings. Her wispy bangs and floral wrap dress added an aura of youthfulness.

"We mustn't waste any time," Jane said.

The night before, Hope called Drew and Jane to arrange a meeting. If she was going to solve Birdie's murder, she needed help.

Drew's superior research skills and access to records Hope would struggle to navigate made his assistance vital. Jane's innate sense of observation of people and their actions made her help indispensable.

Without hesitation, both said yes, and they agreed on a time and place.

For their meeting, Jane set out a tray of blueberry muffins and tea on the coffee table. Hope eyed the teapot and wondered if it was chamomile, a favorite of Jane's. She believed it was the cure-all for everything.

Drew was already there and seated on the sofa, facing the bank of French doors that led to the narrow patio where the inn's guests enjoyed their breakfasts. He twisted around and waved instead of saying "good morning" because he was finishing a bite of muffin.

"I appreciate you both agreeing to help me." Hope slipped her tote off her shoulder and sat next to Drew. From the tote, she pulled out her composition notebook and a pen.

When she'd been a member of Jane's mystery book club, she used a similar notebook to jot observations about the story she was reading. By keeping meticulous notes, she often solved the mystery before any of her fellow book club members.

Now she was using the same technique to solve a real-life mystery.

Drew gave a pointed look at the black and white notebook. "You are serious about doing this, aren't you?"

"Darn right she is." With a cup of tea, Jane settled on an armchair across from Hope and Drew. "All right, let's begin. Unfortunately, because of Birdie's disagreeable personality, she had many enemies. Of course, not all of them would resort to murder. It's our job to figure out which one did."

Easier said than done.

Hope sighed. Jane was right. Birdie had had many enemies. It seemed she thrived on the controversy. How would they narrow down who was the murderer? She leaned forward and poured a cup of tea. She was pleased to find it was black tea.

"I've started digging into Birdie's past. You never know, maybe something from way back when returned and . . . well, you know what they say about karma." Drew broke off a piece of muffin and popped it in his mouth.

"Good thinking! It's likely she was just as disagreeable back then as she was now." Jane leaned back and crossed her legs.

"Last night I filled you both in on what additional information I learned about Zara and Birdie's dispute." Hope sipped her tea and considered a muffin. She shouldn't, but Jane was an excellent baker. Besides, it would be rude not to eat at least one. She reached for a muffin. She pulled back the liner paper and took a bite. It was delicious, as she expected.

Jane smiled with delight seeing Hope enjoying the muffin. She was the resident baker at the inn, though there was a cook to help with the breakfast service. The baked goods she whipped up were family recipes handed down through several generations of Merrifields.

"Mitzi saw Zara push Birdie?" Jane asked.

Hope nodded as she finished her bite. "Yes. But when Zara told me about the incident, she left that part out." She set her plate back on the table and then jotted down in her notebook, *Zara had a heated, physical altercation with Birdie.*

Jane raised her hand. "There's also Cleo."

"I found the complaint Birdie filed against Cleo with the town. She made it sound like Cleo opened a full-blown nursery on her property." Drew ate the last bite of his muffin.

Hope wrote in her notebook. *Cleo forced to close*

flower stand and lose income needed to pay daughter's college bills.

"Oh, Casey told me after the cookbook meeting at the library that she saw Birdie arguing with Angela." After finishing her muffin, Hope wiped her hands on a napkin. She would have a hard time stopping at just one.

Jane sputtered her tea. "I don't think I've ever seen Angela argue."

"Right? She's always as cool as a cucumber." Drew reached forward and grabbed another muffin, earning him a glare from Hope. She'd have to run three miles after their meeting if she had seconds. It wasn't fair.

"But Casey was adamant. She said their voices were low, but their body language left no doubt it was an argument."

"What argument?" Sally entered the parlor carrying a tray of breakfast baked goods intended for the inn's guests out on the patio. Dressed in dark jeans and a lavender striped shirt, her gray hair was sleekly styled. Her usual waves were straightened, and her hair color had a sheen to it.

Hope and Drew looked at each other. Sally didn't approve of their amateur sleuthing, and no doubt would lecture the three of them about its dangers.

"Angela. Did you know she had argued with Birdie before she was murdered?" Jane asked.

Hope's mouth dropped open, and she looked at Jane, whose blue eyes twinkled with mischief. She liked to push the envelope with her sister-in-law.

"Murdered? What are you talking about?" Sally set the tray on the card table. The parlor was set up for multiple conversation groups to encourage guests to socialize. "Who said she was murdered?"

"Detective Reid," Drew said. "Birdie died from an allergic reaction, and they found peanut oil in the muffin she'd been eating."

"Did Angela bake the muffins?" Sally asked.

"No. Hope did." Jane's pink lips set in a grim line.

Sally's gaze narrowed on Hope. "What have you gotten yourself into now?"

Hope shrugged. She didn't know where to start.

"Don't tell me the three of you are playing detective again? Trust me, only trouble will come out of this." Sally propped her hand on her hip. Her frame was lean thanks to her hours of gardening and housekeeping duties. She was of the mindset that if you want it done right, do it yourself. That meant she didn't rely on the housekeeping crew too much. "You're already suspecting Angela? Angela, of all people! Who is next? Me?"

Drew cocked his head to the side. "Well . . . you have had a few run-ins with Birdie."

"Drew! My sister-in-law didn't murder anyone," Jane scolded. She and Sally had been as close as sisters since Jane married into the Merrifield family decades ago. When Jane's husband died, they sold their respective homes and moved into the inn to manage it full-time with the help of their staff.

"Thank you, Jane. However, I'm capable of defending myself."

Sally sat in the armchair next to her sister-in-law's.

"Birdie and I indeed butted heads a couple of times. First, it was over the garden at the library. She wanted to take over the project, and there was no way I would let it happen. The fundraising was under control, and the patrons volunteered to do the planting. Her assistance wasn't needed."

"It's a beautiful garden," Drew added in quickly. Hope guessed he was trying to lessen his suspicion of her only moments ago.

Sally gave him a side glance. Clearly, she hadn't missed his attempt to suck up. "It is beautiful. The only other time we had a disagreement was when she wanted the Garden Club to revamp our Main Street program."

Hope inched to the edge of her seat. She hadn't heard about the incident Sally was talking about. The Jefferson Garden Club was responsible for the planters along a stretch of Main Street. Each season plantings were changed out, and during the holidays wreaths and swags were added for a festive look. A lot of time and effort went into the program. When Sally had been the club president, she'd spent hours preparing and executing all the details.

Leave it to Birdie to want to swoop in and change everything.

"What happened?" In her notebook, Hope wrote *Sally and Birdie had two disagreements. Library garden and Main Street plantings.* Then she gave herself a mental shake. How could she even consider for a second that Sally could have poisoned Birdie? Of course, she wasn't the killer, but maybe Sally knew something because of those two incidents. Maybe there was a library patron upset at Birdie trying to hijack the garden. Or perhaps a member of the Garden Club was upset by Birdie making decisions on her own. Okay, she felt a tad better about what she wrote.

"Birdie felt the plantings the club did were stale, and she wanted to expand out to some side streets. I wasn't opposed to the idea. What I was opposed to was her decision to go ahead without a proper vote. Our discussion turned into an argument, and she stormed off. By the following week, she'd resigned from the club," Sally said.

"Just for the record and to rule you out, where were you the morning Birdie died?" Drew polished off the last of his second muffin and refilled his teacup.

Sally flattened her palms on her lap and squared her shoulders. She didn't look pleased with Drew's question. "Are you asking me for an alibi?"

"He is," Jane said. "If I recall correctly, you left before breakfast service. You mentioned something about an errand."

"I don't believe this. The three of you are meddling into official police business, and like before, you'll wind up with nothing but trouble." Sally stood.

"Well, we can't sit by and do nothing. Hope needs our help. Of course we don't suspect you, but everyone needs to be questioned about Birdie's murder. You may know something you're not aware of." Jane's voice was soothing. Hope sensed that after fifty years, Jane knew how to handle her sister-in-law.

"I'll have no part of this amateur hour. And I strongly suggest the three of you mind your own business." Sally stood and marched to the table, lifted the tray, and exited one of the French doors to the patio.

"I'm sorry we upset her." Hope lowered her pen.

Jane waved away the apology. "She'll be fine. But I sense she's hiding something."

"Who's hiding something?"

Hope and Drew looked over their shoulders and their eyes widened at their unexpected visitor. What on earth was she doing there?

Chapter Nine

"Claire?" Hope and Drew said at the same time. Then they glanced at each other with an unspoken question: What was she doing there? Hope would bet Claire was there to do the same thing Sally had just done—lecture on why sticking her nose into a murder investigation was an awful idea.

"Dear, glad you've dropped by." Jane gestured to the chair Sally had just vacated. "Come, sit over here."

"What are you doing here?" Hope finally asked out loud.

"She's gonna shut this down," Drew whispered to Hope.

"No, I'm not." The delicate ruffles of Claire's dress sleeves flittered as she walked to the chair. When she sat, the hem of her dress grazed her knees. She set her sleek leather satchel beside her feet.

"You're not?" Hope, Drew, and Jane asked together. It was becoming a thing.

Claire's perfectly arched brows pulled together. "Don't be too surprised. Hope's my sister, and there's no way I'm going to let Reid railroad her like he tried to do with me."

Hope's hand covered her heart. Through thick and thin, they were always there for each other. Claire had helped her get back on her feet after her divorce and her very public loss on *The Sweet Taste of Success.* Appearing on the baking competition show had been a spontaneous decision, and she was crushed when she lost. Now, Claire would be there to keep her from being arrested for murder. She had the best sister.

Drew nudged Hope's shoulder with his and gave her a lovey smile. She knew he was thinking the same thing.

"There's no time for mushiness." Claire helped herself to a cup of tea. "Who were you talking about when I came in?"

"Sally," Jane said.

"You think she's the killer? Sure, she's a tough old bird, but she's not a murderer." Claire sipped her tea.

"She's not a serious suspect. But you never know what someone knows." Hope blinked. Did what she just said make sense? "You know what I mean. Someone we have to consider is Ted." Hope scrawled his name in her notebook.

"Ah, yes. The husband." Jane gave a knowing nod. "They always think they're so clever."

"Does anyone know if they were having problems?" Claire asked.

"Every marriage has problems," Drew said. "We just have to find out if the problem was big enough to only be solved by murder."

Claire gasped. She clearly was a newbie at sleuthing.

"Ted left Emily's House the morning Birdie was

killed. We need to find out the time of death." Hope jotted down a note about Ted's mysterious outing. "His assistant, Avery, didn't know where he was off to. She said it was unusual. Come to think of it, she acted a little weird when I told her he'd left. And then there's the passport." Hope wrote those things down as she explained about the passport. "According to Avery, Ted isn't planning any travel."

"Just because he had his passport out doesn't mean he's traveling," Claire said.

Drew looked at Hope and raised his hand to cover his mouth and whispered, "We have so much to teach her."

"I can hear you!" Claire pursed her lips. "This all sounds like conjecture."

"Like we're throwing spaghetti to the wall to see what sticks?" Jane asked.

Claire nodded. "Exactly."

"Welcome to detective work." Hope closed her notebook. "It's not pretty. It's messy. We follow what leads or clues we have. Right now, we need to find out where Ted was the morning his wife died."

"Well, maybe I can help with that," Claire offered.

"How?" Hope, Drew, and Jane said in unison. Yes, it was becoming a thing.

"I regularly play tennis with Robin Delaney. Her husband is on Emily House's Board of Directors and is good friends with Ted. Let me see what I can find out. Besides, we're due for a tennis match." Claire shimmied her shoulders, obviously proud of herself for coming up with a plan.

Jane rose from her seat and beamed at Claire. "Sounds perfect. Make sure you meet up with her ASAP. We don't have time to waste. We're already days behind the police investigation." Jane looked at Drew. "You'll confirm the time of death and continue to dig into Birdie's past. Hope, since you have access to Emily's House, poke around there."

"I'll go over today. First, I'm going to talk to Angela about her argument with Birdie." Hope dropped her note-book and pen into her tote and then stood.

Jane turned her head toward the French doors. "I'm going to find out where Sally was that morning."

"We don't believe she's the killer." You just knew some things in your bones, and Hope knew Sally wasn't a killer no matter how hard Birdie may have pushed her buttons.

"No, she's not. But she is hiding something, and I intend to find out what it is. Well, I need to get back to work. Let's keep each other updated." Jane ambled out of the room.

Claire and Drew both stood and joined Hope by the card table.

"We have a splendid start. So let's try to wrap this murder up before I'm read my rights." Hope linked arms with her sister. "You know, we probably shouldn't mention this to Matt."

Claire pulled back. "You think I'd tell him about this? You know how he felt about your meddling into my case when I was suspected of murdering Peaches McCoy."

"Do I." The memory of Matt's reaction was seared into her brain. Along with the humiliating memory of her thinking he was interested in her. She hadn't known he'd just broken up with his boyfriend and wasn't looking for a new relationship.

"What about Ethan?" Drew slung his messenger bag over his body and linked arms with Hope on the other side. "Does he know what you're doing? What we're doing?"

"He does. I told him last night." Hope felt a powerfulness in not hiding her sleuthing. She wasn't going to be concerned about staying under the radar like her previous forays into investigating. Ethan knew, and if Matt found out, so be it. This was her freedom in jeopardy. She had no intention of sitting on the sidelines waiting to be cleared.

"What did he say?" Claire asked.

"What could he say? We're not allowed to discuss the case." Hope broke free and swaggered out of the parlor. Yeah, she was feeling a whole new sense of independence. Plus, knowing her sister's and best friend's eyes were on her, she embraced the swagger until she tripped and tumbled forward. Quickly she regained her balance and kept from landing on her face. She cleared her throat. Maybe she'd embraced the swagger too much. "I'm okay!"

By the time Hope reached the Jefferson Library, she'd shaken off her embarrassing stumble and was ready to question Angela about the scene Casey witnessed. In the past, she'd try to coyly raise the subject so as not to let on she was sticking her nose where it didn't belong. But not this time.

Inside the lobby, Hope shivered. The thin cardigan she wore did nothing to stave off the cold from the building's air conditioner. Then again, was it really the cooling system causing the chills? She settled the uncomfortable thoughts rolling around in her mind. Since last winter, entering the library had become complicated. Once, it used to feel like a sanctuary; she could get lost in stories in the familiar place. Now, it was the place where she was almost murdered. She squeezed her eyes shut as the scene flashed in her mind.

Her and a killer alone.

She opened her eyes and let out a breath. She'd survived the encounter, and now it was finally time to put the incident behind her. The library was too special a place for her not to enjoy visiting. But she'd take it one step at a time. The library cookbook fundraiser was a big help in getting her back there regularly.

She stepped toward the primary room's doorway. She scanned the space and spotted Angela at the circulation desk. The pink cardigan she wore over a white blouse also added a brightness to her face. She favored layering in the old building because the temperature was forever fluctuating.

Hope walked across the room and noticed a few looks from the early morning patrons seated at the sturdy wooden tables. At first, she didn't think much of it. She was used to being recognized, especially in a town where she was considered a celebrity. Though she considered another reason for the curious stares. Word was spreading—she was a person of interest in a murder.

"Good morning, Hope. What brings you by?" Angela moved a stack of books to the side and leaned her forearms on the countertop.

"I'd like to talk to you about Birdie." Hope stepped closer and rested her clasped hands on the counter.

Angela's lips eased into a neutral smile, and she blinked. "It's still a shock. I can't believe she's dead. I also can't believe you found her. What a horrible experience it must have been for you." She reached out and touched Hope's hand.

"I'm okay, thanks. However, I agree it's a shock." She pulled back her hand. It didn't feel right to have Angela comfort her while questioning her about Birdie's death. Maybe Hope shouldn't be questioning her at all. There was no way the calm, level-headed librarian could be a murderer. Then again, she expected Reid would have thought the same about her. Turns out, she was wrong. "Have you heard she was murdered? Poisoned?"

Shock crossed Angela's face, leaving her speechless. She leaned back and appeared to be processing the information.

"This is news to me. I can't believe someone poisoned her. Do the police know who did it?" So she hadn't heard yet.

Well, they think I did it.

"The police are investigating." At least for the moment, Hope left out the fact the police considered her a suspect. "It's no secret Birdie had burned a lot of bridges over the years."

"No, it's not. Though I can't believe someone would be angry enough to kill her. Then again, people are capable of many unpleasant things."

"Right now, we don't know what the motive was. It could have been anything."

"Why are you interested in this? As you said, the police are investigating. Surely they'll speak to anyone they believe would have information about the matter."

Matter? A polite way to talk about the gruesome crime. Birdie's death wasn't peaceful, it was cruel. The one time Hope had witnessed an allergic reaction, it scared her right down to her toes. It was a co-worker at *Meals in Minutes*, the magazine she was editor of until she left to appear on *The Sweet Taste of Success*. The seconds it took to retrieve her co-worker's epi-pen were the longest moments of her life. The thought of Birdie dying alone on her gazebo sent a chill down Hope's body.

"Two days before Birdie died, someone saw you having a heated discussion with her on the staircase. What were you two talking about?"

Angela shook her head. "I'm not going to get involved in your amateur sleuthing."

"You're not denying the altercation."

"It wasn't an altercation." A flush crept across Angela's cheeks. Hope guessed the mild-mannered librarian regretted the encounter and was embarrassed someone witnessed it. "My goodness, you sound like Jane right now. Fine. The truth is, I'm not proud of the argument. I promise you, it was only an argument."

"I believe you, Angela. I'm sorry that I characterized it the way I did."

Angela gave a nod at Hope's apology.

"Could you tell me what you both argued about?"

"Birdie complained all the time about the distractions here. It was nonstop until she found peace in the Rare Books room. But it was short-lived. A new reading group started, and they were in the room to select a book they wanted to discuss at their bimonthly meeting. Their focus is the classics. It turned out they were too loud for Birdie's liking, and she tracked me down that day to complain."

"She didn't like your answer, did she?"

"No. It's impossible for me to police everyone. Besides, they weren't loud, and they have a right to use the room. I suggested to Birdie she consider doing her reading and research at her home where it's quiet. Most of the books she used can be loaned out."

"She didn't like your suggestion?"

Angela arched a brow. "What do you think? To be honest, I'd gotten to the end of my rope with her demands. But I'd never resort to killing her."

"I know you wouldn't. Do you know if she had any words with a member of the reading group? Perhaps she complained to them before she approached you?"

Angela thought for a moment. "She didn't say, and no one from the book club came to me about her. Check with the group leader, Meg Griffin."

Hope frowned. Of course the book club leader would be Meg. "I will ask her. Thank you for helping me."

"Helping you?" Angela's head cocked sideways.

"It appears I'm a suspect in Birdie's murder. They found the poison in a muffin she was eating, and the day before, I gave her the muffins as a peace offering."

"Oh, no. It's crazy to think you could murder someone. Is it Detective Reid's case? He should know better. Well, whatever you need, let me know."

It was nice to hear Angela wouldn't hold Hope's interrogation against her. "I appreciate the offer." Hope turned to leave but stopped as she remembered the books scattered on Birdie's kitchen table. Something nagged at her about them. She couldn't recall their titles, but she was sure they weren't all garden-related books. She could swear they were business books. She pivoted and looked back at Angela. "There is something you could help me with. Could you tell me about the books Birdie took out the day before she died?"

"Sure." Angela moved over to the computer keyboard

and typed. She stared at the computer screen. "She took out three books on corporate fraud. All the other books she's taken out were about horticulture."

"Why was Birdie interested in that topic?" Hope asked.

Angela shrugged. "I have no idea. She wasn't much of a sharer."

"Hello, ladies." Sally approached the circulation desk. "It's another beautiful day. I'm surprised you're not home working in your garden today, Hope."

Hope knew darn well Sally was far from surprised about seeing her there. Sally was a smart woman and could figure out Hope was following up on a lead about Birdie's murder based on what happened at the inn earlier.

"It turns out Birdie . . ." Hope's words trailed off as Angela gestured to the entrance. She looked over her shoulder and saw Reid standing there with his sights set on the three of them. What was he doing there? Had Casey told him about Angela's argument with Birdie? Maybe someone else had?

"What is the detective doing here?" Sally asked, turning back to Hope and Angela.

"We're about to find out." Hope was glad she'd gotten to talk to Angela before Reid arrived because she expected he would suggest she leave.

"Good morning, ladies." Reid arrived at the counter. He looked relaxed yet alert, as if eyeing every nook and cranny for the unexpected and every facial expression for a weak point. He pushed back his navy blazer with his hands as he slipped them into his pants pockets, revealing his badge. Hope guessed he wanted to indicate that he was there for official business.

"Good morning, Detective. Is there something I can help you with?" Angela asked. Her coolness impressed Hope. If she was worried she was about to be questioned about Birdie's death, she didn't appear so.

"I'm actually here to speak with Ms. Merrifield." Reid's smile was pleasant and disarming. Hope recognized it right away. He was there to question Sally about Birdie's death. Had he really believed that Sally murdered someone over a dispute about flower planters on Main Street or over a library garden? After a moment, she realized people have killed for less.

"Whatever for?" Sally gaped at the detective and then she looked at Hope. She was visibly miffed. "First Drew and now this?"

"Is there somewhere private we can talk?" Reid asked, looking at Angela.

"Yes. Of course. Please use my office." She pointed toward the doorway with the sign "Staff Only" over it. "Sally can show you the way."

"Not until I know why you want to talk to me." Sally squared her shoulders and lifted her chin. She was a strong, opinionated woman who wouldn't be pushed around by anyone. Not even a police detective.

"Why don't we discuss this in private, Ms. Merrifield?" Reid's tone shifted from amiable to firm.

Sally raised her forefinger and waggled it. "I don't think so, Detective. I know Birdie was murdered, and I assure you I did not poison her."

"You're aware of the cause of death?" Reid's gaze landed on Hope, hard. So hard, Hope cringed. He hadn't told her it was a secret. Surely with the highly active gossip mill in Jefferson, the cause of death, including the exact poison, would be public knowledge in no time.

"I know my rights, and if you want to question me, you'll have to do it with my attorney present." Sally turned and walked away toward the Staff Only room. Reid kept his gaze on Sally until she rounded the corner and disappeared.

"You thought this would be easy?" Hope quipped, earning her another glare from the detective. It was time to make herself scarce. "I-I should be going." She stepped back from the desk.

Reid angled and propped a hand on his hip. "I'm curious, what brought you into the library this morning?"

"Ah . . . the fundraiser cookbook. I'm chairing the committee. It's a tremendous amount of work, but it's for a worthwhile cause. Right, Angela?" Hope asked, praying Angela would go along.

"Absolutely. In fact, we're looking for recipes. Perhaps you and your wife would like to contribute one, Detective Reid," Angela said.

Reid looked as if he was considering the offer. "I'll mention it to my wife. I'm sure you have a lot to do today, so don't let me keep you, Hope."

His dismissal of her wasn't very subtle, and she expected he hadn't meant it to be. She murmured a goodbye before hurrying out of the library.

Outside in the bright morning sun, she descended the front steps of the library. It seemed like a lifetime ago she was there confronting Birdie, yet it had only been a few days. In hindsight, it was a bad decision. A very bad decision. If she could, Hope would go back and change it. After learning about the petition, she'd do the sensible thing—go home, eat ice cream, and grumble to Bigelow about Birdie's gall.

Why hadn't she done the smart, sensible thing?

Coming off the last step, she continued along the concrete path to the sidewalk. A lot of things had gone wrong since learning about the petition, but there had been one bright spot. Somehow she'd managed not to have to deal with one pesky reporter in particular. But it looked like her luck had run out.

"Just the person I was looking for." Norrie Jennings hustled from the sidewalk toward Hope.

Slim, pretty, and ruthless. The young reporter was not above sensationalizing a story to advance her career. She'd done it a few times to Hope. The most egregious was when she insinuated Hope had a romantic relationship with a person of interest in the disappearance of Lily Barnhart. Those untrue statements were picked up by other media outlets, and they also caused a problem between her and Ethan. Hope hated holding grudges, but this was one she was having a hard time letting go of.

Hope inwardly sighed as she came to a halt. "Need a recipe?"

Norrie flashed a toothy smile. Wearing a chambray shirt tucked into white cropped jeans and a small red bag slung across her body, she looked relaxed, like she was heading into the library to spend the day researching. Hope knew better.

"I need an interview." Norrie raised her palm. "Before you go all, *Drew is my best buddy ever, so I only give him interviews,* hear me out."

Against her better judgment, Hope agreed to listen to Norrie. It wouldn't be fair to shut her down without hearing what she had to say.

Then again, the reporter was rarely fair to her. Though there was the one time when she did give Hope a heads up about a murder victim's widow.

"Fine. Go ahead." Hope would listen with a healthy dose of skepticism.

"I want to do a human-interest story." Norrie's amber eyes sparkled. "On you!"

"Me? What exactly are you thinking?" That healthy dose of skepticism Hope had increased up to a mega dose.

"What it's like to go from a successful career woman, which you were at the magazine—"

Hope nodded. Norrie was correct.

"To reality show loser. For what it's worth, I think you should have won."

Hope nodded. She agreed with Norrie.

"Then, to a successful blogger who is now coaching other bloggers. Way to give back."

Hope nodded again. It felt good to help other women.

"To murder suspect at risk of losing everything you've worked for."

Hope started to nod until she processed what Norrie just said. "Wait . . . what? Risk of losing everything I've worked for?"

"Too dramatic? See, I don't think so. Let's face it, you're an online entrepreneur, and your image is everything. Being suspected of killing someone isn't going to make sponsors happy. Your fans? Do you really think they'll trust your muffin recipes from now on?"

Hope opened her mouth to respond but closed it quickly. She forced herself to silently count to ten before she said anything. If nothing else over the past few days, she had learned her lesson about making scenes in public spaces. Her head throbbed and her heart rate spiked, and she still didn't trust herself to say anything. She counted to twenty. Then to thirty.

"For the record, I'm innocent." Hope kept a leveled but firm tone. "I believe my sponsors respect me and benefit greatly from working with me. I believe my fans are loyal and understanding. And, yes, I believe they trust *all* of my recipes."

She stomped past Norrie and headed for the parking lot behind the building. What on earth possessed Norrie to propose such an idea for an article? Hope's mouth went dry, and a bubble of foreboding settled in her. Did Norrie know something she didn't?

Hope pulled out her phone from her tote and called Drew. He answered on the first ring, and it sounded like she was on speakerphone because she heard traffic.

"Hey. I'm heading out to Emma Carmichael's house to interview her about her prize-winning pickles. I'm about to get a lesson in pickling cucumbers. Never a dull moment in this reporter's life." He chuckled. The *Gazette* relied on stories like Emma's for their bread and butter. Being a talented writer, Drew would make Emma and her pickles shine. "Enough about me. How did it go with Angela?"

Walking to her Explorer, Hope filled him on her conversation with Angela, Reid's unexpected arrival, and Sally's shutdown of his interview request. Like Hope, Drew found it odd she would be so uncooperative.

"Now, get this. I ran into Norrie, coming out of the library. She wants to write an article about my rise and fall."

"Your what?" Drew sounded outraged, and it warmed Hope's heart. "What's she up to?"

"You tell me." Hope aimed her key fob and unlocked the driver's side door. She slipped into the seat, tossing her tote on the passenger seat. She gave Drew a summary of her conversation with Norrie. She was almost in tears when she repeated Norrie's question about her fans trusting her muffin recipes. "Can you believe she asked me that?"

"Sadly, yes. I think she was trying to get a rise out of you. Your readers love you. Don't let her get to you."

Hope flipped down the sun visor and slid open the mirror to inspect her mascara and liner. So far, neither had gone south.

"You don't think she knows something I don't? Otherwise, why would she want to write such a story?"

"Because we know she can be a witch. Or the other word." He laughed, and in turn, Hope laughed. "Don't worry about her. What are you planning on doing next in our investigation?"

She smiled. *Our investigation*. Knowing he, Jane, and Claire, had her back made her feel invincible despite the small chink in her armor only moments ago.

"Angela confirmed the last three books Birdie borrowed from the library were definitely not her usual reading material. They were all on corporate fraud. Why would she be interested in the topic all of a sudden? It has me thinking there might be something fishy going on at Emily's House."

"Really? From my work so far, everything seems to be on the up-and-up."

"I don't have any proof. What I have is a nagging feeling."

"Like a sixth sense."

"Exactly. It's telling me that it might involve Ted doing something criminal, and he murdered his wife after she discovered what he was up to."

"There's a whole lot of speculation going on in your head." Drew's voice faded out and then returned. "Did you hear me? I just went through a dead zone."

"I heard you." She considered his observation. He wasn't wrong. What she said was purely speculation. She had no proof to back up her theory. There was a chance it was her overactive imagination at work. Though it didn't mean she was wrong.

"Gotta go. I'll keep you updated." She ended the call.

She hated thinking the worst of Ted. He had always been a friendly neighbor, and in his professional life, he helped hundreds of women over the years rebuild their lives. Backing her vehicle out of its space, Hope considered the fact the police were probably looking at Ted as a suspect. By doing her thing, she could help clear his name as well her own. Look at her. Multitasking while crime-solving.

Chapter Ten

On her way to Emily's House, Hope made a quick stop at her house to pack up a container of double chocolate chip cookies. Back on the road, she drove straight to the center. On the drive over, she came up with a plan on how to approach Avery with her questions.

When she arrived at EH, she pulled her Explorer into a space and then grabbed her tote and the cookie container. Would Avery be willing to help as Angela had been? She hoped so. Avery's position gave her full access to Ted and, most likely, all the nonprofit's financial information.

EH was located on an open acre of land. Off to the right side of the house, there was a group of women doing yoga. EH was indeed about helping women—body, mind, and soul.

Her cell phone buzzed. She retrieved it from her tote and read Ethan's message.

How's your day going?

So far, it was okay. She wasn't in handcuffs . . . yet.

Her mom always urged her to look at the bright side of things.

She'd meant to text Ethan after leaving the library but was distracted by her rush to head over to the center and she forgot. Truth be told, she was still annoyed with him, but she loved the guy. Always had. For too long, she'd been too blind or scared to admit it.

In high school, he was the star football player, and she was his little sister's friend who baked and read too many books. Ethan had been cool and she definitely hadn't been. She had a crush on him for years, but he dated cheerleaders and eventually married one. It looked like they'd both made mistakes with choosing a life partner.

Good. At EH. Be home soon. Call me.

She chose not to elaborate on her reason for being at EH, figuring he'd assume it had to do with her workshop. It seemed like a good idea for both to keep their investigations separate. After all, it was what he pretty much said when he told her he wouldn't discuss the case. If he couldn't talk about it, she wouldn't either.

Hope slipped the phone back into her tote and continued into the center. Voices drifted from the parlor, and she glimpsed in as she passed. A small group of women gathered with books opened on their laps and coffee cups in their hands. The book club program often chose self-help, motivational-type books.

She climbed the staircase. So much of the building had been changed, but the carved banister and spindles were left intact. Her hand glided over the smooth, polished mahogany as she climbed the carpeted treads. At the landing, Hope veered right toward Ted's office.

Her footsteps were absorbed by the Persian-motif-inspired carpet runner that stretched the length of the hall.

The walls were painted a soft white, and the original trim woodwork appeared to be intact even though the rooms had been reconfigured to house the offices.

She arrived at the open doorway that led to Avery's small area outside of her boss's office.

Hope peered into the neat and functional space. Sturdy furniture filled the room and colorful artwork hung on the walls. She guessed they were from the art program offered at the center. Erin shared that her art therapy was one of the best programs she'd enrolled in while she was a client.

Avery was seated at her desk with her head tilted downward and the phone receiver pressed to her ear.

"I can't right now," Avery said in a strained voice. "His wife is dead. Jumping on a plane now isn't a good idea. . . . Are you threatening me?"

Hope cleared her throat, prompting Avery to look up. Her face flushed, and she quickly ended the call. With the receiver back in its cradle, she did her best to fix a smile on her face.

"Hi, Hope. I wasn't expecting you today. There's no workshop, right?"

"I'm sorry, I couldn't help but overhear. Is everything okay?" Hope entered the office. Other than the uncomfortable look on Avery's face, she looked more like her professional self than she did the day after Birdie's death. Her turquoise blouse flattered her complexion, and overall she looked rested.

"Yes, of course. Is there something I can help you with?" Avery shifted and positioned her fingers over the computer's keyboard.

Hope didn't believe Avery. Whoever was on the other end of that call had rattled her. She couldn't help but wonder what the person said to make Avery feel it was a threat.

"The police have ruled Birdie's death a homicide."

Avery gasped and paled as she pulled her fingers back from the keyboard. "Are you certain?"

You bet I am.

"One hundred percent."

Avery quickly composed herself. "You are dating the chief of police, so you would know what's what."

Hope allowed the comment about her relationship to slide. She didn't want to explain how she knew about the cause of death. She worried it would hinder Avery from being open if she believed Hope was just trying to pin someone else for the murder.

"I almost forgot. How silly of me. I brought these for you." Hope approached the desk and set the container down. "Double chocolate chip cookies. They're one of the most popular cookie recipes on my blog."

"How thoughtful." Avery pulled the container toward her and removed the lid. She inhaled and then grinned. She appeared to be softening. So maybe Hope could get some information out of her. "I probably shouldn't. I've been stress eating way too much."

"I understand stress eating. When you're a food blogger, there is always something to eat. Over the years, I've learned to turn to yoga when I'm stressed or talk to someone about what's bothering me. Both work wonders." Hope sat on a chair beside the desk, positioning herself as someone available to listen.

"Wonderful advice." Avery lifted a cookie from the container and took a bite. As she chewed, a contented smile formed on her lips. After she swallowed, she said, "These are delicious."

"I can send you the link to the recipe." Hope leaned back and crossed her legs. "The workshop is going well, and I've heard fundraising is on track for this quarter."

"We've had a splendid start to the year, and it's continuing," Avery said between bites.

"People don't realize that success can be nerve-wracking. Sometimes it feels like you're waiting for the other shoe to drop." Hope knew the feeling all too well. When she had her first one-hundred-thousand-view day on her blog, she was sure nobody would return the next day. Luckily, they did.

"Tell me about it." Avery finished her cookie and replaced the lid on the container.

"May I ask you a question about EH?"

"Sure. Go ahead." Avery snatched a tissue out of its container and wiped her fingers.

"Have you noticed any financial irregularities here at EH?"

Avery's eyebrows squished together. "Financial irregularities? Such as what?"

"Perhaps transactions that seem out of sorts."

Avery pushed the container away and folded her arms on her desk. "Those are odd questions. Why are you asking them?"

"I have reason to believe Birdie suspected fraud at EH before her death."

"Are you accusing Ted of embezzling funds from EH?" Avery's voice lowered even though it was only the two of them in the room. "Do you realize even the slightest hint of such behavior could ruin him? And the center."

Hope raised her palms. "I know. I know. I'm not accusing him. It's possible *he* discovered someone doing something criminal and confided in his wife." She prayed her quick, vague accusation of an unknown person would quell Avery's indignation.

"Oh, my goodness. Ted could be in danger."

"Possibly."

Maybe Avery was onto something. What Hope conjectured just now about another person stealing from EH could be true. What if Ted had uncovered fiscal misdeeds and planned to go to the authorities? But why kill Birdie? Why not just kill Ted? Perhaps it was a message to him to keep quiet. Criminals did things like that.

"You said the other day, he hadn't returned from his unexplained outing the morning Birdie was murdered. You thought he could have been meeting with donors, perhaps at the country club. Do you still have no idea of where he went? Or who he might have met with?"

Avery was quiet, her eyes thoughtful as she studied Hope. "No. I don't. Though he's been more secretive. Like leaving without letting me know where he was going. He always told me about his appointments because I managed his calendar." She pointed to her computer screen. "He's also been locking his office door. Even when he steps out to get coffee. He never did that before. After you asked about his travel plans, I checked his calendar and found a confirmation number for an airline."

Hope inched forward on her seat. *It was always the husband.* "Tickets to where?"

Avery shrugged. "I didn't check. I guess I really didn't want to know."

If Ted had purchased a plane ticket, then Hope's theory of him being the one uncovering any financial fraud at the nonprofit went out the window. It was most likely him who was stealing and planning to get out of town.

"Hope . . . there has to be an explanation. Ted isn't a killer." She fell back, and her hands dropped to her lap.

They never are.

"No one is saying he is." Hope leaned forward and rested a hand on the desk. "This information needs to be taken to the police."

"If it gets out, EH will be destroyed."

"I'm sure Detective Reid will be discreet."

"For our sake, I hope he will be. If you'll excuse me, I have to get back to work." Avery dipped her head and tapped on the keyboard.

It appeared their conversation was over. Hope stood and walked out of the office. She descended the staircase. As she reached the bottom, voices drifted from the parlor. The book group was still meeting. She looked in and recognized two of the women from her class seated amongst the six other women.

A tap on her shoulder gave her a start and she spun around. "Oh, Erin. You scared me."

Erin laughed. "It looks like you're snooping. Or should I say sleuthing?"

Hope pressed her lips together. Her new friend had quickly learned about Hope's curiosity. "Caught me."

"Come on. I'll buy you a cup of coffee." Erin smiled and led Hope to the kitchen. "I've heard Birdie's death has been ruled a murder."

"Your sources are correct." Hope dropped her purse on the counter while Erin poured them two cups of coffee.

"I also heard she died from an allergic reaction to peanut oil found in the muffin she was eating." Erin handed Hope a cup.

Hope took a drink. "Who are your sources?"

"When you dig around people's closets for a living,

you hear things. Word is spreading fast." Erin sipped her coffee and then walked to the table. She pulled out a chair and sat. "The muffin she was eating was baked and delivered by you."

Hope's mouth formed an O. "My word, I knew it would get out eventually but so soon?" She made a mental note to call her agent and give her a heads up on what might be coming in the press. She had to get out ahead of this or everything she'd worked for could be ruined. All the more reason to dig into Birdie's murder and find out who was responsible.

"Now tell me why you're here today. There's no class today," Erin said.

Hope carried her cup to the table and joined Erin. "I discovered something unusual when I was in Birdie's house the day I found her dead. I'm following up on it."

Erin sipped her coffee, nodding. "And?"

Hope looked over her shoulder to make sure no one was around. "Has there been any hint of financial problems for the center?"

"Like embezzling? No. No. From what I've observed since becoming involved with EH is that the center has been handled very responsibly." Erin circled the rim of her cup with her forefinger, and she looked like she was working on a memory.

"What is it?" Hope leaned forward, moving her cup. "You're remembering something, aren't you?"

"I'm not sure what it was about. Last week I had to talk to Avery about something. Well, I walked into an argument between her and Ted. Something about . . . oh, gosh, what was the word? Vi . . . Vision . . . Visionary!"

"Visionary? As in someone being able to see visions?"

"I don't think so. It sounded more like a thing. Maybe

a program? Once they saw me, they stopped talking, and Ted went into his office without another word. I'm sorry I can't be more help."

"Don't worry about it." Hope pulled back and lifted her cup. "What was Avery's mood like?"

"I guess a little embarrassed. I caught her arguing with her boss." Erin glanced at her watch. "I have to get going. I have a client consultation to get to. Call me if you need anything. Like bail money." She winked.

"Ha-ha. Talk soon." Hope remained seated while Erin dashed off. She sipped her coffee and then reached into her tote, pulling out her notebook. Opening to a clean sheet of paper, she jotted down what Avery had told her and then what Erin just shared.

She'd finished writing her last thought, *what were Avery and Ted arguing about?* before her cell phone buzzed and she retrieved it from her purse. There was a message from Drew to check out a link.

You were right. Norrie did know something. Sorry.

She lowered her phone to avoid looking at the message. To avoid the ugly link from taunting her. To avoid seeing what the whole freakin' world must have already seen. There was no way to avoid it any longer. She raised the phone, steeling herself for whatever the bad news was.

Chapter Eleven

Drew's link led to an article. Its headline grabbed her attention and her jaw dropped. This wasn't good.

FOOD BLOGGER LOSES IT WITH MURDER VICTIM

Her eyelids shut, and she groaned. Not good at all. She forced her eyes open and tapped the play arrow on the video that accompanied the article. As the video played, Hope brought the phone closer to her face to make sure she was seeing what she thought she was seeing.

"No. No. No. No."

Her shoulders curled forward, caving her chest in and forcing her to suck in her breaths. A sour taste in her mouth made her lips pucker, yet she couldn't take her eyes off the video.

She and Birdie arguing outside the library the day before Birdie died. Someone filmed them!

She squashed the panic stirring inside her. There was no need to panic. None whatsoever.

It was only a disagreement.

A viral disagreement, according to the thousands of shares. Maybe a little panic wasn't out of place. She tapped the video to make it stop. As far as optics went, the video didn't look good for her.

Despite her better judgment, she pressed the play arrow again and enlarged the video. Her face heated as she watched herself and Birdie nose-to-nose while Jane was off to the side, looking on with shock. Hope couldn't blame her. She was shocked at her own behavior.

Something caught Hope's eye. No, not something, someone. She pinched the screen to enlarge the picture. Standing behind the row of evergreen shrubs was a man watching her and Birdie. She thought back to that afternoon. She hadn't noticed him. Not even after Birdie stormed off.

Probably because she was so frustrated and angry with her neighbor at the time.

Besides, she wasn't looking in the bushes for stalkers.

A text notification from Drew popped up on her screen. Hope closed out of the website and navigated back to her texts.

Sorry to send you the video. Thought you should see it. Have any updates?

Breathe in and out.

She repeated the mantra twice as she willed her internal temperature to cool down. A little calmer, she typed a reply to Drew, filling him in on what both Avery and Erin told her. He responded that he shared her thought it was some type of program but would check it out.

Before they ended their conversation, he asked her if she was okay. Her fingers hovered over the phone's keyboard. No, she wasn't okay. Even though she'd told Matt about the incident, seeing it play out in video was a whole lot different. If she ended up on trial, the video would be a damning piece of evidence to her motive. Her stomach quaked. No, she couldn't think about what-ifs.

Instead of pouring out all her fears and doubts into text acronyms, she replied in a way stoic Sally would approve of.

I'm okay. Let's touch base later. Thanks!

Thanks?

What the heck was she thinking? Actually, she couldn't think. Her mind was warbled with snippets of shouting and a never-ending reel of her and Birdie arguing.

With their text exchange concluded, her phone buzzed. She had an incoming call from Jane. She raised the phone to her ear.

"What's up?"

"Dear, Birdie's brother has checked in. He's here for the funeral."

"Brother? She had a brother?" Hope couldn't help but wonder if he was anything like his sister. If he was, Jane and Sally had their hands full.

"Apparently he lives up in Massachusetts."

"Why isn't he staying with Ted?" Hope cradled the phone between her ear and shoulder as she closed her notebook and shoved it into her tote.

"I had the same question."

Hope wasn't surprised that Jane asked him. "What did he say?"

"The family has been estranged for years. He thought it would be best to stay here. Why don't you come over and offer your condolences?"

What Hope really needed to do was make three calls to explain the video. Her lawyer, her boyfriend, and her agent. She was really starting to detest technology.

"Estranged, huh? I wonder why." Hope remembered

how Drew had speculated something from Birdie's past might have caught up with her. Maybe her brother could shed some light on her life before Jefferson. She could make her calls later, after her stop at the inn. "On my way."

Hope arrived back in Jefferson and parked in the adjacent lot for the Merrifield Inn. She hurried to the front door and found Jane waiting for her, frowning. Not exactly the greeting she'd expected, and then it hit her—Jane must have seen the video. And it didn't take an astute police detective to figure out that Drew was the one who sent it to her. Even though Jane had become more active on Facebook, she hadn't mastered following links to websites.

"Hope." Jane shook her head.

Her guess was right. "I know. We can talk about it later."

"Indeed we will." Jane pivoted and led Hope to the parlor. "His name is Gary Oliff, and he's from Beverly."

Hope was familiar with the Massachusetts town because of her antiquing jaunts up north, and she passed through many towns in her travels. Some were more impressive than others, but she often found a beloved treasure in the most unexpected location.

They reached the doorway, and Hope peered in. Jane entered the room with ease while Hope hung back. Intruding on a grieving brother seemed wrong on many levels. *So was being suspected of murder.*

The balding, gray-haired man was seated on the sofa. One arm was slung over the back cushions, and he appeared to be relaxing. As they approached closer, she noticed he looked deep in thought as he stared out the front window. From his vantage point, he could watch passers-by on Main Street.

"Mr. Oliff." Jane reached the chair where she sat earlier that morning with Hope, Drew, and Claire. "I'd like you to meet my good friend Hope Early."

Birdie's brother looked in their direction and gave an appraising look to Hope as her mouth dropped open.

He was the man lurking in the video!

Jane cleared her throat, prompting Hope out of her shock. "I'm very sorry for your loss, Mr. Oliff."

Gary Oliff's bushy eyebrows were dangerously close to becoming a unibrow. His tanned facial skin sagged as if he'd lost a lot of weight fast. Further proof to that assessment was his navy polo shirt, which seemed a size too big and did little for his sallow complexion.

"Thank you." Gary leaned forward and lifted his coffee cup. "My brother-in-law told me you found Birdie's body."

"I did. I'm sure you've also been told I'm a suspect in her death." Hope figured she might as well cut to the chase and address the elephant in the room.

"Of course Hope didn't murder your sister," Jane said quickly and then gave Hope a supportive smile. "I've known her all her life. She's not a killer."

"I believe people are capable of anything given the right circumstances." He took a long drink. "I also believe you wouldn't be here offering your condolences if you killed Birdie. That would take a special kind of black-hearted person."

Hope thought that was the closest to an invite to sit and join him as she was going to get. She settled on the chair next to Jane.

"Birdie and I had our differences, I won't deny it," Hope said.

Gary gave a knowing nod. "Birdie always seemed to rub people the wrong way."

"She had a strong personality," Jane said.

Hope slid her friend a look. Talk about an understatement.

"You're not the only person who had differences with her." Gary set his cup down. "We had a doozy of a falling out twenty years ago and have barely spoken a word since then. Now . . . well, it's too late."

Hope choked with emotion. She couldn't imagine not talking to Claire for two decades. What would her life be like without the one person she'd always leaned on, confided in, and laughed with? Lonely. That's what her life would be like.

"What happened, if you don't mind me asking?" Without any doubt, Hope felt like she was prying, but if he hadn't wanted to talk about the fallout between them, he wouldn't have mentioned it.

"We were raised with morals and values. Our father was a pastor, and we went to church every Sunday. I followed in his footsteps while Birdie ran wild once she turned eighteen." He lowered his eyelids and shook his head.

Hope and Jane exchanged a baffled look. Had they heard right? Birdie Donovan, wild child? Hope couldn't envision it, and she doubted Jane could either. She was challenged to find the words to ask the question on the tip of her tongue in a way not to offend Gary. Then again, he was a pastor, so he'd forgive her, right?

"I have to be honest. I'm having a hard time picturing

Birdie as being wild. She was . . . so . . . rigid." Hope flicked her gaze upward momentarily, hoping for forgiveness from the big guy above for being blunt with the grieving brother.

The corner of Gary's lip tugged upward as a flicker of amusement flashed in his deep-set eyes. Hope sensed it wasn't the first time he heard that comment about his sister. "Lord my God, I called to you for help, and you healed me."

"Psalms 30:2," Jane said reverently.

"Birdie needed healing?" Hope was growing more curious and impatient by the moment. She was dying to hear about Birdie's secret past. And the skeletons in her closet.

"She did. She partied, drank, and ran with a bunch of kids who were godless. We weren't raised to behave in such a manner. The final straw came a few years later when she was working as a bookkeeper . . ." His words trailed off as he seemed to reconsider sharing any further information on Birdie's indiscretions.

"You haven't seen her in twenty years?" Hope asked.

"Correct. There wasn't any point. She chose her life's path, and it wasn't with God."

Hope leaned back and clasped her hands together on her lap. The man of the cloth had just lied. He'd seen Birdie the day before she was murdered.

Gary stood. He was tall, over six feet Hope guessed, based on Ethan's height. She couldn't help but think of what a formidable presence he must have at the pulpit. "If you'll excuse me, I have calls to make." He walked out of the room and turned in the direction of the staircase.

"I don't envy the man. The weight of regret he'll live

with for the rest of his life will be crushing." Jane propped an elbow on the arm of the chair and then rested her chin on her hand. "Now, we need to talk about the video."

"Yes, we do. First, you need to know something." Before Hope could tell Jane that Gary had lied to them about not seeing Birdie before she died, Matt appeared in the parlor's doorway.

"We need to talk." The look on his face matched his severe tone.

"Uh-oh." Hope didn't have to guess why he was in a foul mood. He must have seen the video.

"Jane, do you mind giving us a minute to talk in private? If you stay, whatever we say isn't privileged." Matt entered the room and stood beside the sofa. His expression wasn't softening. What Hope would give to see the lines around his eyes crinkle as his lips curved into a smile. But it didn't look like that would happen anytime soon.

"I understand." Jane stood.

"Wait, she doesn't have to leave. I have nothing to hide." Hope realized she was wasting her time and relented. Matt was trying to help her and she needed to listen to him. If he wanted a private conversation, then that's what they would have.

"Still, we need our conversations to be private. Thanks, Jane." He gave a wink, and Jane smiled. Matt had that effect on women. Tall, broad-shouldered, with sandy blond hair, he was as charming as he was handsome.

Jane scooted out of the room, and Matt's charm must have gone with her because when he turned back to Hope, he was all business.

"The video doesn't look good, Hope."

Tell me something I don't know.

"Did you see there was a man lurking in the shrubs while we had our conversation?" she asked.

"No. Why?"

"He's Birdie's brother, Gary Oliff."

"How do you know?"

"I just met him. He's upstairs in his room now."

Matt looked over his shoulder and then back to Hope. "You talked to him?"

"Yes, me and Jane. He said he hasn't seen his sister in twenty years, yet he is in the video stalking her. He's hiding something."

"By talking to Mr. Oliff and investigating on your own, you're possibly jeopardizing your defense."

"How? I'm innocent! And he lied! He had to be following her."

Matt shook his head. "Look, trust me. I have experience in this area."

Hope took a moment and calmed herself. She accepted Matt's point, somewhat reluctantly. Even with his experience, she was hesitant to place her life entirely in his hands. It wasn't in her nature to sit by and wait for things to happen. Clearing her name wouldn't be any different.

"I hear you. Please know that I appreciate everything you're doing for me." Hope was sincere. She doubted she'd ever be able to express how grateful she was to have him in her corner.

Matt nodded and then stood. "We're still on to meet at your house tomorrow. See you then." He turned and walked out of the room.

Hope picked up her tote and stood. She wanted to find Jane and tell her about Gary. At the doorway, she saw the older woman at the reception desk, on the telephone.

"We'll set everything up for the reception at Ted's

house. Yes, excellent idea, Maretta. We should also include some cut flowers from Birdie's garden."

Jane was arranging the funeral reception at the Donovan house. It meant the house would be empty for a little while between Ted leaving and Jane arriving with her fellow volunteers.

Hope listened for a time confirmation and where Jane would find the spare key to the house.

The front door swung open, and three middle-aged women entered chatting, laughing, and carrying shopping bags. They swept by Hope with a quick wave and hustled to the reception desk. When Jane ended her call, she greeted her guests and was pulled into a conversation about local wineries. Connecticut was becoming one of the fastest-growing wine regions in the country with over forty wineries.

With Jane distracted, Hope slipped out the front door. The telephone call gave her an idea she was sure Jane would disapprove of, even with her penchant for solving mysteries. Yes, it was better not to make Jane an accomplice. Hope hurried along the sidewalk to the path toward the parking lot.

Matt's lecturing her on her investigation cemented her decision. If what he said was true about her jeopardizing her defense by talking to Gary, now there was no turning back. She needed to find out why Gary lied and where he was the morning Birdie was murdered.

Chapter Twelve

During the drive back to her house, Hope's mind churned over possibilities of what had caused the fallout between Gary and Birdie. Had Birdie strayed so far off course that she got involved with drugs? Hope had seen firsthand how addiction was affecting Ethan's family. Her mind was still turning over thoughts about Gary, his lie, and the Oliff family estrangement as she entered her kitchen. She unloaded her tote off her shoulder and quickly lavished an impatient Bigelow with kisses on the head before greeting Josie.

"In the mood for some good news?" Josie asked from her seat at the table. She'd arrived while Hope was at Emily's House and let herself in with her new house key. While Hope had been out snooping around, Josie had edited two videos, scheduled three blog posts, and updated the landing page for Hope's blogger coaching program. The clients she was currently working with were a small group of beta users who got a discount.

Hope rested her hands on the island's counter. "I am definitely in the mood for some good news. Bring it on."

"Traffic is way up. Everywhere." Josie beamed with excitement while Hope sulked. "What's wrong?"

"I think I know the reason why, and it's not a good one." Hope walked to the refrigerator and took out a pitcher of iced tea. After she poured a glass, she joined Josie at the table and filled her in on the viral video.

"You're right. It's not a good reason for increased traffic. All those people are like the ones who drive by accident scenes and gawk."

Yep, that pretty much summed up the situation Hope was in now. She avoided checking her emails because she was certain there was one from her agent. At some point, though, she had to touch base with Laurel. She should also be prepared to be fired as a client.

Hope sipped her tea and filled Josie in on her conversation with Gary. "I wish he'd shared what happened."

"Guess it must have been pretty darn serious for them not to talk for two decades." Josie's mouth gaped. "Maybe she committed a crime. Like a robbery and someone got hurt. Or maybe she was high and got into a car accident and killed someone."

"Do you think Birdie was in prison?"

Josie shrugged. "Anything is possible. Perhaps she was so private because she didn't want to talk about her past. If she was in prison, she probably spent a lot of time in the prison library. Maybe that's why she liked hanging out at the Jefferson Library."

Hope smiled. "You might be right. If she was in prison."

"Not everyone chooses the right life path." Josie shrugged. "What do you plan to do now?"

"I have a coaching call in thirty minutes."

"No. I mean about the murder."

Hope finished her drink. "I'd like to know what caused the falling out between Gary and Birdie. There was something Avery said that has me curious about Ted and the center."

"What did she say?"

Hope hesitated to answer. If she were off base, she could do harm to Ted and the center's reputation. It was better not to repeat what she was told.

"When I confirm it, I'll let you know."

"I have full confidence you'll get to the bottom of the murder." Josie closed her binder. "You probably should call Laurel at some point to discuss the video."

Hope's stomach knotted. "I will. After my coaching call."

An hour later, Hope set her cell phone down and let Laurel's news sink in. Not just one company had put a hold on its partnership with Hope's blog, but two: Graham Flour and Mama Mia Pasta. The companies had seen the video of Hope arguing with Birdie and were aware of her being a suspect in the murder. Laurel cited a clause in the contracts, something about morals and not killing people.

She propped her elbows on the table and dropped her head in her hands. Everything she'd worked so hard for was falling apart. She'd spent thousands of hours creating content, cultivating relationships with brands, and developing a following. Now it was all slipping away.

She spread her hands across her face and slowly lifted her head, dropping her chin in her hands. She wanted to cry. Then a nudge at her arm reminded her she wasn't alone.

She looked down. Bigelow had settled next to her and

rested his head on her lap. Her chin trembled as her heart melted. Gosh, she still wanted to cry but not because of Laurel's news. Blinking, she willed the tears to stop. Even if she lost her career, she still had a wonderful life.

Her phone buzzed with a new text. It was from her nephew Logan.

Coming over, okay?

Hope let out a whoosh of air and lifted her head. Finally, something to smile about. She loved it when Logan came by just because he wanted to spend time with his aunt. It made her feel special. She grabbed the phone and replied.

Need a ride?

A moment later, Logan responded.

Nope. Billy's mom will drop me off.

She'd met Billy's mom a few times at birthday parties. Being around people would be a good thing. Otherwise, she might grab a pint of ice cream from the freezer and hide under her bed covers.

See you soon.

As Hope was setting her phone back down, another text came. It was from Ethan.

Be over in an hour with the girls.

It looked like she was going to have a full house for the evening. Bigelow nudged her again. She rubbed his head, and even though it was soothing to her, anxiety still hummed in her body. "I have to tell him about the video."

Hope had intended to change into some comfy clothes to mope around and hang out with her nephew. When she reached into her closet for her fleece joggers and T-shirt, she suddenly desired a hot shower to wash off the day.

Standing beneath the spray of hot water gave Hope the mental break she wanted. She lathered up with her newest obsession, a shower gel recommended by another blogger. The lively scent was exactly what she needed as she rinsed and toweled dry.

Perked up and ready to face the rest of the day, she reached into her closet for a V-neck top and a pair of twill pants that didn't have an elastic waistband. She would do her best not to have pity because she wasn't ready to give up.

She came off the last step of the staircase and rounded the corner toward the kitchen. Shouts from the family room alerted her that Logan's video watching had strayed from approved viewing content.

He'd arrived before she went upstairs to change clothes and offered to keep an eye on Molly while Becca went with Ethan to get pizza for dinner. When Ethan ushered the girls into the house, he whispered to her he'd seen the video and thought she would like a break from cooking. A moment later, he was back in his truck with Becca and they were off.

She appreciated his thoughtfulness and his decision not to dwell on the video. However, she expected he'd have something to say about the video later when the children weren't around.

In the family room, she found Logan and Molly sitting on the floor in front of the television. On the screen was a video of three bearded men slapping each other on the back.

"Did you see that?" Logan clicked the pause button on the remote control. "That was so cool!"

"What was cool?" Hope looked at the television screen.

The kids weren't watching the cartoons she'd clicked to before going upstairs.

Logan swung around, leaning a hand behind him. "These three guys! They do all sorts of things like pick locks with paper clips. Do you have any zip ties?"

"Zip ties? Yes. Wait. Why?" Hope walked around the sofa onto the area rug where the kids were seated, cross-legged.

"To try to break free." Molly pointed to the television. The six-year-old had her dad's dark hair and the same intensity. She looked determined to reenact what was on the television.

Hope looked at the screen more closely. Logan had frozen the screen in a place where she could see one of the three men had their hands bound by a zip tie.

"Oh, no. You two are not going to try that."

"Come on, Aunt Hope." Logan pressed the play button and the man whose hands were bound demonstrated how to break free. "So cool! We need to practice."

"Practice for what?" Hope asked, staring at the video. She was in awe of how he managed to free his hands.

"In case we get abducted," Molly said. "They're . . ." She scratched her face. "Life skills. Yeah, that's what Daddy calls things we have to learn."

"Well, then we'll wait for your daddy before practicing this particular life skill." Hope took the remote from her nephew, aimed it at the television, and clicked to a cartoon channel. "This is what you're supposed to be watching."

"Cartoons are for babies," Logan protested as he scrambled to his feet.

"Hey, I'm not a baby!" Molly countered, crossing her arms and huffing.

"Cartoons are enjoyable for all ages. Why don't you two watch this show while I prepare the salad?" She was grateful Ethan was getting dinner, but she still wanted something besides just a couple of slices of pizza. A tossed salad with her homemade balsamic vinaigrette dressing sounded like a perfect side dish.

"Salad?" Logan made a face.

"Yes, salad." Hope handed the remote back to her nephew. "Make sure the channel doesn't change."

"Fine," Logan said. He didn't roll his eyes, but his tone implied he wanted to.

Hope's work was done there. She turned and headed to the kitchen, smiling victoriously. Kids were easy. She didn't know what the big deal was.

She tied on her apron and got to work. She retrieved a bag of greens and English cucumbers from the refrigerator. At the sink, she grabbed three tomatoes from the windowsill, and from an upper cabinet, she took out a wooden salad bowl.

Hope busied herself with peeling, chopping, and dicing. When she was done, she had a colorful salad that even Logan would enjoy.

She gave the salad a quick toss. At that moment, her mind wandered back to the subjects she'd been working so hard to stay away from. Her crashing and burning. Personally and professionally. Tears threatened again, but luckily Princess appeared and rubbed her fluffy white body along Hope's legs. Distracted by the show of affection from her feline, Hope wiped the tears and scooped the cat up. They bopped noses. Princess's whiskers tickled her. And just like that, their tender moment was gone. Princess leaped from Hope's arms and slinked out of the room.

"Bye," Hope said, and Princess flicked her tail before she disappeared into the hallway.

A deep woof drew Hope's attention from her cat to Bigelow. The urgent yap indicated to her that the dog needed to go out and do his business. He was at the front door, waiting. She dashed to the entry and opened the door. He trotted down the porch steps, and she followed, stopping at a planter. She deadheaded a few stems while Bigelow sniffed.

Arranging the planters on the porch was as far as she had gotten with decorating the covered outdoor space. Because she'd been so behind with work and chores around the house, she'd only recently set up the outdoor furniture and décor.

A sectional rattan sofa with a matching coffee table filled one end of the porch. It was a perfect spot for lazy days. However, she hadn't had one of those in what felt like forever. Beneath the furniture was a black and white zigzag patterned rug. The rug coordinated with the black front door she'd salvaged. Ethan had hauled it home and installed it for her. But it was she who'd stripped and painted the door, even filling in gouges with putty.

Out of the corner of her eye, she saw Bigelow dart from his "spot" to the edge of the property.

"I'm not in the mood for this." Hope tramped down the steps and went after her dog. She couldn't blame him. It was a beautiful day, and if she didn't have to set the table, she would have stayed outside too. "Come on, Bigelow. Let's go back inside."

Bigelow swung around. His ears flopped, and his eyes brightened with mischief.

Oh, boy.

"After dinner, you'll be out here playing with the kids."

Bigelow tilted his head as if he were considering what she said. But alas, he was a dog and didn't understand what his human was saying. He grabbed a stick off the grass and hunched down.

"Okay, if I get the stick, we're going inside."

Bigelow's tail wagged.

It was on.

Hope lunged forward, and Bigelow spun around and bounded ahead, landing right at the curb.

She advanced, and it must have signaled to Bigelow to take off. He crisscrossed toward the towering oak tree in the center of her front yard and then stopped, waiting for her to chase him. Hope was about to when a car drove by.

It was Alfred Kingston's sensible sedan. The owner of one of Jefferson's most successful real estate agencies lived a low-key existence while his wife was the polar opposite. Maretta was in the passenger seat, gesturing with her hands. It appeared Alfred was getting an earful of something.

Was it about Gary Oliff's arrival in town? Maretta had been close with Birdie, so surely she must have known about the brother. About the estrangement. And she'd definitely have an opinion about it.

"Come on, Bigelow." Hope tapped her leg as she stepped off the curb. Perhaps Maretta had some insight on the feud between the siblings. She crossed the street, and Bigelow quickly caught up.

Alfred's car pulled into the Donovans' driveway and after exiting the vehicle, he walked around the hood as Maretta got out on her side.

"Hope!" Alfred smiled when he saw her. Even with the warm spring temperatures, he wore his trademark sweater vest over a short-sleeved white shirt. What was new was the tan fedora he wore. Hope guessed it was an attempt to hide his thinning white hair. "Good to see you."

Hope felt the same way. She always enjoyed visiting with him and still delivered freshly baked goods to his office when she had extras even though Claire no longer worked for him.

However, it didn't look like his wife felt the same way. Her expression was as neutral as her beige dress and coordinating low-heeled pumps.

"Do you think you should be here?" Maretta asked.

Hope didn't reply to the question, aka accusation. Rather, she opted to get straight to the point. No need to beat around the bush. "Did Birdie ever talk to you about her brother?"

"The one you and Jane harassed at the inn?" Maretta closed the car door.

"Oh, Maretta, I doubt Hope or Jane harassed anybody." Alfred extended a hand behind his wife's back to move her along.

Maretta harrumphed.

"Did Birdie ever share why she and Gary stopped talking twenty years ago?" Hope would not be deterred by Maretta's hostility. After a lifetime of knowing the woman, she was immune to it.

"I have no intention of sharing private conversations with you. I strongly suggest you stay out of the investigation. The town has a very competent police detective handling the case, and he doesn't need you muddying it up." Maretta turned and walked toward the house's front door.

Alfred leaned forward and said in a low voice, "I expect you'll do what you need to do. Good luck."

Hope smiled and nodded a silent thank you for his support.

"Alfred, please, we're here for Ted." Maretta's voice was strained with frustration.

Alfred dutifully turned and hurried to join his wife at the front step. Hope nabbed Bigelow by the collar and escorted him back to their home. Before they reached the porch steps, she glanced over her shoulder and saw the Kingstons entering Ted's house and the door closing. With or without Maretta's help, Hope would find out what had caused the divide between Birdie and Gary. Good thing she had a plan.

Ethan and Becca returned with two large pizzas shortly after Hope corralled Bigelow. One was a plain cheese for the kids, and the other was topped with vegetables for Hope. Ethan was happy eating either. Dinner conversation ranged from a recap of Logan's school day to Molly's plans to become a veterinarian when she grew up because she loved Bigelow and Princess. There was no talk of murder or financial fraud or criminal defense planning. It had been a lovely dinner.

When they were done eating, Hope whipped up sundaes for everyone. She set out the two containers of ice cream, a bottle of chocolate syrup, and jars of toppings. By the time the sundaes were assembled, Hope returned to the table with a mixing bowl of whipped cream.

After dessert, Ethan helped clear the table, and Hope loaded the dishwasher. She asked him how much money he had saved for Molly's education because veterinary school was going to cost a fortune. He gave a good-hearted chuckle and assured her that by next week Molly would be onto a different career. That's when he asked about her day.

She sighed as she closed the dishwasher door. After setting the wash cycle, she recapped her conversation with Laurel, which earned her a sympathetic look from Ethan. Not in the mood for pity from him—she had enough of that all on her own—she sent him out of the kitchen to find a movie for them.

Night had finally settled over Jefferson, and the temperature dipped to a chilly low. Before retiring to watch a movie, Hope dashed outside to cover her tender flowers. Weather in New England was fickle, to say the least.

Back inside, Hope flicked off the kitchen lights and padded into the family room.

Molly and Becca were busy with their coloring books at the coffee table, while Logan was scrunched up on the armchair, playing a video game. Bigelow was softly snoring on his bed in the corner of the family room, and Princess had made herself scarce after eating her dinner.

"Well, I got some news." Ethan pulled her into his arms as he reclined on the sofa in the family room. "I think it's going to be good for all of us."

She snuggled into him, resting her head on his chest and curling her legs up on the cushions.

"I'd love some good news." She could hear the steady beat of Ethan's heart, and it lulled her into a tranquil mood. She felt content, safe, and loved. What more could a gal ask for?

"We don't have to tiptoe around the situation any longer," Ethan said. His lips brushed her earlobe.

"What? Why not?" She craned her head upward and looked at him. Exhaustion and worry filled his eyes. A pang of guilt snapped in her because he was worried about her.

"As of today, I'm on personal leave from the PD."

"Did Maretta make you take leave?" Hope's blood boiled. She wouldn't put it past the inept mayor to do such a thing.

"No. No. It was my idea. I really need to focus on the girls right now as they adjust to their new normal. And it also allows Reid to continue with the case."

"The State Police were going to come in, weren't they? Take the case away from him?"

"Yes. Clifford is now the acting Chief, and Reid stays on the case, and I get to spend time with Molly and Becca. And you." He kissed her on the top of her head.

A lump formed in her throat. If she hadn't let anger get the better of her, she wouldn't have confronted Birdie, and that stupid video wouldn't have been made. She also wouldn't be a suspect, and Ethan would still be working.

"Hey, this isn't your fault. I could have fought the request, but I really should take time off to be more present for the girls. They seem okay, but I heard them crying earlier. They miss Heather." He gently stroked Hope's hair.

"I wish there was more I could do for them."

"You're doing a whole lot by making them feel comfortable here and making sundaes." He laughed. "I'm stuffed."

"I make a mean sundae." Hope shifted around so that she was face to face with Ethan. "I love you."

"Right back at you, babe. And never doubt for one

minute I'm on your side." He studied her face. "You do what you need to do. Got it?"

She nodded. She got it. Oh boy, did she.

He pulled her close and was about to kiss her when the doorbell app on her cell phone chimed.

"Mom's here!" Logan jumped up from the chair and grabbed his backpack off the floor.

Hope untangled herself from Ethan and reluctantly stood. Before walking to the kitchen, she gestured to the girls and gave a wicked smile. "Lucky for us, it's almost their bedtime."

You do what you need to do.

Ethan's words repeated in Hope's head the next morning as she snatched the key to the Donovan house from beneath the faux rock beside the right corner of the patio.

It was precisely where Jane said it would be when she spoke to Maretta on the telephone yesterday. A twinge of guilt reminded her that eavesdropping was wrong. So was being framed for a murder she didn't commit.

Hope scampered across the patio to the slider and then glanced at her watch. She had fifteen minutes before Jane would arrive with her crew to set up the reception. It wasn't a lot of time.

She'd have more if Ted hadn't left for the church so late. While she watched out her living room window for him, she wondered what caused the delay.

Why he was tardy in leaving for his wife's funeral wasn't important now. Not getting caught was the critical thing. The longer Hope stood outside the house, the higher her chance of being discovered. Who knew who could drop by with food for the widower?

Hope unlocked the door and replaced the key under the rock. Her moves were uncharacteristically stealthy.

There couldn't be any sign someone had been in the house.

Inside the kitchen and alone, she could take a better look around, though she couldn't linger. Jane and her helpers would be arriving soon. The first thing she noticed was the table. It had been cleared of the books Birdie had borrowed from the library. The next thing she noticed was how uninspired the kitchen appeared. It lacked character, the kind of hominess she craved in her own kitchen. The countertops were clear of small appliances except for a drip coffee maker. The major appliances looked pristine, like they hadn't been used. Nope. There were no smudged fingerprints on the stainless-steel refrigerator.

At the arched doorway that led to the front of the house, she rested her hands on her hips. She considered what to do next. The next time she broke into someone's house, she needed to have a detailed plan worked out.

Where to look first? It would be easy to decide if she knew what she was looking for.

Down the hall was Ted's study. From what she remembered from her brief time in the room the other day, it hadn't looked like he shared it with Birdie. So where had she worked?

Hope looked over her shoulder. At the kitchen table. That's why the books had been laid out along with notepads. Where were they now?

The layout was almost identical to Mitzi's house, and her laundry room was large enough to include a work area. Hope walked past the island to the white six-panel door and opened it. To her right was the pantry, and to her left was the laundry. She opened the door and entered the organized space. A sleek countertop stretched along the wall and topped the two front-loading machines. Next to the work area was a stainless-steel sink. On the opposite wall was another countertop covered with books, notepads, and photographs of plants.

She'd found Birdie's spot.

She lifted the notepad and flipped through its pages. Not much more than notations about plants, garden sketches, and a long wish list of flowers. Not exactly helpful.

Next, she shuffled through a pile of garden photographs but found nothing out of the ordinary. A stack of hardcover books at the side of the desk caught her attention, and she scanned the titles. None of them were the books on corporate fraud. Where were they? Could Ted have returned them to the library? Or maybe he moved them to his study.

She straightened up and gave the desk one last look over and noticed a torn sheet of paper with "Visionary Media Consulting" written across it.

Ah-ha! That must be what Erin was talking about. Hope pulled out her phone from her back pocket and snapped a photo of the note.

Hope stared at the paper. What was Visionary Media Consulting? Why was Birdie interested in it? Had Hope found a clue? Possibly. Feeling a tad victorious, she went to search the shelves that ran across the end wall until she heard something.

She paused and cocked her head, listening for the sound again.

Maybe it was the cat she saw the other day. She glanced around; he wasn't there.

Hope slipped her phone back into her pocket and

stepped out of the laundry room. The pantry door was still closed, so the cat hadn't gotten into there.

She pulled open the kitchen door and heard footsteps.

Shoot.

"I'll get the oven preheated. We have the baked ziti to reheat."

Hope cringed at the sound of Maretta's voice. She looked at her watch.

They were early!

Chapter Thirteen

Hope gulped as she slowly opened the door wider, careful not to make a sound or be seen. She peered out into the room. Jane swooped around the island with a large casserole in her hand.

"Ted suggested we set the buffet up in the dining room." Jane set the dish on the countertop. "He thinks the sideboard will be long enough."

"Sounds like a good idea." Mitzi dropped a canvas tote on the table.

Hope pulled back into the small hallway so as not to be seen.

Think, Hope, think.

This was not supposed to have happened. Though, when you break into a house, things could go sideways in a blink of an eye. Just like they were doing now. There was only one thing to do. She had to get Jane's attention and help to sneak out of the house.

She opened the door a sliver more. Mitzi bustled out of the kitchen carrying a fruit tray.

At the oven with her back to Hope, Maretta set the temperature. Good, now if she'd stay right there until Hope figured a way to get out of the house, that would be great.

Jane moved to the refrigerator. Perfect. She was close to Hope.

"Psst . . . Jane," Hope said in a strained, low voice.

"We probably should also warm up the rolls." Maretta walked to the island. She removed the lid from a baking dish.

Hope pulled back.

"I got the butter." Jane closed the refrigerator door and carried the butter dish to the island. "We can use the china from the cabinet in the dining room."

Hope leaned forward.

"Psst . . . Jane," she whispered again. "Psst."

Jane twisted around as if she heard something. Good!

"Psst . . . over here." Hope opened the door a little wider so Jane could see her.

Jane looked in Hope's direction, and her blue eyes bulged.

Hope waved frantically toward Maretta and prayed Jane got the message to get the mayor out of the kitchen.

Jane nodded, gesturing for Hope to get back. "I wonder if there are enough dishes for us to use. Maretta, would you be a dear and check the china cabinet?"

Maretta pulled bags of rolls out of her canvas bag. "I'm sure there are. Otherwise, Ted wouldn't have suggested it."

Hope sighed. Of course Maretta would be difficult. It really was no wonder she had been friends with Birdie.

"Well, we don't want to be left scrambling last minute when we have a house full of mourners," Jane said.

"Fine." Maretta folded the canvas bag and then trudged out of the kitchen, muttering something unintelligible.

Hope made her move and darted out to Jane. "You're early."

"You're trespassing."

Touché.

"What on earth are you doing here?" Jane monitored the kitchen's doorway, where Maretta and Mitzi could appear at any moment and catch Hope there.

"Jane, we'll definitely need more coffee cups," Maretta called out. Her footsteps were heading back to the kitchen.

"Good grief," Jane said.

"No time to talk. I need to get out of here." Maretta's footsteps seemed to get closer to the kitchen and Hope had to make a quick exit. "We'll talk later."

"Indeed we will," Jane said with a stern look. She spun Hope around and steered her to the slider. "What were you thinking?"

Hope glided the door open. "I couldn't find the corporate fraud books Birdie took out from the library. But . . ."

"Oh, Maretta, we'll need more dessert plates too!" Mitzi called out as Maretta rounded the corner and entered the kitchen.

Jane shoved Hope out the door, and she stumbled forward. For someone her age, Jane was strong. Hope regained her balance as the door slammed shut. Usually, Jane wasn't so rude, but given the circumstances, Hope understood.

Hope backed away from the door and dodged sideways to stay out of view from the women inside. Her heart was beating a mile a minute. The whole incident could have ended so differently if Maretta had found her. She could imagine the scene, and her heart rate sped up, leaving her lightheaded.

A branch snapped, and her head whipped around. Frozen in place by the sound, she scanned for another reception volunteer approaching. At least now she was outside the house and could come up with a plausible explanation for being there. But there was no one. She stepped to the edge of the patio and heard tree branches bristling. Her gaze traveled along the property line.

Was there someone in the woods? Watching the house? Watching her?

The first person to pop into her mind was Gary. But he would be at the funeral. Wouldn't he?

It could have been a wild animal, like a fox, off in the distance, but Hope didn't want to stay around any longer to find out who or what it was, so she hurried to the garden gate. A couple of times she stumbled, because she kept looking over her shoulder.

While she wanted to believe it could have been an animal creeping around, a little voice inside her said it was a person lurking.

By the time Hope arrived home, her heart rate was back to normal, and she'd shaken the feeling of being watched. Bigelow met her at the mudroom door and followed her into the kitchen, where Princess was busy with a catnip toy. The feline had the mouse toy in the grips of her front paws and was alternating tossing it in the air and biting it. Hope smiled. Princess hadn't a care in the world. Lucky cat.

When Hope reached the center island, she checked her phone again for new messages. During her short trip between the Donovan house and hers, she'd gotten a text from Drew. He was on his way over with news. There was a new email from her agent with an update on a Christmas decorations company's sponsorship. Laurel was trying to salvage the deal. Just in case she couldn't, Hope needed to start brainstorming other holiday content.

Feeling parched, she poured a glass of iced tea. Setting the pitcher back in the refrigerator, she decided to keep her illegal activity from Ethan. Though he had pretty much given her carte blanche to do it.

You do what you need to do.

It's what he said.

She took her beverage to the table and sat. Before she left, she'd been reviewing her notes in her notebook. She opened it to a clean sheet of paper.

She took a long drink of her iced tea before jotting down what she'd found and didn't find at the Donovan house. Her most significant discovery was that she wasn't cut out for breaking and entering. Technically she had a key, but it was a key she shouldn't have used.

Before she could think any more about her decision, her phone chimed, alerting of someone entering the mudroom.

She'd installed the smart doorbell at Ethan's insistence. Over the past winter, when she'd become embroiled in the murder of an old friend, she became vigilant about locking the house tightly. It hadn't lasted long. She'd once again become lax about securing the door, so maybe having the system wasn't a bad thing. Having the heads-up gave her an opportunity to call for help or look for a weapon to defend herself.

Thankfully, she didn't need a weapon. It was Drew at the door.

The kitchen door swung open and he entered, and immediately Hope knew something was wrong. His lips were downturned, and he was missing the usual spring in his step.

"What's wrong? Did something happen?" She braced herself for whatever news he was about to deliver. She let go of her pen and pushed her notebook away.

Drew nodded warily as he joined her at the table, dropping his messenger bag on another chair. "It's Avery. She's dead."

Hope jerked her head back, and her body tensed. "My goodness. How awful. What happened?

"Her body was found on a hiking trail this morning. It looks like she fell."

"An accident?"

"No official word yet. According to her best friend, Avery liked to go out on trail walks to clear her head." He tilted his head in a melancholy way. "Wonder what needed clearing yesterday?"

Hope chewed on her lower lip as she replayed her visit to Emily's House yesterday. "Maybe it was the phone call I overheard when I arrived at her office."

"Though you don't know who she was talking to or what they were talking about." Drew looked to the kitchen. "Got anything to snack on? I'm starving."

"Silly question." She couldn't recall a time when Drew hadn't been hungry. She stood and walked to the counter.

The benefit of being a food blogger was that there was always food in the house. At the cookie jar, she removed the lid and took out five double chocolate chip cookies. After she plated them, she poured a glass of milk for Drew.

"This should hold you over until lunch." Hope set the plate and glass on the table before returning to her seat.

Drew gave her a grateful look. He reached for a cookie and took a bite. "Delish."

Hope grabbed a cookie and sat back down. "When I asked Avery about Ted's travel, and if there were any irregularities at the center, she acted weird."

"From what I've seen in covering the center over the years, Avery was very protective of Ted. She was also loyal to the organization." Drew sipped his iced tea.

"She worked for him a long time. I guess it's possible her death could be a coincidence? Depending upon the conditions, hiking can be dangerous." Hope finished her cookie and then sipped her iced tea. Her cell phone chimed again, and she heard the mudroom door open and close. A moment later, the kitchen door opened, and Jane appeared. She looked none too happy, and Hope figured it had to do with her escapade only minutes ago.

"Hey, Jane," Drew said.

"What were you thinking?" Jane ignored Drew as she approached the table, wagging her finger at Hope.

"Whoa! What did I miss?" Drew dropped the cookie he'd picked up, and his eyes were wide with curiosity, much to Hope's dismay.

"You didn't tell him?" Jane propped a hand on her hip. Her dark floral dress was appropriate for the day, though she preferred brighter colors because they boosted her mood. She often complained that ladies her age tended to wear only black, gray, and white. She detested those dull colors.

"Tell me what?" Drew's voice was spiked with the irritation of being left out.

"She broke into the Donovan house and was snooping," Jane said. "You're lucky Maretta or Mitzi didn't see you."

"No way! You broke in?" Drew pressed his lips together. Hope knew him well enough to know what he was thinking—boring rule follower Hope takes a walk on the wild side.

"I didn't break in!" Hope glowered at Drew, and he dropped his gaze to the plate of cookies and nibbled on the one he had started just moments ago. "The key was under the faux rock," she explained.

Jane looked surprised. "How did you know?"

"I overheard you on the phone yesterday, finalizing the plans to set up for the reception," Hope said sheepishly.

"No!" Drew exclaimed with a mouthful of cookie.

"You eavesdropped on me?" Jane's expression softened, and her hand dropped from her hip.

Hope's brows drew together. Jane wasn't angry anymore. Why? What was going on?

"Why didn't you tell me what you were planning to do?" Jane asked.

"You're upset I didn't tell you?"

"Dear, I thought we were in this together." Jane sat across from Hope.

"We are . . . the idea didn't come to me until . . . I'm sorry I broke into the house without your help." Hope paused for a nanosecond. Had she just apologized for not including Jane in on the crime?

Jane smiled. "All is forgiven."

Hope glanced at Drew, and he looked as confused as she felt.

"I could have helped. Actually, I still can since I'm going back there. Did you find anything?" Jane asked.

"I'm not sure. What I didn't find were the books on corporate fraud."

"Ted could have returned them to the library." Jane helped herself to a cookie. Drew puckered. He was now another cookie short for his snack.

"This may mean something." Hope popped up and grabbed her phone off the island. She tapped the phone and showed them the photo of the notepad she took.

"Visionary Media Consulting. What is it?" Jane took a bite of the cookie.

Hope shrugged. "I don't know. Erin told me she walked in on an argument between Avery and Ted a week ago. They were talking about Visionary. Once they saw her, they stopped talking."

"Interesting. Send me the photo, and I'll see what I can find out." Drew snatched the last cookie.

Hope tapped on her phone again, and a second later, she said, "All done."

"Well, I better get back to Ted's house. I told Maretta I'd be gone only for a few minutes. I will look around." Jane stood and walked to the door.

"Be careful," Hope said.

"Don't worry about me. No one ever suspects a woman of a certain age." She flashed a sly smile.

"Got that right, sistah." Drew winked and then finished his cookie.

"I expect everyone will be too busy gossiping about the fact that Gary wasn't allowed to attend his sister's funeral. You would think such a tragedy would have lessened the animosity between him and Ted."

Hope's phone chimed again, reminding her that Josie was scheduled to work for a few hours. She'd forgotten

Josie was coming over for a couple of hours to work. The door opened and barely missed hitting Jane.

Josie entered, surprised to find Jane standing there. "Sorry. I didn't expect you to be there." She gave an apologetic smile to the older woman.

"No worries, dear. It's what I get for dillydallying. Keep me in the loop," she said to Hope and Drew before leaving.

"In the loop about what?" Josie walked to the table and set her laptop bag down. "Something to do with Birdie's murder?"

"Avery Marshall was found dead this morning." Drew rose and gathered his messenger bag.

"How awful! What happened to her?" Josie asked.

"It appears she fell while hiking. There aren't a lot of details at this time." Drew headed for the door but made a quick detour to the cookie jar and took two more cookies for the road. "I'll let you know what I find, Hope."

"Thanks." Hope reached for her beverage as Drew left.

"Find out what?" Josie sat in the seat Jane had vacated. "What are the three of you up to?"

Hope swallowed her sip as she tried to find a way to evade answering the question. The fewer people who knew what she was doing, the better.

"I get it. You don't trust me enough to confide in me." Josie unzipped her bag and pulled out her computer. While it turned on, she pulled out a file folder. Her silence screamed she was offended.

"I do trust you." Hope heaved a sigh. "There's so much work to do, we should keep our focus on that."

"For how long?"

"What do you mean?"

"Two brands have put you on hold indefinitely because of that video. What happens if more incriminating things come out?"

Hope was taken aback by Josie's question. How could she think that? "There won't be any more incriminating things because I didn't kill Birdie. I thought you believed me."

Josie's gaze flicked from Hope to the family room and back to Hope. "I do. Guess I'm a little scared for you. I keep thinking about worst-case scenarios."

Hope fidgeted with her necklace. It was a small heart pendant Ethan gave her for Valentine's Day. She wished he were there now because she could use his shoulders to lean on. Josie wasn't the only one who was scared for her.

"I understand. Sometimes I find myself caught up in those kinds of thoughts." Hope swiped up her glass and stood to get a refill before her coaching call. Even with her life imploding around her, she looked forward to the time with her clients. So far, none of them had dropped her. "We need to be more positive. We'll have more time to develop recipes and do an audit on the website. Find what needs to be updated and identify what needs to be changed."

"When life gives you lemons, huh?" Josie quipped.

"We make lemon bars."

"Ooh, that sounds delicious."

Hope nodded. She hadn't made them in ages, so maybe it was time to whip up a batch. The bonus of a baking session was that it helped sort out her thoughts, which usually allowed her to see things more clearly.

Josie got to work, and Hope made her coaching call with Bigelow lying beside her desk. Her office was off the kitchen and also served as a photography studio and storage for her expansive cookbook collection. The door was closed while she talked with Annette about the beliefs that kept her back from success. Getting to the core of the issues was difficult. Annette seemed to be the type of person who hadn't wanted to show her weaknesses and vulnerabilities. Still, it was Hope's job as her coach to drill down to those issues.

Forty minutes later, Hope ended the call and returned to the kitchen with Bigelow following behind her. At the island, she gathered all the ingredients for lemon bars. Josie snapped a few candid photographs while Hope prepared the batter.

The whirring of the mixer, the dusting of flour when she scooped out the measuring cup, and the fresh citrus scent that tingled her nose when she cut the lemons pushed away all thoughts about Birdie's murder. In a happier place now, she combined the wet and dry ingredients with practiced ease. The oven timer dinged, signaling the preheating period was done. She poured the batter into her prepared pan and then slipped it into the oven and set the cooking timer.

It was while she was loading the dishwasher she remembered Jane's comment about Gary. He hadn't attended the funeral. She also remembered the sounds she heard outside the Donovan house. Gary could have been there watching the house.

"Hope."

She jumped at the sound of her name, and turned, embarrassed she was jittery.

"Sorry. I didn't mean to startle you." Josie had her laptop bag in her hand, and she was by the kitchen door. "Are you okay?"

"Yeah, I am. It's something Jane said earlier that just clicked."

"What was it?"

"Birdie's brother didn't go to the funeral."

"Wow. I can't imagine not being allowed to attend my brother's funeral. It's a shame. Anyway, I'm heading home. Will you save me a lemon bar?"

"Promise." Hope closed the dishwasher's door and set the wash cycle. When Josie was out of the kitchen, she returned to the table and opened her notebook. She reviewed her notes. Nothing popped out, like the killer's name. Usually, when baking, she got some bit of clarity of things she was trying to sort out. But not this time. All she had was nada. Nothing. All she could think about was Gary. If it was him outside of Ted's house, why was he there? Then another unsettling question struck her.

If it really was him outside the house, would he tell the police she was there? For a moment, she considered telling Ethan, but she'd have to admit to trespassing. It looked like there was only one way to get the answer she was seeking, and that was to ask Gary.

Hope got to work and whipped up a second batch of lemon bars. Once they cooled, she packaged them for delivery. On her way out with the lemon bars, she patted Bigelow and almost tripped over Princess, who had finally emerged from her nap.

Out the door, Hope hurried to the garage and got into her Explorer. Minutes later, she arrived at the Merrifield Inn.

She entered the house, and the part-time receptionist at the desk pointed to the dining room when Hope inquired where Jane was.

Hope looked into the dining room and spotted Jane seated at a table set with a floral teapot and two cups with saucers. The room was identical in size to the living room, minus the French doors. The gleaming hardwood floor continued in from the foyer, as did all the intricate trim work.

Jane's companion had his back to the doorway, but Hope recognized who it was immediately.

A mix of trepidation and unease coursed through her body.

"What's he doing here?" she muttered as she plastered on a smile. It wasn't as if she could turn and run out of the inn. Jane had already spotted her.

"Good afternoon, dear." Jane beamed. "What have you brought?"

"Lemon bars." Hope walked to the table and set the container down. "I'm sorry to intrude."

Reid lifted his teacup. "No problem, Hope. I'm glad you dropped by. You were next on my list."

Chapter Fourteen

"Really? Why?" Hope willed her voice not to waver and her body not to tremble as she stared at Reid, who observed her over the rim of his cup. He knew about her entering and searching the Donovan house. She was certain.

How would she explain her presence in the house? Her mind raced, double-speed, for a plausible explanation, and then she remembered Matt's advice. She shouldn't speak to the police unless he was present.

"You were seen entering Ted Donovan's house earlier today. Mr. Donovan didn't give you permission to be there." Reid's eyes narrowed even more as he studied Hope. "Would you care to explain?"

Hope's heart thumped against her chest, hard. Hiding behind her attorney was so out of character. Yet admitting she trespassed while being suspected of a murder would probably get her arrested.

"Detective, there's clearly a misunderstanding." Jane refilled her teacup. "I'd asked Hope to do me a favor before we arrived to set up for the reception. When we arrived, we had plenty of hands to do the work, which allowed Hope to return to her home. As you see, she didn't break into the house."

Reid's expression was neutral, so Hope couldn't read whether he was buying Jane's claim. Though Hope could see no reason not to believe Jane because she sounded very convincing.

"Were the other ladies aware of Hope's involvement?" Reid asked.

"I don't believe so. It was one of those last-minute things. Maretta is very busy with town business, and Mitzi is a little flighty. She's often late, you know. Sometimes it's easier to make a decision without a lot of discussions."

Reid nodded. "I see. Well, it appears this matter is all cleared up."

"It is?" Hope asked, earning her a searing look from Jane. "It is. It's all cleared up."

"You were helping a friend." Reid stood. "I suggest from now on you stay away from the Donovan house."

"I intend to," Hope said with a nod.

"It's good to have a loyal friend," he said in a low voice as he passed by on his way out of the dining room.

Hope's hand flew up to her chest and rested over her heart as she exhaled and dropped onto a chair, setting the container on the table. "He knows I wasn't there to help you with the reception."

"He *knows* you're innocent." Jane sipped her tea. "I wonder who told him you were there."

"I think it was Gary. When you shoved me out of the house," Hope paused midsentence.

Jane gave an apologetic smile. "What choice did I

have? Maretta was marching into the kitchen. Could you imagine the scene if she found you skulking around Ted's home?"

Hope sighed. She wanted to argue, but there were three reasons why she couldn't. First, she could imagine the scene, and no doubt it would have included the police. Second, she couldn't argue with Jane's characterization of her skulking around the house because she had. Third, Jane had done the right thing. She would have done the same if the roles were reversed.

"Anyway, outside, I heard noises. Like someone was there, though I didn't see anyone. You mentioned Gary wasn't at the funeral. Maybe he was going to try to break into the house."

Jane opened the container and helped herself to a lemon bar. "You know these are my favorite."

Hope smiled. Everything she baked was Jane's favorite, but she didn't point that out. She accepted the compliment and reveled in the joy that came from spoiling a lifelong friend.

"Is Gary here?"

Jane swallowed her bite before answering. "No. I haven't seen him since he left after breakfast. I thought there was a chance he'd show up at the funeral, despite Ted's decision. After all, Birdie was his sister."

"Well, it sounds like he put his beliefs above family, so it couldn't have come as a big shock not to be invited to the funeral."

"I suppose so. When he comes back, I'll give you a call." Jane took another bite of the lemon bar.

"Promise me you won't confront him about his whereabouts today? For all we know, he could have snapped and come here to kill his sister." Hope stood.

"You have my word. Now go and do what you need to do. Remember, we're in this together, so be sure to report back." Jane continued eating her pastry.

Hope nodded and then stood to leave. On her way out the front door, she decided to take a drive and visit the trail where Avery had died. She didn't think she'd gain any new information, but she felt the pull to see where Avery had spent the last minutes of her life.

Hope reached the start of the trail when her phone chimed. The ringtone belonged to Corey Lucas, the former producer of *The Sweet Taste of Success*. The reality baking show that changed her life. She made it to the final round but lost the competition and the six-figure prize. Instead, on the night of the show's finale, she was unemployed and divorcing her husband. The bright side was that the exposure helped her fledgling blog, and by the end of the year, she was a full-time blogger moving back to her hometown. Her grandmother always said things happened for a reason. It looked like Grandma had been right. Hope now had a fulfilling life and a career she loved.

The ringtone chimed again, taunting Hope. Was there more bad news? Corey no longer worked in television. He worked for her agent now. His job title was still a mystery to Hope. He wasn't intentionally vague; he was just a get-to-the-point kind of person who didn't chitchat.

Reluctantly, she tapped on the phone to take his call.

"What's up, Corey?"

"We're in crisis mode. Geez, what have you gotten yourself into this time? Murder suspect?" A blaring horn drowned out whatever he said next. "Be assured, I'm doing everything I can to keep your career from crashing."

Corey had a dramatic flair. She guessed that was why he'd been so successful at producing reality television.

He had a knack for stirring drama and then exploiting it. Which gave her pause. Was he the right person to protect her career? Maybe a quick call to Laurel wouldn't be a bad thing.

"I appreciate anything you can do. And for the record, I didn't kill anyone."

"Yeah, yeah, of course not. You're innocent."

I am.

"Anything else?" she asked.

"No. Geez! These bicycles! It's like they own the street."

Corey lived in New York City, where he roamed the streets looking for coffee shops to work. Hope wondered if he had an office at Laurel's midtown location. He never said.

"Thanks for the update. Have a good day." She disconnected the call. Usually she'd feel bad ending a call so abruptly, but she was dealing with Corey, and he didn't stand on ceremony.

She slid the phone into her back pocket and continued on the trail. She did her best to concentrate on why she was there. The expansive vistas of woodlands all around her captivated her. The nature trail was gorgeous. As far as she could see, there was pristine, undeveloped land—a perfect spot to sit and reflect.

Or die.

She swallowed hard.

Had Avery been thinking the same thing when she set out on her hike the other day? A quiet respite from the stress of life? Like discovering her boss was an embezzler and murderer?

Hope reminded herself there was no substantial evidence against Ted. All she had was speculation. But her theories in the past had been pretty spot on for solving murders.

Up ahead, she saw the curved incline. There was no turning around now. She wanted to see the spot where Avery had fallen. She wasn't expecting a neon sign at the exact place, but Drew had texted her what he'd learned from the local police, and it should get her to the location.

Hope proceeded. Her attention was torn between the scenery surrounding her and keeping an eye on her footing. The trail was rocky and littered with fallen branches from past storms.

Up ahead, there was a section that narrowed before it widened out again to allow hikers going different directions to pass easily.

A few feet more, she reached the spot where she believed Avery fell. Off to her left were a steep ravine and a familiar figure staring at her.

Hope stopped and propped her hands on her hips. "What are you doing here?"

"I could ask you the same question." Ethan stood with his arms crossed, and when he grinned, her insides quivered. The man had an extraordinary effect on her. And she loved it.

Hope shrugged. "I wanted to see where Avery died."

"Same here."

"Why? You're on personal leave, and this isn't your jurisdiction." She crept to the edge of the trail; a break in the growth appeared to be where Avery slipped. Had she been doing what Hope was? Looking at the babbling brook beneath them?

"Reid's right. You do ask a lot of questions." Ethan moved closer to her and put a protective hand on her shoulder.

"You're talking to Reid?" She looked over her shoulder. Did that mean Ethan also knew about her snooping around Ted's house? "Does the acting chief know?"

"What do you think?"

Hope moved back from the edge. "Tell me the truth—are you investigating? Couldn't you get into trouble?"

"There are varying degrees of trouble, and I know how to stay under the radar. Officially, I'm here to hike." He glanced at his trail boots. Rugged and worn, they'd been on countless trails. "Looks like you're here to hike, too."

Hope looked at her newish hiking boots. She'd replaced her old pair last fall after a long stretch of weekend hikes. "It's a beautiful day for a walk."

"Shall we?" He took her hand and led her along the path. "According to the police report, Avery fell up ahead."

"Not here?" Hope gripped his hand tighter as she navigated around a cluster of rocks. "You read the report? How's that staying under the radar?"

"The detective handling the case is an old friend. Trust me. I know what I'm doing."

Hope trusted him completely with her safety and with her heart. She'd follow him anywhere. When she returned to Jefferson, she'd been uncertain about many things until she reconnected with him. He'd been a shoulder to lean on when her life was turned upside down, leaving her unsteady and unsure. He was also a friend to celebrate the successes with and eventually the person she knew she wanted to spend the rest of her life with.

They continued forward in silence for about thirty feet when they reached another narrow curve with three boulders positioned as steps. With the aid of Ethan guiding her, Hope climbed them. She kept her gaze on her feet, making sure she was secure as she ascended the rocks. Her thoughts drifted off to her worries about Ethan. He could be risking his career to help her. As if her mind wasn't jumbled enough with worries, another thought flickered in her mind. What would Matt say if he found out Ethan was helping her?

She lost her footing and slipped, but Ethan caught her and kept her upright. The misstep instantly focused Hope's thoughts. She and Ethan were doing what they needed to do. If it upset Matt, then so be it.

"Why aren't I surprised to see you?" Matt stood sturdy in his boots and looking comfortable in a plaid shirt and worn jeans. His position on a higher rock gave him an unobstructed view of the hills and valleys that were blooming.

"What . . . what are you doing here?" Hope wasn't sure what was going on. She climbed the final rock and quickly rooted herself back on the dirt path.

Matt smiled. "It's a beautiful day, so I thought I'd take a hike. Thanks for suggesting it, Ethan."

"Suggesting it?" Hope looked to Ethan and then back to Matt. "I thought you didn't want me to talk to Ethan about the case?" she asked Matt.

"I can only give advice. It's ultimately my client's decision whether to take it." Matt leaped off the rock and shoved his hands into his jean's pocket. "You don't take advice very well."

Hope's mouth gaped. She started to defend herself, but Ethan stepped between her and Matt and pointed to the break in the brush. Staggered down the hillside were old logs and sparse bushes.

"According to the police report, Avery left her house around five, and her body was found the next morning by a group of sunrise hikers." Ethan glanced at Hope and Matt. "She could have stopped to look around and slipped."

"Or she was pushed." Hope swallowed. She was staring down at the spot where Avery had died. She couldn't help but wonder what Avery's last thoughts were. Did she think she'd survive the freefall? "Someone could have followed her. Or she could have been walking with someone she trusted mistakenly."

"Do we know if she was with anyone? Who saw her leave for the hike?" Matt asked.

"A neighbor was outside in her garden when Avery waved before getting into her car." Ethan shielded his eyes with his hand and looked across the landscape.

"There's no way to find out what cars came into the parking lot?" Hope asked.

"No. Permits aren't required." Matt stepped back as two women approached. They smiled as they passed by and Hope pondered if they knew a woman died there.

"The police are satisfied that Avery's death was an accident?" she asked when the hikers were out of earshot.

"Pretty much. Unless something comes to light that shows foul play." Ethan dragged his fingers through his hair. Hope had noticed a sprinkle of graying at his sideburns and thought it gave him a distinguished look that was a little sexy. "I agree with you, Hope. It seems too much of a coincidence."

Ethan agreed with her about the case? Hope was tempted to pull out her cell phone and snap a selfie of them to mark the date.

"Do you know if she talked to Reid before she left the office?" Hope kept her phone where it was. She didn't need a photo to seal the date in her memory bank.

"Why did she need to talk to the detective?" Matt asked.

Hope gave them a recap of her conversation with Avery at EH. They weren't surprised by her probing. In fact, it turned out they were expecting it. However, both concurred she was basing her theories on nothing more than hunches.

"I wouldn't say they're total hunches." Hope chewed on her lower lip. She'd like to think she had more skill than just being lucky at guessing from time to time.

"Ted's passport could have been out for several reasons," Ethan said. "Perhaps it needed to be renewed. Did you check it?"

"No." Hope fretted at Ethan's good point.

"It's possible Ted became secretive because he was working with an anonymous donor. I have a few friends who donate a big chunk of change but want to remain private," Matt said.

"Okay." Hope held her hands up in surrender. "I get your point. Ethan, did she talk to Reid?"

Ethan shook his head.

"She probably came here to help get some clarity of what to do." Why hadn't Avery done what Hope said to do? Probably because Avery was in a denial stage. She couldn't fathom Ted being an embezzler and murderer.

Hope's gaze fixed on a hawk soaring above. Would Avery still be alive if she'd gone to see the detective before coming to this hiking trail? Now they'd never know.

The three agreed there wasn't anything further to learn on the trail. Whatever evidence had been there had either been collected by the police or disturbed by hikers. They turned and walked back to the parking lot.

Matt said goodbye and then got into his Lexus. Together, Hope and Ethan walked to her Explorer. She leaned against the vehicle's side, and Ethan planted himself in front of her, taking her hand in his.

"Thank you." She squeezed his hand and tugged him closer.

"For what?" He leaned in, pressing his body against hers. His mouth was mere inches from hers.

"For being on my side. For helping me."

"I'm always on your side." He covered her lips with his and kissed her for a long moment. He pulled back as if he remembered they were in public. "We don't need another viral video."

She giggled as she pushed him away. She surprised herself by being able to laugh at his joke. An hour ago, she probably would have cried. But now she saw the light at the end of the tunnel. With Ethan doing his thing while she was doing her sleuthing, she felt confident Birdie's killer would be discovered. Then her life could return to normal.

"No, we don't. What are you going to do next? Any surveillance? A stakeout?"

Ethan chuckled. "No. If there was, I wouldn't take you. I have to pick up the girls." Molly was in first grade and Becca was at preschool. He was trying to keep their schedule as routine as possible. "I want you to promise me you'll be careful. You were one of the last people to have talked to Avery before she died, and she confided in you."

"Though she really didn't tell me anything."

"Nonetheless, I want you to be careful. Understand?"

"Absolutely. I have the workshop at EH, and then I'm going home."

"Why don't you cancel the workshop until we know who killed Birdie?"

Hope considered postponing the class. Then quickly dismissed it because then she wouldn't be privy to any gossip or access to Avery's office. Basically, teaching gave her a cover for snooping.

Ethan kissed her on the cheek and then headed to his truck.

In her vehicle, Hope set her phone to an episode of a podcast, her new obsession. She'd been listening to the show since the end of winter. She was then introduced to true crime podcasts when an old friend from high school returned to Jefferson. She was a podcaster who focused on cold cases. Her show was no longer on the air, but hooked and intrigued by the medium, Hope found a new one. *Dear Husband* was the one she stumbled upon a couple of months ago. The host delved into the murders of wives at the hands of their spouses. At times, the episodes were chilling.

She tapped on the fourth episode of the current season before driving out of the lot. She chose to take the shortest route to the center. Once she merged onto the byway, she turned her attention to the podcast. The episode picked up from the last, recounting the husband's motives for murdering his wife. Top on the list was financial gain.

Just like Ted.

But she had no proof he was stealing from the center.

The podcaster moved on to a second motive: another woman.

Hope hadn't considered the possibility, though an affair would have explained his mysterious absences from the center.

Again, she had no proof. Maybe Avery had evidence, but she was dead.

Chapter Fifteen

Hope entered Emily's House, and the weight of grief and sadness of everyone inside enveloped her. The emotions were also palpable among her students when they filed into the classroom. Maybe she should have postponed the session until next week. Then again, the women gathered around the table were all survivors. Strong and determined, they would be able to push aside their mourning for Avery and focus on why they were there—to ensure a better future for themselves and their families.

Their topic was how to write a business plan. Most thought only brick and mortar businesses needed a business plan, and they were wrong. For the first part of the class, Hope drove home all the reasons why their online business also required a plan.

The lesson took longer than Hope expected, prompting one of the ladies to run downstairs and make fresh coffee for them. They worked through the pot of coffee and the official closing time of the center. Finally, Hope dismissed the class, and the ladies exited, still somber.

As Hope packed up, EH employees passed by the room on their way out. Kimmie Jensen, the administrative assistant, appeared in the doorway.

"I'm surprised you're still here." Kimmie was fresh out of college and ready to change the world. Well, that's how Avery had described the young woman after she was hired. When Hope was the editor at *Meals in Minutes*, she had worked with many editorial assistants who were exactly like Kimmie. Hope reflected further back and remembered being Kimmie. Now, Hope wasn't looking to change the world; she was looking to bring a killer to justice.

"The workshop ran over. I'm almost ready to head home." Hope closed her laptop. "How are you doing?"

Kimmie shrugged. "It doesn't seem real that Avery is dead. All day I expected to see her, to hear her ask if I wanted to order Italian or deli for lunch." Her lips twitched.

"Understandable. Guess it'll take time." Hope set her laptop into her tote bag. "Did Avery mention to you her plans to go hiking yesterday? Was she going with someone?"

"The detective handling the case asked me the same question." She lifted, then dropped her shoulders. "Avery didn't say. She hiked a lot on her own." Her cell phone buzzed. "Geez, that's my boyfriend. He's looking for a new place, and we're supposed to meet his real estate agent in thirty minutes. Are you going to be much longer?"

"You go on. I'll be right behind you." Hope closed the spiral notebook she used during class to jot down notes. She glanced up and noticed that Kimmie looked torn. The policy was not to leave a non-staff member alone in the building. "I'll make sure I lock the front door. Go on. Don't keep your boyfriend waiting."

"I don't know. . . ."

"It's fine. I won't tell." Hope smiled.

"Okay. Thanks. See you later." Kimmie swung around and practically bounced out of the room.

Hope quickly gathered her things and stuffed them into her tote. She grabbed the leather handles and walked out of the room. She looked to her right and then to her left. No one was in the house. She went to the staircase and climbed up to the second floor.

Kimmie's office door was opened, as were all the other offices on the floor. Hope made her way along the hall to Avery's workspace.

She hesitated at the entrance, her hand resting on the doorjamb as she considered what she was about to do. If anyone had asked her a week ago if she'd willingly break the law, she would have said "no way." Standing there knowing she could find something to prove her innocence left her no choice to make a different decision. Heck, she'd already searched Ted's house without permission. What was one more transgression?

She entered the outer office and went to Ted's closed office door. She turned the knob. It was locked. Not much of a surprise. Avery had mentioned he'd been locking his door lately. She turned and walked across the room to Avery's desk.

Rifling through a dead woman's workspace was something she never thought she'd do. *I'll add it to my list of things I'd never do but have done.*

Hope set her tote down and wiggled the mouse. Shoot. The computer was off, and she didn't know the password.

She could try to guess the password and waste time because she wouldn't know where to begin.

She scanned the desk. Avery kept a neat work environment. A blotter, a pencil cup, a file holder, and a landline. Hope fingered through the file holder and saw what she would have expected—documents about EH programs, events, and meetings.

She pulled open the drawers one by one and only found office supplies. It was official. Searching the office was a bust. Disappointment settled in Hope.

She expected to find something tying Avery's so-called accident to Birdie's murder. There was nothing. She reached for her tote and caught a glimpse of a piece of paper, sticking out from beneath the blotter.

Hope let go of her tote and lifted the corner of the blotter. It was a document. A contract. Between her appearance on *Sweet Taste of Success*, her business, and purchasing her home, she was familiar with contracts.

She skimmed the document between EH and Visionary Media Consulting for creative content services. According to the contract, they were in the last year of a three-year agreement.

"Holy bananas! EH paid how much?" The cost of Visionary Media's services was exorbitant. But it was the signature at the bottom of the contract that had Hope doing a double take. Avery had signed the agreement, and her title was listed as Assistant Director.

Hope worked her memory for the name of the center's former assistant director. It finally came to her. Douglas Draper. He'd resigned a year ago, so why hadn't Douglas signed the contract? And why had Birdie been interested in Visionary Media?

Hope bent over and fished in her tote for her phone.

She really needed to use a purse organizer if she continued sleuthing because she was wasting valuable time. When she finally found the phone, she took a photo of the contract. While closing the app, she saw the time. She needed to get going, but first she carefully replaced the contract in its original location, grabbed her tote, and walked to the doorway.

She popped her head out to make sure the coast was clear. Not seeing anyone, she stepped out of the office and rushed for the stairs. Her thoughts were still churning over Douglas Draper.

Why had he resigned? What happened to him?

Her hand grabbed for the newel cap when she reached the staircase, but a noise broke through her thoughts. It sounded like a floorboard squeaking.

"Hello?" Hope leaned back and looked around but didn't see anyone. She shrugged it off to being in an old house. They made noise. She began down the stairs, her palm gliding along the handrail until the hairs on the back of her neck prickled and her spidey senses went on high alert.

Someone was behind her.

Before she could react, turn to see the person, she was pushed forward.

She tumbled, tripping over her feet while frantically grappling the banister to keep from plummeting down the staircase.

Hope regained her balance; her pounding heart competed with the burst of relief surging in her body. Steadied on her feet, she turned around.

Whoever pushed her had disappeared.

This time "holy bananas" wouldn't cut it. She muttered an expletive her mother wouldn't have approved of.

Considering she could have broken her neck falling down the staircase, a few colorful words seemed reasonable.

Knowing she'd have more satisfaction saying those words to the person who pushed her, Hope turned and sprinted up the stairs.

She reached the landing and looked in both directions of the hall. Where on earth had the person gone?

The back staircase!

She zagged to her left and raced along the hall, passing empty offices to reach the narrow staircase. She paused and listened.

She heard heavy footsteps below.

Aha!

Hope tramped down the steps, her tote bouncing against her back. She'd probably have a bruise tomorrow because the bag was heavy with her laptop. When she reached the bottom of the stairs, she didn't see anyone in the kitchen.

But the back door was open.

She darted to the door and stepped out onto the porch. In the distance, she heard an engine roaring and then the sound of a car driving off.

Darn!

She pivoted and stomped back into the house. Her gaze scanned the grounds as she locked the door. Finally, she exhaled the breath caught in her throat. It was a good thing because it made way for a scream to be unleashed when a hand grabbed her shoulder.

Hope swung around with her arms in the guard position, and her hands balled into fists. She was ready to swing.

"Whoa! What's the matter with you?" Drew had his hands up in surrender mode as he jumped back.

"What are you doing here?" Adrenaline pumped through her body. "You scared the daylights out of me."

"Same here! Were you really going to punch me?" Drew dropped his hands and walked around to the door, giving Hope a wide berth.

Hope realized her arms were still up, ready to spring some jabs. She lowered them. "Sorry."

"Did something happen?" He looked through the door's window.

"I was coming down the front staircase, and someone pushed me."

"Seriously?" He spun around. "Are you okay? Wait, you were about to deck me, so you're okay. Did you see who it was?"

"No. Whoever it was left through that door," she said, pointing. "The house was empty when I went upstairs. Well, I thought it was. Did you see anyone on your way in? A car passing?"

Drew shook his head. "No. Sorry. When you were upstairs, did you find anything? I hope you did, seeing as you almost broke your neck on the staircase." He moved away from the door, closer to Hope.

"I think I did. But first, why are you here?"

"I wanted to get some quotes from Avery's co-workers. Looks like I'm late for that."

The sound of a door slamming shut had them freezing in place. They cocked their heads toward the doorway to the hall that led to the foyer and listened.

"Did you hear that?" Drew asked.

"I did. Someone is here."

"You think, Sherlock?"

Hope squinted. "I do. Now let's find out who's there." She stepped forward.

Drew grabbed her arm. "Wait. You're just going to walk out there? It could be the killer. You need a weapon."

"What do you suggest? The broom?" She gestured to the one hanging from a hook by the back door.

Drew shrugged. "It'll work."

Hope sighed. "Come on, let's find out who's out there."

Before following her, Drew grabbed the broom. She gave him an *are you kidding me* look, and he shrugged again. "If we need it, you'll be thankful I grabbed it."

Hope continued out to the narrow corridor and crept as quietly as she could with Drew behind her. Would they come face to face with the person who pushed her on the staircase? It seemed unlikely the person would have returned. Unless they wanted to finish the job. She swallowed hard. Maybe having the broom handy wasn't a bad idea.

"We need a plan," he whispered.

"You need to stop breathing on my neck," Hope hissed. A few more steps and they reached the foyer. There they found a woman standing beside the staircase with her hand resting on the newel cap and looking up to the second floor.

"Hello! Is there anyone here? Hello!"

"Norrie?" Hope and Drew said at the same time.

Norrie pivoted. When she saw Hope and Drew, she glowered.

"What are you doing here?" Hope broke from Drew and approached the reporter.

"What are you *two* doing here? And what's with the broom?" Norrie pointed to Drew's weapon. "Have you taken a job as a janitor?"

Drew frowned, and he quickly discarded the broom before joining Hope. "I'm here to interview Avery's coworkers."

"Huh." Norrie didn't look pleased, and Hope guessed

she'd planned to do the same thing. "It appears nobody is here."

"The center is closed. We were just leaving." Hope turned to go back to the kitchen and nudged Drew to move.

"Too bad you're late." Drew shimmied his shoulders as he walked away with Hope. "You snooze, you lose."

Norrie puffed.

"That wasn't very nice," Hope said.

"Neither is she." Drew wrapped an arm around Hope's shoulder. "Let's get out of here."

As they reached the kitchen, they heard the front door close. Drew threw his hands up in the air. "Thank goodness she's gone. Now, tell me what you found." Drew leaned against the counter.

Hope moved to the table and grabbed the handles of her tote. "A contract between EH and Visionary Media. Avery signed it."

"She was a secretary. Why did she sign the contract?"

"According to the document, she was the assistant director. And you need to find Douglas Draper because he resigned last year, remember? I wonder if he discovered Ted and Avery embezzling from the center."

"Wow. You think Avery was in on it?"

"We can't rule anything out." Hope lifted her tote bag.

"I'm on it. Where are you going?"

"To the country club."

"Must be nice. I'm slaving away, and you're lunching with the ladies."

Hope grabbed her tote from the kitchen chair. She definitely wouldn't be lunching at the country club. The last time she was there, she kind of made not one scene, but two. She wasn't sure she'd get in the door.

Chapter Sixteen

Hope smiled at the nice man dressed for an afternoon of golf as he held the door of the Jefferson Country Club for her. So far, so good. Inside the lobby people were coming and going from the golf greens and tennis courts. Clusters of members engaged in conversations and shared drinks, while others filed by on their way outdoors.

She spotted Claire in the restaurant, seated at a table with Robin Delaney.

Wearing a white tennis dress with a pink jacket, Claire looked ready to hit the courts. As did her friend and opponent for the day. Robin's zipped top had a pricey designer label and the quilted tennis bag set by her chair hadn't come from a discount store. She took her game as seriously as Claire and spared no expense.

They looked relaxed and in good spirits, which meant they hadn't played yet. As Hope approached the table, she overheard their conversation about someone named Margot and her showy Tesla.

Was there any other kind? Hope had a hard time not rolling her eyes.

"Hope?" Claire set her glass of lemonade on the table. "What on earth are you doing here?"

"I was in the neighborhood," Hope lied. She was nowhere near the country club but didn't want to miss out on the conversation with Robin. It was Claire's first foray into sleuthing and she might be needing some help. "Hi, Robin."

"Good to see you, Hope. How's the blog business treating you?" Robin's plumped lips eased into a smile. Her glossy auburn hair was tamed by a headband and her angular face was smooth and line free. She wasn't beautiful, nor was she unattractive. She was average. She was also a socialite who hadn't needed to rely on her looks for anything in life. While Claire had earned her own money to afford the club's fees, Robin inherited hers as well as her membership. There were never any waiting lists in Robin's world.

"It's going great. Do you mind if I join you?" Hope pulled out the empty chair without waiting for a reply.

"Well, we're going to play in a few minutes," Claire said.

"I've been thinking of joining." Hope looked around the club. "It would be nice to have somewhere to go and decompress for a bit."

"Is blogging stressful?" Robin reached for her glass and took a sip of her drink. Her diamond tennis bracelet sparkled, mesmerizing Hope.

"It can be." Hope reached for a grape from the fruit plate. "What I didn't realize when I started the blog was the number of opportunities I'd get to expand my platform."

Or how many I'd lose so quickly.

"Really?" Claire asked dryly.

"How so, Hope?" Robin sounded genuinely curious.

"I've started coaching other bloggers to help them build their businesses. I'm also teaching a workshop on how to start an online business at Emily's House." Hope leaned back.

Claire glowered at her sister. She wasn't pleased with Hope's insertion into what should have been her questioning of Robin. Hope offered her sibling a weak smile and then turned her attention back to Robin, whose face was clouded with sadness.

"It's such a shame. First, Birdie's death and now Avery's. Tragic." Robin lifted her fork and pierced a cucumber from her salad bowl.

"Indeed," Claire said. "EH does so much good."

"They have changed countless lives—saved, even." Robin set her fork down. Her gaze drifted toward a group of women entering from the locker rooms, and then she glanced at her pricy watch. Hope worried she was losing interest.

"Your husband is on the board of directors, isn't he?" Hope asked.

Robin's perfect posture, thanks to years of Pilates, perked up with pride. "Has been for ten years."

"It's admirable he's given so freely of his time to EH. You know, I was thinking earlier about the center's upcoming anniversary celebration, and one name popped into my head out of the blue. Douglas Draper." Hope grabbed another grape. "Do you remember him? He was the assistant director. I'm sure your husband had dealings with him."

Claire cleared her throat as she pushed back her chair.

"May I have a word with you in private?" Not giving her sister the chance to answer, she tugged Hope up from her chair.

"Excuse us." Hope slapped at her sister's hand as she followed Claire. "What's the matter with you?"

Claire released the grip on her sister when she came to a stop by the entry of the restaurant. "Why are you checking up on me?"

"I'm doing no such thing." Hope crinkled her nose. It was a little white lie. Teeny, really. "I am thinking about joining the club."

"Good for you. Applications are at the front desk." Claire pointed.

"Okay. Fine. I'm here to help you. You're new at this sleuthing thing. Getting information out of someone can be tricky."

Claire tilted her head sideways. "I'm an experienced real estate agent. Do you really think I can't get information out of people?"

"Point taken."

"Now tell me why you're asking about Douglas Draper."

Hope leaned closer to her sister and lowered her voice when she explained the contract she discovered under Avery's blotter. She left out the part about being pushed down the stairs. There wasn't any need to worry Claire since she wasn't hurt.

"Now that's interesting. It's a shame you won't be able to ask Douglas about what happened."

"Why not?" Hope stepped aside when a party of four gentlemen passed by to join another group already seated.

"He died last year after a long illness. That's why he resigned from EH. I sold his house, and his widow now lives in Florida. I need to get back to Robin. You can show yourself out." Claire returned to her table.

Hope, frowning at the news about Douglas, made her way to the restaurant's entrance.

Not being able to talk to him was disappointing, just like not speaking with Robin. She looked over her shoulder. Sure, Claire had experience communicating with people. Still, she wasn't trying to find out if Robin wanted a second-floor laundry room or a good school system.

"You should watch where you're walking." Meg's harsh tone snapped Hope's head forward.

The temptation to come back with a snarky reply was hard to resist. Meg always seemed to push the wrong buttons. Even so, Hope refrained from creating a scene since they were in public and everyone carried a cell phone.

She wasn't about to make the same mistake twice.

Meg was dressed in a pair of wide-leg pants and a fitted sleeveless top. Dark sunglasses topped her head, and she carried a rattan bag in the crook of her arm. She appeared to be going for the ladies who lunch look.

"You're a member?" Hope asked. It seemed like a safe question.

"No. My aunt is. Not that it's any of your business." Meg strode pass Hope, heading toward the dining room.

"Wait, Meg." Hope spun around. "I need to ask you something."

Meg stopped, tilted her head, and huffed. She was always so dramatic. She probably should have gotten the lead in the school play they'd been arguing over for decades. For some reason, Meg thought the part had been hers before the casting decision was announced. When Mrs. Collins made the announcement that Hope was the lead, Meg got it in her head that Hope had cajoled their teacher for the part. Hope wondered if deep down Meg thought that landing the lead in the school play had something to do with Hope appearing on the reality baking show and getting her fifteen minutes of fame.

Meg turned around and gave Hope a blank stare. "What is it?"

Hope wasn't going to be put off by Meg's less than enthusiastic attitude. "Did anyone in your book club have a problem with Birdie? I heard Birdie had complained about the club coming into the rare books room when she was working there."

"Birdie complained about a lot of things. She acted like she owned the library and could tell us where to go. I think she shushed more people than Angela ever has."

"Did she ever confront anyone in your group?"

"Not really. She griped when we were in there, but other than that, she left us alone. She didn't track down people on the street and yell at them." Meg snickered at her little jab to Hope. "However, I know she gave Angela an earful. Are you playing detective again?"

Meg was trying to bait Hope, but she wasn't taking it. She'd gotten what she needed from Meg.

"Have a nice day." Hope pivoted and walked away. Since elementary school, Hope had tried to be friends with Meg. When Meg's aunt died last year, Hope thought they'd had a chance to finally move past their silly rivalry. She had been wrong.

"Though I did see Birdie arguing with someone a couple of weeks ago at the library," Meg said.

Hope stopped and turned on her heel. "Who?"

Meg blinked and gave a satisfied smile. She had something she knew Hope wanted. Childish.

"If you saw the argument, I'm sure someone else also

did. Thanks for the tip." Hope made a move to turn. It probably was the same argument Casey witnessed between Angela and Birdie.

"Sally. They were outside in the garden. Birdie was going on and on about how she would have done a better job with the design."

Sally?

"What happened?"

"Sally stormed off after telling Birdie to 'stuff it.'"

Stuff it? That sounded like Sally. It also reminded Hope of how defensive Sally got when she was asked her whereabouts when Birdie was poisoned. She also had been uncooperative with Reid at the library. Why hadn't she welcomed the opportunity to prove to him she hadn't murdered Birdie? Sally definitely was hiding something.

"Thanks, Meg."

"For what it's worth, I don't think you poisoned Birdie. A lot of people didn't like her. I always wondered what her deal was. You know, what made her so mean. And how the heck did Ted ever marry her?" Meg asked.

Hope suspected what happened twenty years ago that caused a falling out between Birdie and her brother had a lot to do with her sour disposition, though she wouldn't be speculating with Meg any time soon.

"Thanks again for your help. Enjoy your lunch." Hope swiveled around and headed for the exit. Things were adding up on her to-do list, but there was one action item she had to do ASAP—find out what Sally was hiding.

Hope was greeted by Bigelow at the door when she arrived home. She patted him on the head before seeking out Princess. She found her feline lying on the ottoman in the family room. As Hope approached, Princess slit her eyes open and stretched her long body. Hope sat on the floor and rubbed the cat's belly. She was rewarded with purrs of contentment. Not wanting to be left out, Bigelow settled next to Hope and rested his head on her leg. This was precisely what she needed—a big dose of unconditional love.

Her phone dinged with a notification alerting her to comments coming from followers. She'd scheduled a garden video to go up on her social media. She pulled the phone out and checked.

"These garden videos are always popular," she said to Bigelow and Princess. "Too bad, it looks like I won't be planting a vegetable garden this year. Next year, for sure." Hope scrolled through the comments. That warm and fuzzy feeling she had a moment ago faded as she came to a section of not-so-nice comments.

You might not get to plant your veggie garden if you're in the slammer, one person wrote.

It looked like not all her followers were loyal. Like the troll who left that nasty comment.

Maybe you can work in the prison garden, another person wrote.

Hope shook her head. What was wrong with people? And why was she reading those comments?

Princess rolled over. She leaped off the ottoman and slinked out of the family room. Clearly, she was done bonding with Hope. Bigelow lifted his head and tilted it. His big brown eyes stared up at Hope.

Hope swallowed the lump in her throat. She was about to get emotional if she didn't do something . . . anything. As if reading her mind, Bigelow stood and trotted to the front door. She liked what he had in mind. Standing up, she grabbed the novel she'd been trying to finish for a month off the coffee table and headed for the front porch.

Hope left the door open but closed the screen door behind her as she stepped out onto the porch. She inhaled a deep breath of sweet air as Bigelow darted down the steps. On the front lawn, he started sniffing earnestly. It seemed like every time he got outside, he discovered fresh scents. The activity would keep him occupied for a while.

A breeze rolled through, rustling the old oak tree in her front yard, and the clusters of daffodils planted throughout the garden beds also swayed.

She glanced at the book she carried and couldn't wait to pick up where she left off. Reading on the porch seemed decadent, considering all the work waiting for her and the big, fat dark cloud hanging over her. Some would argue if there was ever a time for such decadence, now would be the time.

An approaching car's sound drew her attention from her book, and she moved to the porch railing. She recognized the green minivan and wondered what brought Casey by.

"Hey, Hope!" Out of her vehicle, Casey grabbed her purse before closing the driver's side door. "I'm sorry I didn't call before dropping by."

Hope set her book on the sectional and then walked to the steps. "No problem. It's nice to see a friendly face."

She forced herself to shake off those mean comments because they were a part of the job that would not go away. People had opinions about everything she did. She guessed she needed to develop a thicker skin.

"I'm sorry. I heard about Birdie's cause of death and the fact the police consider you a person of interest. Anyone who knows you doesn't believe you'd do such a thing. Hang in there."

"I appreciate the support. What brings you by?" Hope descended the steps.

"I wanted to run this by you." Casey dug into her purse and pulled out a piece of paper and a photo. "This is a recipe for my grandmother's pound cake. It's a family treasure, and it means a lot to all of us. This is me and my brother, Parker. Every Christmas, Granny made the pound cake, and Parker and I would tear down the stairs to see what Santa left. My parents had a rule. We could open only one gift, and then we'd have to eat breakfast."

"Sounds cruel," Hope joked.

"It was! Deciding what gift to open first, would it be the one we were hoping for? Then having to take a break to eat? But the bright side was that breakfast included a slice of the pound cake with whipped cream and a sprinkle of cinnamon. Which meant we were hyped up on sugar to open the rest of the presents."

"And certain to crash later to give your parents a break."

"Exactly. Do you think we could include this recipe in the cookbook? I'd love to share my family's Christmas tradition."

"I don't see why not. May I?" Hope gestured for the recipe.

"Of course." Casey handed the sheet of paper to Hope.

"You two were cute kids," Hope commented on the photo. "Look at all the snow outside the window."

"Yeah, winters were brutal up in Massachusetts. I guess it's the same down here." She stared at the photo. "It's a shame the very next year after we took this photo,

Christmas was different. Our mom was gone." Casey's voice was melancholy, and she looked sad.

"I'm sorry." Hope rubbed Casey's arm. "You know, I was about to go inside and pour a glass of iced tea. Would you like to join me?" Her book could wait a little while longer.

Casey shook her head. "No, thank you. I have to get over to the school for a PTO event. Some days I feel like I live at the school. Thanks again for including the recipe." She turned and dashed back to her minivan. A few moments later, she was pulling out of the driveway.

Hope looked at the recipe and had a thought. She could publish a few recipes that would go into the library's cookbook on her blog. It would give added exposure to the fundraiser, and possibly more sales since her website was already set up to sell products.

Happy with the idea, she bounded into the house to write down the details while they were still fresh in her mind. Her book could wait a few more minutes. Bigelow followed but detoured into the family room to settle on his bed.

At her desk, Hope wrote her ideas for the cookbook. She opened the computer file where her notes and timelines for the cookbook were stored. She added in the recipe and then put the notepaper into a file folder. When she was done with her brain dump, she closed the folder and patted it, confident she'd be organizing dozens of recipes for the book. Having a pleasant distraction was welcomed. To think she'd dreaded the project only a few days ago. It was amazing how quickly things changed.

It was also nice to see Casey becoming involved in the community, her new hometown. She seemed to be making friends, jumping into volunteer projects, and exploring Jefferson. Like she was doing the day Hope dropped off the muffins to Birdie.

Hope leaned back and recalled the incident. Birdie had spotted Casey jogging by, and in a flash, her demeanor became more unpleasant. Thinking back to the exchange, Hope zeroed in on Birdie's tone. At the time, she hadn't thought much of it since she was there trying to make amends. Now, revisiting it, Hope realized that Birdie's tone had turned from annoyed to bitter and cold.

Had Birdie really thought she owned the street? Or was there something about Casey that Birdie despised?

She flipped open the folder and looked at the recipe. Casey said she was from Massachusetts. Birdie had been from that state too. Coincidence? Possibly. Yet could Casey have had something to do with whatever caused a wedge between Birdie and Gary?

Chapter Seventeen

"Good night, girls." Hope flicked off the light switch and stepped out into the hall with Ethan behind her. He pulled the door closed and grasped Hope's hand. "They're exhausted."

Not too long after Casey left after dropping off the recipe, Ethan and his daughters arrived. Hope wasted no time in putting all three to work in the kitchen. Ethan grilled, Molly and Becca buttered the homemade rolls before they went into the oven, and Bigelow gave his best *I'm a starving dog, please feed me* face. Hope knew better and shooed him away.

While on the patio out of earshot of the girls, Hope told Ethan about the incident at EH. She assured him she wasn't injured, only a little shaken afterward. Their conversation was cut short because Molly came out to help grill. After dinner, the four of them played a board game and then watched a mermaid movie until bedtime.

"They'll sleep tight." Ethan led Hope downstairs and

into the family room. Bigelow was seated by the French doors, looking outside. He'd stare out there for hours, occasionally woofing when he heard the resident raccoon. Princess couldn't be bothered to keep a night watch. She was curled up on an armchair, gently snoring. "I see someone else is sleeping tight."

"Swatting at Bigelow all day takes a lot out of her." Hope dropped onto the sofa, and she tugged Ethan down with her. "I have to admit, this day took a lot out of me."

"Are you sure you're okay?" he asked.

"I'm sure. I only lost my balance for a split second." She thought back to the minutes before she went upstairs to Avery's office. "I'm certain there was nobody else there. I saw the staff leave. Kimmie was the last to leave."

"It's possible one of them returned through the back door." He propped an elbow on the back of the sofa. "There's something we need to talk about."

Hope studied his face. While he told everyone he was fine, the deep creases on his forehead, the fatigue in his eyes, and his missing smile told a different story. So it pained her to say, "If it's about me investigating, don't waste your time. I'm not stopping." She grabbed the remote control and pressed the on button.

Ethan took the remote and pressed the off button. "It's not about you investigating."

"Oh."

"I'm concerned Heather won't be in the position to take back custody when she's released from rehab. At least right away. This means I'll have full custody of the girls, and it's got me thinking about the future. *Our* future. What do you think about moving in together?"

"Move in together? Live here? Together?" Hope's words were jumbled in her brain and she couldn't make a complete sentence. She'd hoped they would have the conversation someday but now seemed too soon. Their first getaway as a couple only happened in March. Ethan had been staying over more, though, and she was getting used to waking up beside him. It was becoming the best part of her days.

"We're practically doing it now."

"You and me?" Hope wasn't sure how she felt about living together. The only person she'd lived with besides college dormmates was her ex-husband. Neither experience had been overwhelmingly positive. When she moved into the farmhouse by herself, it felt liberating. She came and went as she pleased. There was no one to answer to or check with before doing any projects. If she wanted pizza for breakfast that's what she had.

Ethan reached out and stroked Hope's arm. "Maybe get a house with a pool for the girls."

"Sell my house?" She pulled back and leaned into the cushion. After all the work she'd done with the renovations and upgrades, could she sell her home? The blogger in her considered that a new home could serve as a new project to write about. It would also be a lot of work. She wasn't sure she wanted to do it again. At least, not for a few more years.

He shrugged. "It's clear your neighbors aren't thrilled with you."

Hope's mouth dropped open.

"I'm joking." He chuckled, but Hope wasn't amused. "It would be nice if we could get a place of our own big enough for the girls and maybe some more room for you. You've complained the kitchen isn't big enough for all your filming needs. Maybe we can find a house with a separate building that can be converted into a studio."

Now there was a point she couldn't argue. A separate studio kitchen would be a dream come true. She could leave the lighting and cameras set up and be able to close the door on her workday. Working from home was a luxury but work often crept into her personal time.

But moving in together was a big step, a big commitment. Add in Molly and Becca, and it wasn't something to decide too quickly about. She loved Ethan, and he loved her, but were they ready to live together? Then again, Molly and Becca were being shuffled between two homes right now, and when Heather was released, it would be three homes.

Also, was now the right time to make a life-altering decision? Birdie's murder case loomed over her, and until she was cleared, the smart thing to do would be to hold off making any significant changes.

"I thought you'd be more excited about the idea. I just asked you to move in with me. For us to live together." Ethan sounded disappointed.

"I am excited. I'm also surprised. There's so much going on. Heather's treatment, me being a murder suspect, and I love my home. You know how much it means to me." She leaned forward and cradled his face in her hands. She needed for him to understand her reasons for being hesitant. "It's more than just a house. It's my home."

"I do. I'm hoping the home we buy together will mean more to you."

Her heart squeezed. Of course *their* home would mean the world to her, but the home she was living in at the moment was far more than only a shelter. It represented her independence, her hard work, and her strength.

"Am I moving too fast?" Ethan asked.

"You're moving in the exact direction I'd been thinking of." She sighed. "I don't know. Maybe it's the murder case. . . . I'm having a hard time focusing on anything else. It's also a lot to think about. Finding a new home will be a lot of work to get what we both want."

"I know. You'll at least think about it?"

Oh, there wasn't any way she wouldn't be thinking about it. "Yes." She leaned forward and kissed him.

The next morning, Hope and the girls waved goodbye to Ethan as he strode down the porch steps, heading to his truck. He had an appointment with his attorney to shore up the details of the new custody arrangement. Not sure how long he'd be tied up, Hope offered to watch the girls. "Come on, let's finish breakfast."

"Chocolate chip pancakes!" Becca suggested.

"No! Banana pancakes!" Molly countered.

Bigelow slid down to the porch floor and rested his head on his front legs. He seemed to take the girls' bickering in stride.

"How about chocolate chip and banana pancakes?" Hope's question was answered by two sets of wide eyes. "Sound good?"

Becca and Molly nodded as they hurried to the front door. Bigelow popped up and joined them as they entered the house. Inside, Becca broke free and skipped into the kitchen while Molly chided her for not walking like a lady. Hope suppressed a giggle. The two of them reminded her so much of herself and Claire when they were little.

The girls settled at the table with their coloring books while Hope whipped up the pancakes. She scooped out a cup of mini–chocolate chips and mashed a ripe banana. Within minutes, she flipped perfectly browned pancakes onto two plates. Molly liked only butter while Becca preferred maple syrup. Lots of maple syrup.

While the girls ate, Hope fed Bigelow. She made him a special treat: his very own pancake minus the chocolate chips.

After serving him, she took a few minutes to pour a cup of coffee and review her to-do list for the day.

It was a long one, and now that she was babysitting, she wasn't sure how she'd get everything done.

"What are we doing today, Hope?" Becca asked between mouthfuls of pancake.

"I want to play outside. Do you think Poppy will play with us?" Molly asked.

Hope looked up from her planner. "Poppy really doesn't play. But sure, you both can play outside." She made a note in her planner about buying a swing set. There was only so much tag and kickball the girls could play.

"Maybe we can make some friends here," Molly said to her sister.

Becca shrugged. "We have friends."

"But not here. We have friends at home and at Dad's house. We need friends here." Molly drank her milk. She was the social butterfly of the siblings. She made friends quickly, while Becca held back a little around strangers. "Hope, are there any kids here?"

Hope thought for a second and remembered Zara had kids close to Molly and Becca's age. "Yes, there are. Let me make a call." She reached for her cell phone and found Zara's contact information. While waiting for Zara to answer, she realized the playtime would allow her to find out if Zara had pushed Birdie during their dispute.

An hour later, Hope walked the girls to Zara's house. Becca and Molly were excited to meet new friends, and so were Zara's children. In the front yard, introductions were made, and then they all went running to the backyard. There was a massive swing set, an in-ground trampoline, and a soccer net for them to enjoy.

"They're adorable." Zara led Hope to the back deck, where they'd have a full view of the playdate. "I have lemonade. Would you like a glass?"

"I'd love some." Hope followed her up the deck stairs. The morning was warming up with a hint of humidity, giving them a summer preview. The change in weather prompted her to pull her hair into a ponytail to keep the frizz down.

Zara reached the wooden table with chunky legs and poured two glasses. "So will the girls be staying with you a lot?"

"Yes, they will. It's nice that they can make friends here." Hope took a glass as she sat on a chair. She sipped the beverage. "This definitely hits the spot."

Zara nodded and raised her glass. She pulled out a chair beside Hope and sat. "I wish I could say it's freshly made, but . . . I scooped it out of a container and added water. These days I have little time for anything from scratch."

"There's no shame in shortcuts." Hope craned her head to look at the kids. Becca was on a swing and Molly was kicking a soccer ball with Zara's eldest. "Looks like they're getting along."

"Sure does. It gives us some downtime. Trust me, you'll learn how important it is, even if it's only a few minutes here and there."

Her glass was halfway to her lips when she paused.

Last night Ethan talked about moving in together, and now Zara was giving her mom advice. Her palms got sweaty, and her stomach churned. It seemed everything was moving so fast. In a matter of days, she had a ready-made family. Not that she wasn't happy about it. She loved Ethan and his daughters. So why wasn't she more excited about the changes?

"Thanks for the advice. I'll keep it in mind." Hope sipped the lemonade. It was time to shift the conversation from parenting tips to Birdie. "I'm going to enjoy this break. A lot has been going on."

Zara barked out a laugh. "Well, if that isn't an understatement. You're a murder suspect."

Hope stiffened. Even though Zara's tone was light, her words stung.

"Of course you're innocent." Zara's words were rushed, probably because she saw the hurt look on Hope's face. "I'm certain there were a lot of other people who were angrier with her than you were. Though if I found out she had started a petition to get me to move, I would have been furious with her."

"You were pretty steamed with her about the shrub she cut down." Hope set her glass down. A burst of giggling drew her attention to the play area. They'd been through so much because of their mom. Seeing Molly and Becca enjoying themselves filled her heart with happiness.

"I'm sensing this visit wasn't just about the kids playing together." Zara set her glass on the table with a clang. "Let me guess. Mitzi Madison. Neighbors love to gossip, don't they?"

"You don't deny your altercation with Birdie was a little more intense than you told me?"

"Are you trying to make me out to be Birdie's killer?"

Zara folded her arms across her chest. "You have a lot of nerve. I invite you and your boyfriend's kids over to play with my children, and you accuse me of murder?"

"I'm not accusing you of anything." Hope sensed her welcome was wearing thin.

"I disagree." Zara uncrossed her arms. "Birdie and I argued. She was indignant, as always. There was no reasoning with her. Our tempers flared, and I pushed her. After all, she was on my property."

High-pitched squeals filled the midmorning air. With a quick look behind her, Hope found the kids playing tag.

"I think you should leave." Zara stood and swiped up Hope's glass. "Playtime is over. It's time to go inside! Come on. Molly and Becca have to go home."

"Please, don't do this." Hope raised her hand in surrender. "I apologize. I was out of line."

"You most definitely were. I won't be accused of murder in my own home." Zara marched toward the children, who were voicing their unhappiness with the sudden change of events.

Hope inhaled and shook her head as she stood. She'd made a mess of things, and this time it affected not only her. It affected Molly and Becca. She climbed off the deck toward the kids.

"Why do we have to go?" Molly asked.

"Yeah, why?" Becca pouted as she propped her hands on her hips.

"I forgot we have something to do back at the house," Hope lied. Now she had to figure out what they were going to do. It had to be something extraordinary, or she'd have two miserable girls.

"You can come back," Zara's youngest said as Hope took each girl by the hand.

Zara shot Hope a look that showed there was no open invitation for her or the girls to return. Hope had no idea of how to handle the situation. She'd have to call Claire for advice once she got home.

While Becca and Molly chatted amongst themselves about their new friends, Hope couldn't help but wonder why Zara had gotten so upset. All she had to do was admit to pushing Birdie and say she hadn't killed her neighbor. Instead, she got all hot about it and threw Hope and the girls off her property. She looked over her shoulder back at the Meyers' house.

Zara had moved to the top of her suspects' list.

"Ah . . . Ah . . . baking," Hope suggested when the girls asked what they would do next

"Baking? We can bake anytime," Molly said.

"We can, but I need the cake for my blog, so I have to make it today." Hope hated lying, especially to children. "I'll need your help."

Becca and Molly looked skeptical.

"What kind of cake?" Becca asked.

"Well, I need help deciding. What do you both suggest?"

Becca and Molly looked at each other and then said, "Princess cake!"

Hope nodded. What on earth was a Princess cake?

It turned out a Princess cake, based on Molly and Becca's description, was a two-layer white cake with a buttercream filling and pink frosting sprinkled with edible sugar pearls. Hope photographed the final product before cutting two slices of the cake. While the girls ate, she snapped photos, careful not to get their full faces in the photos.

Hope was enjoying a bite of the cake when her phone rang. It was Matt, and he sounded somber. *Again.*

"What's up?" Hope stood from the table, carrying her plate to the dishwasher.

"We need to talk. I'm on my way over."

"Sure. Becca and Molly are here."

"Put on a video for them to watch. This can't wait. Be there in ten." The line went silent.

Hope set her phone on the counter. She chewed on her lower lip as the slice of cake she just ate settled in her stomach like a brick. It didn't take a rocket scientist to know that when your attorney said a conversation wouldn't wait, it would be bad.

She gave herself a mental shake. Being all doom and gloom would not help whatever situation had arisen. After setting the phone down, she clapped her hands, prompting the girls to look up.

"It looks like we're going to have company. How about a video?"

Both girls nodded and blurted out suggestions.

"Okay, here's what we'll do. Becca, we'll put yours on now, and after dinner, Molly, we'll put yours on," Hope hurried her words to ward off a mini-meltdown from Molly. She thought her game plan was reasonable.

Molly's face scrunched, and it was clear she disagreed with Hope's plan. "Why can't we watch my choice now?"

"It's a compromise." Hope walked to the table and picked up the plates and empty milk glasses.

"What's a compromise?" Molly asked.

"It's what we're doing by watching my video first and then yours," Becca answered. "Come on, let's go watch it."

Hope heaved a sigh of relief. The battle wasn't as bad

as it could have been. She did a quick cleanup of the kitchen before Matt arrived.

She had a few minutes, and she used it to check her email. It turned out to be a mistake because there was one from Laurel.

Dread consumed her as she hit the subject line to open the email. As she read, it turned out she was right to feel apprehensive. Lily-Frye, the premium paint company she'd had a working relationship with for two years, was taking a break from her.

Laurel cited the morals clause in their contract. Yadda, yadda, yadda. Hope knew the drill by now. She didn't need it all spelled out. Being a murder suspect wasn't good for their business. Or hers.

Matt arrived and she settled him in the living room. There they could talk without worry they'd be overheard. Her nerves were on edge and she hadn't been in the mood for small talk.

"I'm having a hard time believing Reid can't find another suspect in Birdie's murder. I mean, I have!"

"What do you have so far?"

Hope hurried back to the sofa and sat, tucking one leg under her body and slinging an arm across the sofa's back.

"Ted. He rushed out of EH the morning his wife was murdered, and no one knew where he went, plus he had his passport out and an airline confirmation for a trip. Gary, who claimed not to have seen his sister in two decades, is lying because there's a video of him skulking in the shrubs outside the library the day before she died. Zara had a physical altercation with Birdie, and Zara is still upset by the incident. See, three people off the top of my head."

"Warning you off investigating at the start of all this seemed to have been a wasted effort." Matt sipped his coffee.

Hope shrugged. "You didn't seriously think I'd stay out of this. Besides, you and Ethan have had your heads together."

Matt grinned. "He had no intention of not helping you. Look, my gut tells me Reid doesn't want to arrest you. I suspect he believes you're innocent, but if Clifford or the State Police put pressure on him, he'll have no choice. I need you prepared for it. Just in case."

Matt's words sunk into Hope, and they had the same chilling effect as the words her ex-husband said to her when he told her he wanted a divorce. It felt like a rug had been pulled out from under her, leaving her reeling. What followed next was an overwhelming sense of insecurity. The not knowing was the hardest thing to deal with then, and now she was facing it again.

"I appreciate the heads up. I'm not sure how to prepare for being arrested, but I'll do the best I can."

"Know it's not personal. Reid would only be doing his job. And given that Ethan is the chief of police, as many courtesies as possible will be extended to you. At least, that's what I think from my experience. Try not to worry."

Easier said than done.

Hope stood and walked to the window and looked out. She had no choice but to kick her investigation up a notch. Three suspects weren't enough. She needed a lead, some evidence, or a Deep Throat. Any one of those would come in handy since she was determined to hand-deliver the killer to Detective Reid.

Chapter Eighteen

Hope waved to Matt as he backed his Lexus out of her driveway. She couldn't say she felt better after their conversation. Still, at least she knew where she stood regarding the police investigation.

She glanced at her watch. There were fifteen minutes before the girls' video would be over. That was enough time for her to grab her trusty planner and jot down ideas for recipes. She might have lost her sponsorships, but she still had her blog. Besides, keeping busy was a good thing.

She turned around at the sound of Molly and Becca at the front door. They were done with the video earlier than she calculated. Bigelow joined them, and he had that familiar look on his face.

"Can we take Bigelow for a walk?" Molly was already holding the harness and leash.

"Sure. Let's go." Hope harnessed her dog and gave the leash back to Molly. They jogged down the porch steps and set off for a quick walk up and down the street.

The girls chatted while Bigelow displayed his best behavior while walking. Hope was sure if any of her neighbors were looking out their windows, the whole scene looked normal. Normal was something she craved. Would she ever experience it again?

"Who's he? He's looking at you funny, Hope." Becca pointed to Ted, who was walking to his mailbox.

Hope grimaced. She couldn't very well explain her relationship with him to Becca. "His name is Ted Donovan. I want to talk to him for a moment. Can you both stay right here?" When the girls nodded, Hope broke away and sprinted toward him.

"Hope." Ted's gaze drifted back to his mailbox, and he removed a thick stack of envelopes. She guessed they were condolence cards. Hers was probably in the bunch.

"How are you doing?" As soon as the question escaped her lips, she knew it was a lame question.

"As well as you'd expect. My wife was murdered." His voice was harsh, and it matched his stare.

"Of course, I'm sorry. The other day I met Birdie's brother. He said he hadn't seen her in twenty years. That's a long time."

"That's true. They had a falling out, and he, being a holier-than-thou man, couldn't forgive his sister." From the tenor of Ted's voice, it was clear there was no love lost between the men.

"He saw her the day before she died."

"What are you talking about?"

"At the library. There's a video of Birdie and me talking, and when I enlarged it, I saw Gary in the background. Why would he lie?"

Ted's jaw hardened. "I'm sure the police will find out. I'd appreciate it if you stayed out of my family business."

He slammed the mailbox door shut. "Also, under the circumstances, I think it's best to cancel the rest of the online business workshop at the center."

"We're almost at the end."

"My mind is made up." Ted stalked back to his house.

"So is mine," Hope muttered. She propelled forward, determined to get some answers. "Ted!"

He stopped, turned around, and gave a look that dared her to continue—a look he probably expected to force Hope to cower and turn away.

She rooted herself in place; she wasn't about to back down, not when she knew that Ted was hiding something.

"Why was Birdie researching corporate fraud?"

"How do you know she was?"

"I saw the books when I went into your house after I found her to call the police. The library confirmed she took those books out. Why was your passport out? You have an airline confirmation. Where are you going?"

Ted's eyes narrowed, and his nostrils flared. "How dare you? My wife was murdered. According to the police, you are a suspect, and you're interrogating me? You're trying to lay the blame for her death on me?"

"I'm trying to find the truth. Like why did Gary lie? Why did he suddenly show up a day before his sister was murdered? Don't you want to know? Or are you satisfied with the thought of me being the killer?"

"I'll be satisfied when the police make an arrest, and a jury convicts the person responsible. If it's you, then so be it." He pointed a finger at Hope. "Stay away from me and stay out of my house!" He swung around and marched to his front door and then disappeared inside.

"Hope! Can we finish our walk?" Molly cried out.

Hope looked over her shoulder and then back to Ted's

front door. She wasn't going to get any more information from him. If she stood there any longer, he'd probably call the police. It was time to head back home.

"Sure." She pasted on a smile and darted back to them. She took Bigelow's leash and led them on a quiet stroll.

The leisurely walk and listening to Molly and Becca chitchat lulled Hope into a moment of normalcy. Until the girls started talking about missing their mom. Her heart ached for them. She was tempted to change the subject to something more cheerful, but instead let them share their feelings. When they arrived back at the house, they settled in the living room with their coloring books and a new video.

Hope used the quiet time to jot down ideas for future blog posts. The bright side of not creating content for the companies that had let her go was that she had more time to devote to recipe development. And to her blog coaching business. She created another list of ideas for expanding that venture. Which reminded her, she had to check in with Annette by the end of the week.

"Daddy's home." Becca jumped up from her spot on the sofa, dropping her coloring book and green crayon.

Hope stood from the armchair and walked to the window where Becca had been looking out. "What on earth?"

Two Jefferson PD vehicles pulled into her driveway, followed by what looked like Reid's black SUV. Her stomach flip-flopped. She stepped back from the window and then chased after Becca, who ran out of the living room to the front door.

"Maybe he can take us to the park." Molly followed behind Hope.

"It's not your dad. It's his co-workers." She did her

best to keep her voice level as she opened the door. "I need to talk to his friends, so you two stay here, okay?" When the girls nodded, she stepped out onto the porch, pulling the door closed behind her.

Reid had exited his vehicle and climbed the porch steps. He didn't look happy. In fact, it was the grimmest Hope had ever seen him. "We're here on official business."

Those five words sent Hope's head spinning and a wave of nausea through her, making her feel as if she had to vomit. She knew what kind of business he was there for.

"Sam, Ethan's daughters are in the house," she said in a low, pleading voice.

Regret covered Reid's face. "We're going to do this by the book. I promise you we'll be respectful and cause the least amount of disruption. Ethan is on his way over to get the girls."

"He knows?"

"I called him once I got the search warrant. Because the girls are in the house, we'll start in the barn and garage." He reached into his blazer's breast pocket and pulled out the legal document. "You should call your lawyer."

Hope nodded and then took the search warrant.

She jogged up the porch steps and returned inside with Reid behind her. She knew why he was following her inside—he needed to make sure she didn't destroy evidence. If it weren't for the girls hurling a slew of questions at her, she would have been seething. How could he possibly think she'd destroy evidence? In fact, how could he believe she had evidence to destroy? It was maddening.

Hope did her best to tamp down her frustration and explain to the girls what was going on, but nothing she said seemed to satisfy them. Finally, she told them the officers were on a scavenger hunt out in the barn. Molly and Becca got excited and set off on their own even though Hope needed them to pack up their overnight bags. She noticed Reid hadn't followed them, probably due to the fact he hadn't been worried about their unsupervised activities. He at least had the decency to give her a little privacy when she called Matt.

She explained to him what was going on and did her best not to cry. He said he was on his way back.

Within minutes, Matt arrived back at the house. Hope greeted him outside and handed over the search warrant. While he reviewed the legal document, she peered into her garage. The officer assigned to search was being considerate of her belongings, though he was searching through everything. Lucky for him, she had all of it organized and labeled.

"I can't believe they're searching my home." She combed her fingers through her hair as she continued casting sidelong glances at the barn. A shiver wiggled through her body. "Are they going to touch everything?"

Matt looked up from the warrant. "That's the least of your worries. This is serious."

Hope threw her hands up in the air. "I know. But I didn't kill Birdie. What about Gary? He lied about seeing his sister, and they had a twenty-year-old feud."

"Then why wait so long to kill her?" Matt asked.

"I don't know. I would think Reid would ask him that question. But I guess it's up to me!"

"No. Now you need to be a criminal defense client. And you need to listen to me." Matt rubbed the back of his neck.

"Seems like sound advice," Reid said as he approached

carrying an evidence bag. "We found something behind the barn."

"What?" Matt tucked the search warrant into the pocket of his blazer.

"A bottle of peanut oil. Do you know why it was there, Hope?" Reid asked.

The discovery had her blinking. How on earth could they have found a bottle of peanut oil by her barn? She hadn't used that kind of oil since last summer when she made batches of fried chicken for a picnic. And she'd recycled the bottle. Since then, she hadn't restocked the item in her pantry.

"Do you know why it was there?" Reid asked again.

Before Hope could answer, Matt stepped forward. "My client doesn't know where the bottle came from or who put it there."

"Does this mean you're done with your search?" Hope asked, earning her a scowl from Matt. Wow. He really didn't want her saying anything.

"No." Reid looked toward the farmhouse. "We still have your home to search."

Those words hung in the uncomfortable silence between the three of them. Reid cleared his throat before turning and walking away toward a police vehicle.

The fact that Reid looked far from victorious about finding a piece of incriminating evidence on Hope's property was of little consolation to her.

"Looks like there's nothing we can do until they leave." The urge to let defeat overwhelm her was powerful, but she couldn't succumb to the feeling. Too much was on the line. Someone had planted that bottle of peanut oil behind the barn, and she intended to find out who it was.

Matt rested his hand on her shoulder, and he gave a reassuring squeeze. "It's going to be okay. Come on, let's get Bigelow."

"The girls should be done packing up their things." Hope sighed. She wondered if they would confiscate her notebook, where she jotted her thoughts on the case. "Have you ever heard of Visionary Media Consulting?"

"No. Why?"

"I think it has something to do with why Birdie was researching corporate fraud. Avery and Ted were overheard arguing about the company. Birdie's murder could be connected with Emily's House."

"I understand why you're investigating on your own and why Ethan has supported it, but you have to stop now."

"I can't. We have the police here searching my home rather than tracking down the leads I was able to find. And I'm a food blogger. Matt, the Jefferson Police are incompetent. I'm not trusting my life to them." She spun around to face Matt but seeing Ethan behind him nearly knocked her off balance. "Ethan. I'm so glad you're here."

"Hey, good to see you," Matt said as he turned to face Ethan. "Reid has executed the search warrant. They're going in the house as soon as the girls are gone."

Ethan's jaw tensed, and he glanced at the house. "I'll take them to my place." He pulled back and turned toward the porch.

"Wait! Ethan!" Hope propelled forward, chasing after him. She was surprised he hadn't hugged her, offered her any sort of comfort. Then she realized he must have heard her comment about his police department. "I didn't mean what I said about your officers. I'm . . . I'm scared and upset, and they found something."

"What was it?"

"A bottle of peanut oil behind the barn. Someone put it there for your officer to find." She thought back to the previous days. She'd been out at the barn doing the chores every morning and evening. She couldn't remember the last time she did a complete walk around the structure. Possibly when she did a spring cleanup on the property.

"Not good," Ethan muttered. He surveyed the officers, who had moved to the house. "I'll check the doorbell's video to see if we can get a lead."

"Good thinking! That should show us who was here." That bit of good news cheered Hope up. It was exactly what she needed.

"Even for the chief of an incompetent police department, huh?"

She quickly closed the small space between them and reached out to him. "I'm sorry. Sam and your officers are being very courteous. And it's helping with the sense of violation I'm feeling."

Ethan dipped his head down and kissed her. "I understand. It's forgotten. Do you want to come with us back to my house?"

Hope considered his offer. Running away sounded pretty darn good at the moment. "I probably should stay here. Go on inside, the girls are waiting for you. Oh, can you bring Bigelow out?"

"Sure." He turned and climbed the porch steps and then disappeared inside the house.

Hope turned and marched back to Matt. "Ethan will review the video from my smart doorbell to see who dropped the bottle of peanut oil behind the barn."

"It captures that area too?" Matt's glance bounced between the front door and the barn.

"It would capture a car pulling into the driveway. The back doorbell could capture someone walking from the driveway to the barn. Also, if someone approached from back there." Hope pointed. Her three acres weren't completely cleared. Behind her landscaped acre, there were a lot of dense woods.

For the first time in days, she felt hopeful. When they got the person planting the peanut oil, they'd have the killer.

Drew showed up after Reid and his officers departed Hope's property. He helped put things away. True to Reid's word, the search wasn't horrible, but the officers looked everywhere. The most infuriating part was tidying up her clothing. The officers had gone through her dresser drawers, closet, and bathroom. She had no idea what they expected to find in her bathroom. She considered herself lucky that they left her laptop. Then again, they already had "evidence" on video, so why bother with her computer.

Claire called with an update of her tennis game with Robin—she won the match.

When Hope told her that wasn't the update she wanted, Claire huffed and then told her about Robin's conversation. She said her husband expressed no concerns with EH's finances and suggested Claire was barking up the wrong tree.

Hope didn't share the same sentiment but didn't interrupt her sister. Though maybe she should have because

Claire enjoyed sleuthing so much, she asked whom she could interrogate next.

Not feeling as enthusiastic as her sister, Hope felt fatigued by the whole situation and made a vague promise to let Claire know whom she could question next.

"She's hooked, isn't she? You've created a monster." Drew rubbed Bigelow's head in between sips of his coffee.

Before Hope could confirm his assessment, her phone rang again. It was Ethan calling, and she put him on speakerphone.

"I reviewed the doorbell's video feed." His voice was flat, and Hope knew he found nothing helpful. "It didn't show anyone who wasn't supposed to be on your property, Hope. There's Casey, Matt, Drew, Mitzi, Claire, and Josie. Plus me and the girls."

It wasn't the news Hope wanted to hear.

"However, there seems to be several minutes missing from the video in the app's history section. There was a notice of motion detected by the mudroom door, yet there wasn't any video accompanying it," Ethan said.

"Someone could have hacked your system and deleted video of themselves planting the evidence." Drew straightened in his chair, his full attention on the phone now. "What can you do about it, Ethan?"

Hope jotted the information down in her notebook, which was spared being bagged as evidence against her.

"I have someone looking at it as we speak." Of course Ethan had someone looking at it. Before coming to Jefferson, he worked in the Hartford Police Department. He had connections throughout many departments and the State Police. Hope didn't doubt that someone owed him a favor. "I'll let you know what I find out. Love you, babe. Don't worry, okay?" He disconnected the call.

How could she not worry? The evidence against her was piling up. The oven timer dinged. After she finished tidying her home, she made a quick pasta bake for her and Drew. She hadn't much of an appetite when she put the pasta on to boil but cooking gave her something to do. Besides, Drew was always hungry and she loved feeding him. She stood and walked to the double ovens.

"It could be possible to get the footage from the company." Drew popped up from his chair and quickly set the table for their meal. Hope wasn't sure if it was lunch or dinner; all she knew was that suddenly she was starving. And by the looks of Bigelow, with his snout working overtime at the cheesy pasta dish's aroma, he was hungry too.

"It seems Ethan has it under control. Oh, I didn't get a chance to tell you what Claire said. Robin's husband isn't aware of any problems at EH." Hope pulled a serving spoon from a drawer. "Did you find out anything about Visionary Media Consulting?"

"Yes, I did. I've been dying to tell you." Drew opened a utility drawer and took out a wine bottle opener. Hope had selected a pinot noir for their meal. He undid the cork and poured two glasses. She noticed he added a little extra to her glass. Bless him.

"Tell me." Hope carried the Le Creuset baker to the table and served.

Drew set the wine glasses on the table. "You won't believe it!"

Hope forced a smile so that way she wouldn't scream. She wasn't in the mood for twenty questions. Her house had been searched, planted evidence was found, and she'd stuck her foot in her mouth with the stupid comment about the JPD. No, she wasn't in the mood for guessing games.

She reached forward and yanked back Drew's plate. "Tell me, or I give this to Bigelow."

Bigelow's ears perked up while Drew made a face as he jerked his plate back. "Sorry, boy," he said to the dog.

Bigelow's ears drooped, and he gave a confused look to Hope. Feeling guilty, she stood and went to the container on the counter where the homemade dog treats were stored. Two of them did the trick and lifted Bigelow's mood instantly.

Back at the table, she sat and waited for Drew to swallow his bite.

"It took a lot of digging. Shell companies are notorious for having firewalls."

"Shell company?"

"They are used for financial maneuvers, sometimes legit. Most of the time, they're not. Visionary is a shell company. It has no apparent business operation or generates any real assets. It has one client, Emily's House."

"Avery was the one stealing?"

"I don't think so. You wouldn't believe all the digging I had to do, but I finally came up with two names." Drew took another bite of the ziti and made a yummy noise.

"Drew! Can we focus?"

"Sorry. It's delicious. Okay, back to work. Delores Jameson is listed as the CFO."

"Who's Delores Jameson?"

Drew shrugged. "No idea. But it's a different story with the CEO. It was Berta Oliff."

"Birdie?" Hope let that piece of information sink in as she drummed her fingers on the tabletop.

"I'm going to keep digging, but we could be looking at an embezzlement scheme. Ted could have set up the company to funnel money to it and ultimately through an offshore account."

"Do you think Birdie knew about it?"

"Maybe not. You said she borrowed books on corporate fraud from the library."

"Ted could have gotten her to sign papers without her knowing what they were really for."

Drew pointed a finger at Hope. "Exactly what I was thinking. Then something raised a red flag, and she started her own digging. We have to fill Jane in."

"And I'll update Claire." She leaned back, and Bigelow came to her side. Finished with his snack, he rested his head on her lap. She patted him. "It's possible Birdie figured all of this out and confronted Ted."

"To keep her quiet, he had no choice but to kill her." Drew stood and walked over to the counter where he'd hooked up his phone for charging. He removed the cable and checked his phone before slipping it into his jeans' back pocket. "New charging cube?"

"It's Josie's. I misplaced the one I was using. Never mind that, what about Avery?" Hope asked.

"From what Erin told you, it sounds like she was suspicious."

"Ted killed her, too?"

"It's possible." Drew sipped his wine. "You need to be careful. He lives right across the street."

Hope's gaze drifted to the French doors. Drew's warning sent a chill through her. Did she have a killer as a neighbor?

Chapter Nineteen

The next morning, Hope sipped her coffee while reviewing her notes on the porch. Her day was off to a slow start. While waking up and getting dressed, she moved at half her average speed. Even feeding the chickens and letting them out to free roam for the day took longer than usual.

Princess was curled next to Hope on the sectional, her eyes shut and her head slightly tipped up. The cat's comfort was welcomed after yesterday. No. She stopped those thoughts in their tracks. There would be no dwelling on the officers traipsing through her home and touching her belongings. It was over. Her mind needed to be clear to concentrate on the most important thing—finding the killer.

After Drew left yesterday, she updated her notes on the case.

Thanks to Claire, Hope knew that EH's finances looked good. If she and Drew were right about Ted, he had successfully taken money from the nonprofit to pay a shell company he created with no one the wiser.

Except for Avery. Somehow, she must have found out about the contract with her signature on it. Beneath those notes, Hope added that Birdie must have discovered the deception and that she was linked to the shell company. Hope drew an arrow pointing to a previous note about Ted skipping out of EH the morning Birdie died.

Further down on the sheet was the name Delores Jameson.

Was she made up like the company, or was she involved in the fraud?

The last note she made before going to bed last night was about the time gap on her doorbell's video feed.

There was no doubt in her mind that those few minutes captured whoever it was who planted the empty bottle behind the barn, aka the killer.

She reached forward for her coffee and drained the mug. Princess objected at the disturbance of her morning nap but quickly shifted and went back to dozing.

Hope contemplated making another coffee but decided to go to the Coffee Clique for two coffees on her way to Claire's shop. Instantly, she felt perked up.

Then a familiar car pulled into her driveway, and her perkiness vanished. She stood, gathering her notebook and mug, and then walked to the porch steps.

Norrie exited her vehicle. "Good morning, Hope. My sources tell me that the Jefferson Police Department executed a search warrant here yesterday. Care to comment?"

Oh, Hope had a comment for Norrie alright, but she gave a curt nod instead. "I have no comment."

"Don't you want to get your side of the story out

there? Maybe bring back some brands that dropped you like a hot potato?" Norrie grinned.

Hope wouldn't be baited into giving Norrie what she wanted—a statement she could twist to make Hope look bad.

"I have no comment. Have a nice day, Norrie." Hope turned and entered her house, closing the door on the pesky reporter.

Hope entered the Coffee Clique, and the aroma of freshly brewed coffee and pastries welcomed her like a warm hug. Then came the cheerful greeting from Jenny, the newest barista. Barely out of her teens, Jenny had mastered the fine art of cappuccinos and lattes and always seemed disappointed when Hope asked for a simple coffee with milk. Hope walked across the wide plank floor to the counter and gave her order.

"Nothing for the chief today?" Jenny filled two to-go cups, one with hazelnut and one regular, and then secured a lid on each.

"No. I'm on my way to Claire's shop." Whenever she visited Ethan at the PD, she usually brought him a coffee.

"Here you go." Jenny set the cups on the counter and rang up the sale. "It's a beautiful day. Fingers crossed the weather holds out for the weekend. I'm going camping with my girlfriends."

"Sounds like fun." Hope swiped her credit card and approved the payment. "Have a good day."

"You too." Jenny's attention was already on the customer behind Hope. "What would you like?"

When Hope turned to step away from the counter, she

caught a glimpse of Gary in line. Instead of going to the door, she approached him.

"What do you want?" Gary scowled at her as he stepped forward as the line moved up.

At first, his crusty greeting took Hope aback, but it helped clarify that he wasn't interested in chitchat. Good. Because neither was she.

"I'd like to know where you were during Birdie's funeral."

"I don't see how it's any of your business." He moved up in the line again.

"You were at your sister's house, weren't you?" She followed. "Lurking like you were at the library."

"You have a very active imagination," he said without looking at Hope.

"You're on video outside the library. Why didn't you want to be seen by her? Why were you at her house on the day of the funeral?"

"Hope!" Cleo's voice had Hope twisting around. "How are you doing?"

"I have nothing to say to you, so stay away, or I'll have you charged with harassment." Gary stepped toward the counter to place his order.

"Is he Birdie's brother?" Cleo hurried to Hope's side and leaned close. "He seems upset with you."

"He is, but it's okay." She gave a dismissive wave. There was no reason to explain to Cleo.

Cleo looked disappointed that she would not learn why Gary was angry. "How's the hosta doing? Have you planted her yet?"

"The other day. I found the perfect spot for her over the weekend. Thank you again for the plant."

"You're welcome. I never thought I'd say this, but I owe Birdie a big fat thank-you. Too bad she's no longer with us."

"Are you talking about your arrangement with Timmy's Garden Supply?"

"You bet I am." Cleo's smile was wide. She looked pleased with herself. "Selling through them, I'm making more money than I did on my own, and I don't have to worry about keeping an eye on the flower stand at the road."

"Though at the time they shut you down, you didn't know you'd be able to sell through the nursery. Birdie had caused a big problem for you," Hope said.

Cleo's eyes narrowed. "What are you saying? Are you suggesting I killed her because she turned me in to the town?"

Hope opened her mouth to answer, but Cleo cut her off before she could utter a word.

"Now I see why that man was miffed at you. Did you accuse him of killing Birdie too?"

"I'm not . . ."

"Next!" Jenny called out.

Cleo marched toward the counter, looking over her shoulder once to give Hope the stink eye. Hope frowned. In a matter of minutes, she got told off by two people. A record? She wasn't sure. But she was convinced that they were two people who had motives to kill Birdie.

Her coffees were getting cold, and she needed to hit the road. She walked along Main Street, nodding to familiar faces as she made her way to Staged with Style. When she entered the shop, her sister was in a deep conversation with a stylishly dressed woman. Hope glanced at her outfit and sighed. She was far from stylish herself in her cropped jeans and floral top. She kept promising herself she'd dress better but working from home afforded her the luxury of being comfortable after years of professionally dressing when she worked at the magazine. Maybe she should let Claire take her shopping for a new wardrobe.

"Good morning, Hope." Lola was behind the sales counter and searching through a makeup bag. She had a determined yet slightly worried look on her face. "Claire will be a few minutes. She's wrapping up a consultation."

Hope moved to the counter right as Lola pulled out a tube of lipstick and smiled victoriously.

"How long were you looking for it?" Hope asked.

"Long enough to make me think I'd have to buy another tube. I love this shade. Glad it's safe." She dropped the lipstick in the bag.

When Lola zipped the pink-striped bag, Hope noticed the monogram. It was the letter D. "Pretty bag. What does the D stand for?"

Lola turned the bag around and ran her fingers over the embroidery. "It's the initial of my first name. Delores. But everyone calls me Lola. It's shorter and cooler, don't you think?" The shop's phone rang, and she excused herself to answer the call. She disappeared to the back room.

Delores? Was it a coincidence?

"Is that for me?" Claire had come up behind Hope as her client exited the shop. She reached for one of the coffees in Hope's hands.

"Yes."

"What's up? You look funny." Claire sipped her coffee as she walked to the shop's window. "I think I'm going to redo the display. Any ideas?"

Hope joined her sister and, in a low voice, asked, "Did you know Lola's first name is really Delores?"

"Of course I did. Remember, she's an employee and filled out paperwork. Why are you asking?"

"Because Drew told me last night that Visionary Media Consulting has Birdie and another woman, named Delores Jameson, listed as the as board members."

"You think Lola is Delores Jameson?"

"I don't know. She could be."

"Her last name is Granger."

"Isn't she divorced? Maybe Jameson is her maiden name."

"Maybe she's not involved." Claire walked back to the counter and set her coffee down. "You know I'm on board with doing whatever I can to help you find the real killer, but Lola is a great employee. The best I've had since I opened the shop, and I don't want to lose her. So don't go accusing her of murder unless we have solid proof. Understand?"

"Fine."

"Well, that was easy." Claire looked suspicious.

"Because finding out her maiden name will be easy for Drew. Gotta go." Hope turned and hurried out of the shop. Back out on Main Street, she juggled her coffee cup while pulling her phone out of her purse. Then she juggled writing a text to Drew. She gave him a recap about Lola, and he replied with a thumb's up emoji.

If Lola was indeed Delores Jameson, then what was her connection to Ted?

Passing by the driveway that led to the communal parking lot behind the row of shops, she spotted Lola outside, with her back turned, talking on her cell phone. Hope looked over her shoulder. There was no one around to see what she was about to do. She inched forward, keeping light on her feet so not to be heard. When she reached the back corner of the building she paused. She jutted out her chin, angling her head so she could listen to what Lola was saying.

She couldn't hear Lola. Shoot.

Hope had no choice. She had to get closer yet remain undetected to hear what Lola was saying. How hard could it be?

"Don't put me off. We haven't seen each other in days. I'm tired of waiting. We were supposed to be out of here by now." Lola's head dropped back, leaving Hope to guess the person on the other end of the call wasn't saying what Lola wanted to hear. "Yes. I can get away. . . . See you there."

Hope scurried backward to put some space between her and Lola. But she wasn't quick enough. Lola turned around and saw her.

"Hey, Hope. Is there something you need?" Lola approached Hope as her lips curled slightly.

Think fast, Hope.

"Yes. I wanted to ask you where you got your makeup bag from. It's pretty, and I think Hannah would like to have one with her monogram on it." Hope wasn't sure how Claire would feel about her tween daughter being given a makeup bag since there was a strict rule about wearing cosmetics, though Hannah could keep her lip balms and other items in the bag. She could even use it for tech storage. Which reminded Hope, she needed to buy a new charging cube since she couldn't find hers, and she didn't want to keep Josie's.

"I don't remember. I've had it for years. I'm sure you can find something similar. Have a good day." Lola turned and walked back into the shop.

Hope waved goodbye and turned. Speed walking back

to the sidewalk, her mind churned to come up with a plan. A plan that would allow her to find out who Lola would be meeting and where. Though there was a glitch in her plan even before it was fully formed—she didn't know when Lola was leaving, and she didn't have a vehicle to follow Lola. Her Explorer was at home. Between rushing back there and returning in her SUV, she could miss Lola.

There was only one option and one person close by who would be her wheelman. She pulled out her phone again.

Minutes later, Drew's sleek sports car pulled up to the curb, a few stores from Staged with Style. Approaching the vehicle, Hope noted it wasn't the best option to follow someone, but beggars couldn't be choosers.

Hope slid into the luxurious leather seat. The long stretch of wintery weather in New England made Drew's beloved vehicle impractical for daily use. Still, it sure was a pleasure to sit in.

"Is she still in there?" Drew removed his Ray-Bans.

"Yes, she is. Unfortunately, Lola didn't repeat the time the other person said." Hope fastened her seatbelt.

"So we're on a stakeout."

"Looks like it. Did you have any luck finding out what Lola's maiden name was?" Hope adjusted the seatbelt in preparation for the drive.

"No. I got called into an unplanned meeting. The *Gazette* is bringing back the home and garden quarterly feature. The first issue will be out in the fall."

"Good news, right?"

"Yes, and no. It's going to mean extra work for the features editor because while the budget is there for the feature, there isn't one for any extra staff. At least not yet."

"Was that person named at the meeting?" Hope had an

inkling of who the person was, but she didn't want to spoil his big moment.

Drew turned to face her, and his big broad smile revealed she was right. "Me! I'm the editor of the home and garden quarterly. In addition to my regular reporting duties."

Hope reached out and patted Drew on the shoulder. "Congratulations. I'm so proud of you. You're going to do an outstanding job."

"I will, won't I?" Drew was nodding and smiling bigger. "Tomorrow, we have our first meeting to brainstorm the issue."

"Well, I have some ideas." She rattled off her list. It was the magazine editor inside of her, and she couldn't help herself. And because of their distraction, they almost missed Lola's metallic blue Jetta pulling out of the driveway. "Drew! That's Lola!"

"What?" His gaze returned to the road ahead. He slipped his sunglasses back on and shifted his sports car into drive.

"Hang back, so she doesn't spot us," Hope said.

Drew gave her a sidelong glance. "No back seat driving tips on tailing someone."

"You're an expert? Since when?" She gave him a pointed look.

"Who's the reporter here? Of course I have more experience."

Drew's skill at tailing a vehicle impressed Hope and made her wonder how many times he'd followed someone. His attention was on the Jetta two cars ahead of them and never wavered. He maneuvered his car at a steady pace as to not draw Lola's awareness to them.

At Pilgrim Landing, the Jetta took a right turn and

cruised along the serpentine road shaded by towering maple and oak trees on both sides. The side road led to Mill Lake, a favorite picnic spot in the warm weather and skating destination in the dead of winter.

"Do you think she's going to the lake?" Hope asked.

"Probably. Let's see if she turns off up ahead. Crosby Road is a back way to a corporate park. She could be meeting the person there."

Hope kept her gaze locked on the Jetta and worried Lola would realize she was being followed. She barely talked herself out of eavesdropping on Lola's phone call earlier. How would she explain them following her?

At a stop sign, Lola breezed through without coming to a full stop. Drew obeyed the rules of the road and stopped to look before continuing through.

"Don't lose her." Hope noticed Lola had picked up speed after passing the stop sign.

"I got this. Did you see her blow through the stop sign? She's a little speed demon."

"It was more like she rolled through it." Hope noticed the left blinker flash on Lola's car. "Looks like she's going to the lake."

The Jetta disappeared around the corner as Drew's car approached the turn. He flicked his blinker on and made the turn onto Mill Lake Road. While there were no turnoffs to other streets, there were hidden driveways scattered along the road, and Lola could easily have turned off into any one of them. But she hadn't. Her vehicle came into sight as it traveled the narrowing road.

Halfway down the road, the blacktop turned into a rocky dirt lane that wound around a dense copse of brush and trees. Despite having traveled that path countless times since she was a kid, Hope had a heightened watchfulness, examining every branch, rock, and fallen log she could see. She wasn't sure what she was expecting to see, but she didn't want to be surprised.

Finally, the road opened to a large parking area and the expansiveness of the still lake. Lola's Jetta continued driving to the makeshift parking lot at the farthest end, where it came to a stop beside a Cadillac Hope recognized.

From their vantage point, they could see cottages and boathouses dotted along the beautiful stretch of wooded shoreline on the lake's opposite side. At the south end was a protected area, home to a large assortment of bird species. Birders spent hours out there all year long. Bald eagles were often spotted in the winter months.

"It looks like Ted's car." Hope pointed as Drew stopped just feet away from the wooden sign welcoming visitors to the lake.

"Are you sure?" Drew reached around to the backseat and grabbed his camera.

"I see it every day. Look, a man is getting out. I'm sure it's Ted."

"Let me look." Drew angled his camera and adjusted the lens. "You're right. It's him."

Hope leaned forward, resting a hand on the dashboard. "They're hugging!"

Ted had his arms around Lola and then kissed her.

"I'd bet my Le Creuset Dutch oven that Lola is Delores Jameson, who is listed on Visionary Media Consulting's website." Hope looked at Drew.

"I think it would be a sound bet." Drew snapped a flurry of photographs.

"She pulled away from him . . . look how she's jabbing at his chest. Hard."

"Lover's spat?"

"It sure looks like one." Hope watched as Lola's body language changed markedly from delighted to furious. "Look what he just did!" Ted grabbed Lola's hand, and it looked like he was shouting. "I wish we could hear what they're talking about."

"Oh, no! They're looking in this direction. Get down!" Drew slid down in his seat, and Hope followed.

"Do you think they saw us?" Hope asked.

Chapter Twenty

"Don't know." Drew peeked over the dashboard. "Uh-oh. She's walking back to her car. We should get going."

"I think you're right. I'll stay down until we're in the clear."

"Good idea." Drew handed her the camera, and he shifted his car into reverse and made a U-turn to drive out of the parking area. He traveled along the same road he drove to get to the lake. Hope emerged from her slouched position. "It looks like they had a lover's spat."

"It does, doesn't it? This leads me to believe we're right in thinking Lola is Delores Jameson. I wonder if she knew about Ted's plan to murder Birdie." Hope looked over the seat to see if the Jetta was behind them.

It wasn't.

"My guess is that Ted acted alone," Drew said.

"Oh, no!" Hope grabbed Drew's arm and squeezed, causing him to lose control of the steering wheel momentarily.

"Geez!" Drew swerved and then righted the car. "What's wrong with you, woman?"

"Ted could have acted alone."

"Right. I said that. Don't you listen to me?"

"Lola could be in danger."

"You think he lured her here to kill her?"

"If he thinks she would go to the police to tell them about their affair, that means she's a loose end. . . . That's why he wanted to meet at the lake!" She pointed to the rear window.

"He's going to drown her." Drew made a sharp turn into the next driveway and then a reckless U-turn, kicking up dirt and gravel. He floored the accelerator and sped back to the lake. In a matter of seconds, he was navigating his car to the spot where they'd just left.

Ted and Lola's cars were still parked in the same location, but now Lola wasn't in her vehicle.

"Look!" Hope shouted as she spotted Ted, grasping Lola by the arm and leading her to the water.

The lake was tranquil, mesmerizing almost. The water lazily lapped up on the sandy beach. Hope undid her seatbelt and pushed the car door open.

"He's taking her to the water!"

"Holy cow! He's really going to drown her!" Drew turned off the ignition. "Wait for me!"

"We have to stop him." Hope sprinted toward the water. "Lola! Stop!"

"Let her go," Drew shouted.

Ted halted and turned around.

"What on earth is going on?" Lola asked. She looked confused as Hope and Drew ran toward her.

"You heard, Drew. Let go of her!" Hope stood a few feet from Ted and Lola. Surely with witnesses Ted wouldn't go through with his plan to kill her. "We're not going to let you murder her like you did Birdie and Avery."

"Murder her?" Ted let go of Lola's arm. His sharp gaze seared into Hope. "You're insane."

"Murder me?" Lola recoiled, pulling away from Ted.

"No. I'm not insane. We know everything. You set up a shell company, Visionary Media Consulting, to funnel money from EH, and you listed Birdie and Lola as the principles." Hope's chin lifted, her posture straightened, and she anchored a hand on her hip. She'd caught a killer. "Drew, call 9-1-1."

"You did what?" Lola's shock had diminished, and in its place was fury. Her skin flushed, and her arms flailed with gestures that made Ted back up. "What have you gotten me messed up in? Stealing money? Murder?"

"Don't listen to them. They don't know what they're talking about," Ted said.

"Oh, no. Don't you lie to me. Again! All your promises. Nothing but lies!" Lola lowered her hands. They were shaking. She looked at Hope and Drew. Her eyes were wet, and a pained look covered her face. "Believe me, I had no idea what he was doing."

"You're having an affair with him," Hope said.

"Yes. Yes, I am, and I'm deeply ashamed of my behavior. I didn't intend to fall in love with a married man." Lola shifted her gaze to Ted and her face twisted into disgust. "You were going to kill me?"

"No! Don't listen to them. Hope's just trying to clear her name, and her sidekick is looking for a front-page story," Ted said.

"Sidekick?" Drew gaped. "I'm nobody's sidekick."

"Focus," Hope whispered. "Lola, did you know Ted bought a plane ticket?"

Lola shook her head no at Hope's question.

"Well, that's not surprising, is it? If he didn't bring you here to kill you, when his embezzlement was finally noticed after he was long gone, everything would lead back to you."

"How could you?" Lola's face twisted with disgust when she looked at Ted. "Stealing? Murder? I was next?"

"You don't understand. . . . Alright. Fine. I'm guilty." Ted sounded and looked defeated. He was caught, and there wasn't any way out. Hope presumed the best he could wish for was to admit his guilt in exchange for a lighter sentence. Smart move.

Lola gasped loudly at her lover's confession.

"Did he just confess?" Not waiting for an answer, Drew pulled out his cell phone and tapped on the screen. He used a recording app all the time for interviews. "I can see the headline now."

"I set up Visionary Media as a way to embezzle funds from EH." Ted dipped his head, breaking eye contact.

"Birdie learned about your scheme, didn't she? And Avery had suspicions about Visionary Media. You had no choice. You had to keep them quiet," Hope said. "When you left EH the morning Birdie died, you went home and laced her muffin with the peanut oil. Then you followed Avery to her hiking trail and pushed her off the edge."

"You're a monster!" Lola swooped forward and slapped Ted. She then rushed to her vehicle and got in.

"We have to call the police," Hope said to Drew.

"Already did. When you leaped out of the car, I called Ethan."

"There wasn't any time to waste. We had to stop him from drowning Lola." A rumble of a vehicle approaching had Hope looking over her shoulder. She recognized that rumble.

Ethan had arrived.

The green pickup truck came to a hard stop, and Ethan exited with speed and jogged toward them. "Are you two okay?"

Hope and Drew nodded.

"Good. Now tell me what's going on." Ethan's voice was stern. He was in full cop mode.

"Ted just confessed to embezzling funds from Emily's House," Hope said. "He arranged to meet Lola here so he could drown her."

"But I didn't kill my wife!" Ted shouted.

The sound of an engine drew their attention to Lola's vehicle.

"Where the heck is she going?" Hope asked.

Ethan sprinted to the Jetta and gave a signal to turn off the ignition. When Lola didn't comply, he did it again as he approached the driver's side. Lola shut off her car. Ethan opened the door and assisted her out of the vehicle.

"Hey, do you think she had something to do with Birdie's murder?" Drew leaned in close to Hope. "Maybe she planned to off Ted."

Hope shrugged. "I guess it's possible." She watched Ethan questioning Lola. She would have loved to know what Lola was saying. Too bad she never learned how to read lips.

Ethan escorted Lola back toward his truck. Passing Hope and Drew, he pulled out his cell phone from the pouch on his belt. "I'm going to call this in. Lola and Ted will be going to the PD to straighten out this matter."

"You're not going to arrest him?" Hope pointed to Ted as she followed Ethan. "He confessed."

"We all heard him." Lola backed Hope up and it looked like the love affair was over.

"Drew, Hope, I need for you two to go back to the PD and wait there for me. You'll give your statements." Ethan lifted his phone to his ear. "Lola, Ted, you're both going in for questioning, and you'll be able to call a lawyer if you choose to."

"I most certainly do want my lawyer," Ted replied. "You can't use anything I've said against me!"

"We'll see about that," Ethan said.

"I did nothing wrong, so I don't need a lawyer," Lola said with confidence.

Hope slipped next to Lola and, in a low voice, said, "You may want to rethink your decision. It appears Ted has set you up to take the fall for embezzling money. If what he said earlier isn't going to be admissible in court, then you need to protect yourself."

Lola gave Hope a curious look as if she didn't trust what Hope was saying. "You really think so?"

"I do. Don't say anything else and get a lawyer. Trust me." Hope saw the doubt in Lola's eyes. The man she loved had betrayed her and was probably a murderer. How could she trust anything anyone ever said again? As much as she wanted to, she couldn't force Lola to take her advice.

"Hope, you and Drew should leave now." Ethan guided Lola away from Hope.

Hope nodded and joined Drew at his car. He had the driver's side door open and had one hand resting on the roof.

"We did good today." His eyes gleamed with satisfaction. "We caught a murderer, and I got a front-page story. Come on, let's get out of here."

Hope pulled opened the passenger door. Drew was right. They did do good today. So why didn't she feel like they did? Was it because the adrenaline that pumped through her body when confronting Ted was crashing, leaving her feeling exhausted? Most likely. While all she craved was a nap, she couldn't. At least not until she gave her statement and was dropped off at home.

The weight of the past couple of hours had taken its toll on Hope. Her shoulders drooped, and her eyelids were heavy with fatigue. Depleted and fatigued. Yep, that pretty much summed up how she felt. She wasn't even sure she'd be able to stand once she got the okay from Reid to leave the Jefferson PD.

She'd given her statement, reviewed it, and then signed and dated the document. Now she waited in the department's lobby. Seated on a bench, her gaze was locked on the brochure rack. There were pamphlets on various topics, including opioid abuse. A twinge of guilt pinged inside her. She hadn't asked Ethan how Heather was doing in rehab. In fact, they hadn't spoken much since she went lukewarm on his suggestion to move in together.

"Hope."

She looked up at the sound of her name. Reid emerged from the interior offices, where she'd given her statement.

"Can I go?" She stood, relieved her legs held sturdy and she wouldn't be face planting in front of the detective.

"Yes. Thank you for your statement."

"I'm happy to help. When you questioned Ted, did he confess about embezzling money from Emily's House?"

"I'm sorry, but I'm not at liberty to share that information with you." Reid turned toward the locked door and punched his code onto the keypad.

"Do you have enough to investigate him and find his connection to Visionary Media Consulting?"

Reid looked over his shoulder. "Hope, we got this. Go home and bake something." He smiled and then opened the door. A moment later, he was gone.

Go home and bake something?

Not a bad suggestion since it appeared Birdie and Avery's murders were all wrapped up. Ted confessed to stealing money from EH, and that gave him a motive to kill both women. Though she thought Reid would have given her a thank you for helping to wrap up his case. Then again, what did it really matter? As Drew said, they did good today, and knowing she'd played a role in finding justice for two victims was thanks enough.

"Okay, then I should get going," she said to no one. Hope turned and waved goodbye to Freddie, the dispatcher who was on a call but nodded.

She walked out of the building and inhaled a deep breath. While she loved the crisp, cold air of autumn, spring was her next favorite season. The mingling of fresh grass, flowers blooming, and rain showers made for a sweetness in the air that made her happy. Right now, she wanted to feel happy. She'd feel even happier if she baked something like Reid suggested.

She passed the sitting area in front of the police department. Two colorful flowerpots anchored a bench that was shaded by a Japanese maple. At the end of the concrete path, she stepped onto Main Street and continued toward home. Drew left after giving his statement. He had to get back to the newspaper and file his story. Ethan had to pick up the girls from a playdate. She was on her own.

At the curb, she paused and looked up and down Jefferson's primary thoroughfare. Life looked normal. Nothing showed that Ted Donovan, a once upstanding member of the town, had been stealing money from a charity, cheating on his wife, and lying to everyone.

This wasn't the first time someone had duped her. Was she too gullible? Too trusting? Perhaps. What was the alternative? Suspect every person's motives? Question their character? Harden her heart and wall people off? Was that any way to live?

She shook her head. It wasn't. Even though Ted had disappointed her, she wouldn't lose faith in people. Especially the people in Jefferson. There were too many good ones.

A loud barking drew her attention to Federal Drive, a side street off Main Street lined with residential homes on small lots, and she saw a woman walking a small dog. The dog was no bigger than Bigelow but far more vocal than Bigelow was while walking.

Her gaze moved from the pair to a woman walking at a quick pace. It was Sally. Hope raised her hand to wave, but Sally wasn't looking in her direction. Instead, she was focused on a black sedan parked at the curb. The driver's side door opened, and Jeffrey, the mail carrier, got out and dashed around the vehicle's front.

He said something. Sally laughed and then leaned forward and kissed Jeffrey. On. The. Lips.

Hope gaped.

"You little minx. You have a boyfriend." Now she knew why Sally had been so secretive about her whereabouts. And she'd bet her limited-edition Kitchen Aid mixer that the morning Birdie died, Sally and Jeffrey had been together.

The big question now was why Sally was keeping her relationship a secret.

It looked like Hope had a new mystery to solve.

Hope cracked three eggs, one at a time, and added them to her stand mixer, which was churning at a slow speed to incorporate the eggs. When she returned home, she'd changed into a pair of cutoffs and a pink T-shirt with a graphic heart design. Ethan had given her the shirt and a bottle of her favorite perfume for Valentine's Day over a romantic dinner. She couldn't help but think that her less-than-enthusiastic response to his proposal of living together had shifted their relationship into a gray area. Suddenly the tea she'd made tasted bitter on her tongue and she set the beverage aside. She didn't want to be in a gray area with Ethan. She wanted the white picket fence, the carpool duty, and the happily ever after.

So why did she practically toss cold water on his suggestion?

Because she was scared. Plain and simple.

Scared of being vulnerable, scared of screwing up another relationship, scared of not being worthy of Ethan's love.

The whiz of her mixer drew her back to the recipe she was developing. Last winter while talking to a friend, she had an idea for a cookie recipe but hadn't pursued it.

Maybe it was because she wasn't sure how it would turn out but hey, she had all the ingredients on hand and Reid did tell her to bake something.

It was a little early to begin developing recipes for the holiday season, but she figured this year she'd need to self-publish a baking guide complete with tips and recipes to help offset the loss in revenue from the brands that had dumped her.

As the eggs incorporated into the other wet ingredients, she jotted down the number of eggs in her recipe notebook. Her sleuthing notebook was tucked away since there wasn't any need for it now. Even though Ted hadn't confessed to the murders, she didn't have any doubt in her mind about his guilt.

She reached for the bowl where she'd sifted together flour, sugar, and other dry ingredients. Slowly, she added the flour mixture into the wet ingredients.

The paddle attachment worked its magic on the dough and gave Hope a few moments of reflection and allowed her to recognize that she'd been on an emotional roller coaster from being suspected of murder, to being asked to make a major life change, to confronting a criminally deceptive man.

A low growl had her head turning toward the family room. Bigelow was at his canvas tote cubby trying to unearth a squeak toy buried beneath a layer of Kongs and balls. He was persistent and finally pulled the plush toy from the tote and carried it to his bed. She'd purchased the tote a few days after adopting Bigelow. It had a paw print and his name stenciled onto it. Ethan had pointed out that Bigelow couldn't read, but she ignored the silly observation. What she was wanted was cute storage for the messy toys.

She checked her cookie dough. It was time to add in the chocolate chips and give one last final whip. When it reached its perfect consistency, she turned off the mixer and lowered the bowl. After disengaging the paddle attachment, she carried the bowl to her workstation to form the dough into a disc and then wrap in plastic wrap. The dough went into the refrigerator to chill. She estimated two hours for this first test.

Hope started to clean up. Being a type A personality, she couldn't walk out of her kitchen while it was still messy. As she wiped the counters, her mood started to lift and change. While she kept reminding herself all along that her blogging career was salvageable, she finally now believed it.

With the kitchen tidied, she grabbed her recipe notebook to finish jotting her thoughts about the gingerbread chocolate chip cookie recipe. Her cell phone's ping alerted her to an incoming text.

She grabbed the phone and read Ethan's message.

Got the girls and dropped them off at their aunt's. Want to show you something.

Show her something? Now? She glanced at the refrigerator. She had at least two hours to spare.

What is it? She typed and sent the reply.

You'll want to see it. Trust me.

She glanced at her baking outfit and wondered if it would be okay to wear out in public. Her first instinct was that it wasn't. Her second was, who would care? Ethan wouldn't. In fact, he liked her cutoffs.

Okay. Where?

He texted back with an address. Turkey Hill Road. It was way on the other side of Jefferson. Oh, boy. It was a house. A part of her was thrilled that he was still interested in taking the next step in their relationship after what she said about his police department yesterday. Another part of her still wasn't sure she wanted to take the next step right now.

She leaned forward and, with all her might, lifted her body from the sofa. Halfway up, she paused. Ethan had replied with a heart emoji. He usually wasn't an emoji kind of guy. Maybe he just wanted to make extra sure she knew he wasn't upset with her. She replied with her own heart emoji and then went upstairs to change into a pair of jeans. She opted to keep the T-shirt on, and she slipped into a pair of sneakers.

Behind the steering wheel, she typed in the address to her GPS and then backed out of her garage. Turkey Hill Road was on the border of Jefferson and was far more rural than where Hope currently lived. If she remembered correctly, the homes in that area were situated on several acres of land. Out there, she would have a lot of privacy from prying and gossiping neighbors.

Hope arrived at the address but didn't see Ethan's truck in the driveway. She eased her Explorer into the gravel driveway and shifted it into park.

She leaned forward on the steering wheel and stared at the Colonial-styled house.

Not bad.

The home appeared to be set on a good-sized property—definitely more room for the girls to play and to add more animals in the future. Mature trees dotted the expansive front yard, and a low stone wall ran the length of the walkway leading to the home's entrance. The second-story windows were accented by charming window boxes, while stunning potted urns bookended the front door.

Her gaze flicked across the landscape. A large red barn with a side shed, set back from the house, looked to be in good shape. There was plenty of room for a riding ring. Molly and Becca had enjoyed the few lessons they'd taken, and Hope could imagine owning a couple of mares.

She pulled out her phone from her purse and sent a text to Ethan letting him know she was there and asked how long he'd be. When the text was sent, she got out of the vehicle and walked toward the house. As she inspected more closely, she considered if this was somewhere she could see herself living.

The location was far from town. A part of her liked being able to walk to Main Street to grab a coffee at the Coffee Clique or pop into Claire's shop. Also, a quick trip to the general store was easy to do when she needed something at the last minute. Out here, she'd have to drive more, and there weren't any close neighbors with kids for Molly and Becca.

But it had privacy. Lots of privacy.

Hope walked around the side of the house, noting the new-looking central air conditioning unit, to check the backyard.

It was immaculately maintained like the front. The gently curved garden beds were in full bloom and gave definition to the outdoor living space. The large slate patio looked to be in good shape; she envisioned all the entertaining possibilities.

Her high-end grill would fit perfectly out there. She could see Ethan grilling and her walking out from the kitchen carrying a tray of food while the girls played on the swing set not too far away. The only thing missing was a pool, but there was plenty of space to put one in.

She sighed. She really hadn't wanted to like the house.

Hope glanced at her watch. Where was Ethan? And the real estate agent? Otherwise, how would she be able to tour the inside? Then it hit her; Claire must have told him about the property. Even though Claire wasn't working as a real estate agent any longer, she still had her license and kept her pulse on properties in town.

Hope stepped onto the patio, and as she passed the outdoor dining table, her hand glided over the top of a chair on the way to the slider door. She hated to admit it, but the place was growing on her.

When she reached the door, she cupped her head with her hands and peered into the combination family room and kitchen.

The cathedral ceilings were impressive, but she didn't like the stark white cabinets or the current stainless-steel appliances. She'd have to gut the kitchen and start from scratch. But the room was a good size. Other than remodeling the kitchen, it looked as if she'd have no projects to tackle, unlike her current home.

Being project-free would give her extra time to develop recipes, maybe even tackle writing a cookbook. In her daydreams, it was filled with delicious recipes and stunning photography. Those things took time. She'd also be able to work more on her coaching program. Considering how fast her sponsorship deals had gone away with only the hint of scandal, having another stream of income would be a wonderful thing.

A sound like a snapping branch pulled Hope out of her thoughts. *Great. Ethan's here*. She couldn't wait to tell him she liked the house so far and was eager to tour inside. She stepped away from the slider and started to turn when something hard struck her on the back of her head.

She yelped and teetered for a moment as she tried to grasp the slider's handle to steady herself but missed it as she collapsed to the ground. Her body hit the slate hard, and everything faded to darkness.

Chapter Twenty-One

"What . . . where . . ." Hope tried to piece together why she was lying on the ground with a crushing headache. Where was she? A jagged streak of pain shot through her head. Perhaps it was better not to think too much. She lifted her hand to her temple and rubbed.

"Hope!"

Ethan?

"Hope! What happened?" Ethan's voice boomed, and in a flash he was beside her.

"I don't know. I was looking in the window. My head." She winced as she touched a sore spot. "I think someone hit me."

"Let me see." Ethan pulled her close to his chest and parted her hair. "You're not bleeding. We need to get an ice pack on it. I have a first aid kit in my truck. Do you have any idea how long you've been out?"

"Not really. I didn't pay attention to the time as I was

looking around the house. The inside looks nice. I was looking in, and I heard a noise. Actually, I thought it was you arriving. I went to turn around, and then I was hit . . . yes, I remember. Someone was behind me. I heard breathing."

"Did you catch a glimpse of the person?"

"No. It happened so fast. Why would someone hit me on the head?" She looked up at the exterior wall next to her. It was the barn. How did she get behind there? "Wait . . . I was on the patio. How did I get over here?"

"I have to call this in and get an ambulance." Ethan helped situate her against the barn's wall before he pulled out his cell phone.

"No. I don't want an ambulance."

"You were hit on the head and knocked unconscious for an undetermined amount of time. You're going to the emergency room." Ethan's voice was firm.

"Okay, I'll go to the ER but not in an ambulance. I can walk." At least she hoped so, otherwise, he'd be strapping her onto a gurney in a heartbeat.

"Fine. Let's get you to my truck."

He stood, assisting her up. She wobbled before finding her balance. "I'm okay. Where's my purse? Oh, I left it in the car. Can you grab it for me?"

"I will." Keeping a tight hold on her, he guided Hope to his truck and settled her in the passenger seat. He then called 9-1-1 to report the incident.

Hope leaned back against the bucket seat and closed her eyelids. The tension in her shoulders dissipated but the throbbing in her head ratcheted up a notch. The pain was making it difficult for her to recall the moments leading up to being hit.

She remembered hearing a branch break but nothing else. No, that wasn't true. She'd heard breathing. Too bad she couldn't identify someone by his or her breathing pattern.

Wait.

She had a split second between turning around at the noise and getting hit. She touched the back of her head again, and she felt for the sore spot. Whoever struck her wasn't any taller than she was. Otherwise, whatever was used would have hit her higher on the head. Her hand flew down, and she pushed open the door to tell Ethan, but he was gone.

"Ethan?" Panic swelled inside of her as she swung her legs around and her feet pressed down on the running board. She was about to climb out of the truck when she spotted Ethan walking back to the truck from the shed. "Ethan!"

He broke into a run and reached her in seconds. "What? What's wrong?"

"Where did you go?" She wrapped her arms around him and held him close. "I thought something happened to you."

"I'm sorry. I went back to the barn to look around. I should have told you. I found a board nearby. It might be the weapon. I'll have it collected for evidence."

Hope nodded. "I also think whoever hit me was around my height based on where I was hit."

"Okay. That's good. Things are coming back to you." He stroked her back.

"I don't know why anyone would want to hurt me. I mean, Ted is still in custody, right?"

"Unfortunately, I don't know his status."

"Of course." She chewed on her lip. "I'm sorry our viewing of this house turned out like this."

"Hey, don't worry about it, babe. We can come back if you want."

She shook her head. "I don't think so. I like it, but after what happened, I don't think we should start our new life together here. But I'm glad you still wanted to look at houses considering my earlier hesitation."

"I admit I was a little surprised when you texted me you were out here." Ethan caressed her cheek.

"Wait . . . what? You texted me to meet you here."

"Babe, I didn't text you."

"You did. I got a text from you, and you even added in a heart emoji after I said I'd go to the house."

"I don't use those things." His eyes clouded with unease.

"I know, but I just thought you were thrilled I agreed to look at the house. Wait. When I went to text you after I got here, I had to start a new text string. The one we were using about the house was gone. How's that possible?"

"Are you sure? Be right back." Ethan jogged to the Explorer and pulled out Hope's purse. He returned to his pickup truck and took out the phone. He tapped on the screen.

"Ethan, if you didn't send me the text, then who did?" It only took a nanosecond for Hope to figure it out and it left her a little shaky. "Someone who wanted to hurt me. But who?"

Two days later, Hope was doing her best to follow the doctor's orders. Recuperating from the mild concussion wasn't as easy as it sounded because she was told to rest and not drive. Sure, it sounded simple enough to do, but she wasn't the type of person to sit idle. And while she loved her home and had a ton of work to catch up on, knowing she wasn't allowed to do much or go anywhere was a struggle. The lingering headache and foggy brain that came from the head injury kept her from rebelling too much.

"This peach cobbler is to die for." Josie scooped up her last forkful.

"Wait until you make it when peaches are in season." Hope looked up from her recipe notebook. With the help of Josie, she whipped up the dessert. Despite her assistant's praise, there were a few tweaks Hope wanted to make to the final recipe.

"You look a little better today. More alert." Josie stood from the table and took her fork and plate to the dishwasher. "You're rebounding quickly."

Hope tapped her pen on the table. Since yesterday, her sensitivity to light and sound had improved. It was a sign she was on the road to a full recovery. She hoped it would be a speedy one too.

Earlier in the morning, she had a call with her agent. Laurel had done her magic and gotten both Mama Mia Pasta and Lily-Frye Paints to renew their agreements with Hope. Graham Flour was taking a lot more work to woo back. And that's why Laurel earned the big bucks. Hope was confident her agent could get the job done.

Whether she'd continue with the sponsorships after the current contracts ran out was up in the air. She realized she was much happier creating recipes than creating content for a paint company.

"I heal fast," she quipped.

"Don't go making light of what happened. It's scary that you were attacked in broad daylight by some random person."

"I don't think it was random."

"You don't? Do you know who attacked you?"

"I can't prove it, but I've been giving it a lot of thought, and I think it was Gary." Hope closed her notebook and reached for her glass of water.

Josie leaned on the island countertop. "You've suspected him all along, haven't you? Did you ever find out what happened between him and Birdie?"

"Yes. Twenty years ago, Birdie had an affair with a married man. He confessed to his wife, and she was angry, and they argued, vases were broken, and then she stormed out of the house. She shouldn't have been driving. She was far too upset. Not a mile away from her home, she got into an accident and died."

"How awful." Josie pushed off the counter. "The poor family. Two young children losing their mother. How did you find out?"

"During Ted's interview with Detective Reid—by the way, he still maintains his innocence in the murder—he finally shared what caused a wedge between Birdie and her brother. I guess Gary is a highly moral man and couldn't forgive his sister's part in an adulterous relationship." What Hope couldn't figure out was what his motive for killing Birdie would have been. It'd been twenty years since the affair. Why wait so long to kill her? And why hurt Hope?

Hope stared at her notebook as a memory struggled to push its way to the front of her mind, but then disappeared. It was so frustrating since she believed it had to do with the murder investigation.

"Are you okay? You look a little funny," Josie said, drawing Hope out of her thoughts.

Hope nodded. "Yeah, I'm okay. It doesn't seem to fit."

"What doesn't?" Josie lifted her computer bag.

"For some reason, I don't see him spoofing a text message from Ethan." She'd gotten a quick course on the creepy technique. It allowed a person to send a message impersonating another person. While it wasn't hard to do, it took some tech savviness, which she didn't feel Gary had. "Something doesn't feel right. I can't quite put my finger on it.

"Perhaps you should do something besides work and think about the incident. Maybe read a book. But not a mystery." Josie smiled. "Take your mind off the question, and you'll have an answer sooner than you think."

Hope considered the advice. It sounded good. "Thanks. And you don't have to come over tomorrow. I'll be fine."

"Okay. But call me if you need anything." Josie turned and left the kitchen. A few moments later, Hope heard her doorbell's app jingle, letting her know Josie had exited the mudroom and was on her way home.

Hope took another sip of her water before going back to her notes about the peach cobbler. The dessert was a springboard to another recipe idea—peach chili sauce. She jotted her thoughts until her cell phone interrupted her.

She reached for the phone and saw the incoming number was unknown. Considering the spoofing text she received, Hope hesitated to accept the call. But if it was Gary, she wanted to talk to him. She tapped on the phone to take the call.

"Hello," Hope said.

"Hi, it's Casey. I hope I'm not disturbing you."

Hope let out a relieved breath. "No. Actually, this is a delightful distraction. What's up?"

"I'm going through all the submitted recipes for the library's cookbook, which are making me very hungry." Casey laughed. "There are so many. I know I offered to fill in for you until you're feeling better, but it's kind of overwhelming."

"There's a lot of enthusiasm. Would you like some help?"

"I'd love some, but only if you're up to it."

"Actually, I'm going stir crazy. I've only been outside to feed the chickens and to read on the front porch. I need to do something else."

"Wow. You really are type A because it's only been two days."

"Two very long days. Let me change, and I'll meet you. Where are you?"

"I'm at the library. Angela is popping in and out when she has a free moment to help."

The library wasn't too far and getting some fresh air and exercise would make her feel better. Decision made.

"I can't drive yet, so I'll be walking. I won't be long." She ended the call and stood. She took her glass to the sink and glanced out the window. The sunny day had darkened. Gray clouds had rolled in, and the forecast was for rain showers later in the day. Just in case, she would drop an umbrella in her tote. If it were raining when she left the library, she could call Claire or Drew for a lift home.

She walked out of the kitchen, toward the hall. When she reached the staircase, she grabbed the newel post, and as she raised her foot on the first step, a wave of dizziness hit her. Her hold on the post tightened as the dizziness passed. She sucked in a deep breath, then exhaled. Maybe she should stay put. But she'd been staying put for two days. Granted, that wasn't a long time, but she hated being housebound. Being treated like a patient was the worst feeling. Another deep breath in and out, her head cleared, and she could climb the stairs.

Changing out of her yoga pants and T-shirt into jeans and a button-down shirt made her feel instantly better. She ran a brush through her hair and then swept it up into a loose ponytail.

Back downstairs, she tossed an umbrella into her tote as she exited the front door. She descended the porch steps, holding onto the railing just in case another dizzy spell struck her.

Gosh, she hated feeling feeble.

She reached the brick path that led to her driveway and breathed in the fresh air. A sweet, pungent zing hit her nostrils. Rain was on its way—all the more reason to get moving.

She continued to the top of her road at a leisurely pace. She wouldn't overdo it and risk fainting. Ahead, she spotted a group of three moms, including Zara, waiting for the school bus. She waved and was ignored by her still irritated neighbor. Another mom, who Hope recognized but didn't know, said something to Zara, and they laughed. Hope noted it wasn't a good-hearted laugh; no, it was more of a snicker. She'd read about mommy cliques in books, even enjoyed a chuckle or two at their antics. Now she wasn't laughing. Maybe she should move.

Hope was tempted to lower her head, but instead kept her chin high and swept her gaze back to the road ahead.

She wouldn't allow Zara or her mean-girl mommy friends to see that her snub was hurtful.

Luckily, the clique was on the other corner, so Hope wouldn't have to wait near them to cross the street.

A plop of cold wetness landed on her head, and then another. *Great*. It had started to rain. She reached into her tote for the umbrella. All the while, she felt the judging eyes of the mommies. Never shy in public, she was surprised by the pressure building from being gawked at by those three women. It was rattling her nerves.

Clumsily, she opened the umbrella, and even though she didn't want to look, she did, and noticed the smirks on their faces.

She picked up her pace and quickly made it to the intersection of her road and Hartford Road. There she paused and waited for a break in the traffic. She wouldn't have thought twice about dashing across the street any other day, but the fact she felt like she was teetering on a seesaw caused her to be extra careful before stepping out into the road. Especially since the big, fat raindrops had started to come down harder and faster.

When the coast was clear in both directions, Hope crossed the street and stepped up onto the grass. Hartford Road didn't have a sidewalk, so it was either walk on the very edge of the front lawns of the tidy Cape Cods or on the pavement. Once safely across, she breathed a sigh of relief. Somehow, she'd have to make things right with Zara. But that was for another day.

She did her best to shake off the unpleasant encounter but was hindered by a stabbing pain in her head and a harder downpour of rain. She should have slipped on her rain jacket before heading out. A gust of wind swept by, yanking her umbrella hard, and she struggled to keep it in position over her body. Now her arms were wet and cold.

A large truck passed by, spraying up water and hitting her legs. Great. Her trek from home to the library was going to end with her being soaked to the core.

Her pace slowed as her head pain intensified, and another round of dizziness hit. It was mild, but enough to make her reconsider the decision to go to the library. She ought to turn around and go back. Then she'd have to pass by the mommy clique again. That wasn't going to happen.

She mentally regrouped, determined to make it to the library. If she still felt ill, she'd ask Casey to drive her home.

She passed the Cavanaugh house. The lovely Cape Cod still had its Christmas lights hung along its roof.

Hope appreciated efficiency but drew the line at keeping holiday decorations up all year long.

Christmas.

A memory pushed its way to the front of Hope's mind. She remembered what Casey said about her family. Her mother had died suddenly. And she had a brother. Two children.

I can't believe I forgot.

Casey.

Could Casey's father be the man Birdie had an affair with twenty years ago?

It was unlikely.

Hope continued walking.

What if it wasn't so unlikely? There was Birdie's odd reaction to seeing Casey out jogging past her home. Casey was from Birdie's home state, and her mother was dead.

It had to be a coincidence.

A sweep of wind slammed her hard. The rain shower that was predicted was turning into a raging storm.

What if it wasn't a coincidence?

What if it was true, and Casey held Birdie responsible for her mother's death?

But why frame Hope for the murder?

Hope's grip on the umbrella handle tightened as anxiety rippled through her body.

Whoa.

Her head spun, forcing her to stop. Hope rode out the unpleasant sensation, and when it passed, she turned around to go back home. She no longer cared about Zara and her friends. They could snicker and glare all they wanted. She needed to get home.

Her feet slogged through the wet grass, and her breathing increased. Fear built up inside her.

Would she pass out right there on the side of the road, or would she make it back to her house?

She felt woozy again. She stopped and bent over, resting one hand on her thigh. She inhaled and exhaled deeply.

A honking caught her attention, and when she looked toward the road, she saw a familiar car and felt a flush of relief in her body. She straightened up as Josie darted out of her vehicle and around to the side of the road.

"Hope, my goodness, are you okay? What are you doing out?" Josie reached and grabbed Hope's arm and led her to the car. "Get in."

"I got dizzy. . . . I don't feel well." Hope slumped into the passenger seat.

"Don't worry. I'll take care of everything." Josie buckled Hope's seatbelt and then walked around the front of the car and got inside. "You never know when to stop, do you?"

"I have to call Ethan." It was hard for Hope to concentrate. Her thoughts were jumbled. She fought the feeling of passing out. "I don't think Ted or Gary killed Birdie." Her eyes fluttered closed, and her head dropped to the side.

"You're right. They didn't."

Chapter Twenty-Two

Hope's eyes opened with a start. Where was she? Coldness seeped through her body as her nose wriggled at the scent of mustiness mingled with mothballs. Why was she was lying on a concrete floor? And why was there a zip tie binding her hands and a gag in her mouth? She looked around the unfamiliar space.

Where am I?

A basement. Whose?

The last thing she remembered was walking past Zara and her friends at the bus stop. Her thoughts were jumbled. Frustration bubbled inside her. Why couldn't she remember how she got to this basement?

Focus, Hope. Focus.

She looked around the space again.

Dingy drywall covered the walls and dim fluorescent light fixtures hung precariously from the ceiling. A workbench was set against a wall beneath a casement window.

Rain battered the grimy glass surface. There was nothing recognizable about where she was.

Fighting despair, she shifted gears and concentrated on how she got there.

Again, she tried to remember what happened after she crossed the street away from Zara and her mommy friends.

Her mind began burrowing, mining to unearth the smallest bit of memory it could recover.

Rain.

It had started to rain, and she felt dizzy when she pulled the umbrella out of her tote.

Where was her tote?

Her gaze searched the basement, and she spotted it beside the staircase. A glimmer of hope sparked in her. Her cell phone was in there. She could call for help. The phone's location service could identify where she was for the police.

She directed her thoughts back to walking to the library. Yes! She remembered. She was going to meet Casey.

Oh, no.

Casey had lured her out to the library. Her mind whirred with all the information she'd pieced together since the murder. A sickening feeling settled in her stomach. Casey was the killer.

A whisper gnawed in her head.

Life path.

"She chose her life's path." That's what Gary had said about his sister. She'd heard it again later.

"Not everyone chooses the right life path."

Life. Path.

Hope's eyes widened with a terrifying realization that it hadn't been Casey who stopped by the roadside to help her.

"I'll take care of everything." It had been Josie's voice.

It was Josie!

Hope's mind churned over snippets from the past few days. Josie always said she was from Florida, but she shared details about living through a blizzard that hit the Cambridge area twenty years ago. Josie also had access to Hope's house thanks to the key Hope gave her. She could have poisoned Birdie's muffin and then planted the peanut oil bottle by the barn. She was tech savvy enough to manipulate the doorbell video and spoof a text message.

And she had a brother.

No, it couldn't be her.

The killer couldn't have been Josie.

I have to be wrong.

The creaking of a door opening drew Hope's gaze upward. The next sound was a slam. She winced. When her eyes opened, she glimpsed navy sneakers descending the steps. With each footfall, the person came into view.

Jean-clad legs.

A white T-shirt.

Then *her* face.

"You're awake." Josie came off the last step and walked toward Hope. "I guess it's time for our heart-to-heart, don't you think?" She lowered the gag from Hope's mouth and assisted Hope up to a sitting position. She leaned Hope's body against a support column.

The quick movement sent a bout of nausea rolling through Hope's body. She lowered her eyelids to ride out the unpleasant surge and the feeling like she was going to vomit. She prayed to God that when she opened her eyes Josie wouldn't be there.

Her prayer wasn't answered.

"What have you done? Why am I here?"

"Are you telling me you haven't figured it out yet?" Josie stood and stepped back away from Hope. "Come on. You solved this mystery puzzle. You know it was me who killed Birdie."

"And Avery."

Josie tilted her head. "No. I didn't. That death isn't on me. And Birdie's death won't be on me either." Her voice was unemotional, chilling Hope to the bone.

"You won't get away with this. The police will find out that you killed Birdie and have me held here." Though Hope wasn't sure how, considering no one knew where she was. She hadn't even told anyone she was going to the library. Except Casey.

"You'll be amazed at what I can get away with. Like planting the peanut oil bottle. A few minutes of hacking and poof, the video of me doing that disappears."

Even though the enormity of the situation Hope was in had hit her once she regained consciousness, hearing Josie's admission astounded her.

"Josie, listen to me. I can help you."

"Let me guess. First, I have to let you go. It's a game to you, isn't it?"

Hope blinked. Tears welled in her eyes, and her throat tightened with fear. "I don't know what you're talking about. Josie, this is serious. You killed two women, and you've abducted me!"

"I did not kill two women! Only Birdie! And she deserved it." Josie planted her hands on her hips and bit her lower lip. Her gaze drifted to the dirty window that was being pelted by rain. She appeared to be regrouping.

Josie's confession should have appalled Hope, yet relief ebbed through her knowing her employee was responsible for only one death. Now, to keep it that way.

"Why did you kill Birdie? Because she had an affair with your father twenty years ago?" Hope wasn't looking for an explanation, at least not there in the basement. She didn't care about Josie's reasons why. What she wanted was to escape. By keeping Josie distracted, Hope had a chance of escaping.

Josie dropped her hands from her hips and stomped back to Hope and squatted down to eye level. Her lips pulled back and she bared her teeth. "You really don't know when to stop, do you? No worries, I'll play along with you. At least for a little while. Guess I can do that, considering you've been a good boss. One of the best, actually."

"Then why don't you let me go?"

"Because you'll go running to your boyfriend and tell him everything. I won't go to prison. I shouldn't have to go to prison for doing what I did. Birdie deserved to die!" The kind-hearted, perky woman Hope had hired last winter was gone. In her place was an enraged, dangerous woman who had no remorse for taking a life and displayed little hesitation to take another.

"What happened?"

"I told you. Birdie ruined my life. My mother died in that car accident, and nothing was the same after that. Our father dragged us to Florida after the funeral. Gosh, how I hated it down there. All my friends were in Massachusetts. Our home was there. All of that was gone because of Birdie!"

"I'm so sorry you and your brother had to go through that."

"Yeah, everyone was sorry. Sorry my mom died. Sorry my dad started drinking. Sorry my brother got sick. Sorry. Sorry. Sorry. You know what *sorry* really means?" Josie got into Hope's face. "It means better you than me."

Hope's head jerked back, away from the distorted and unfamiliar face of her employee. "No. No. That's not what I mean at all. Josie, you went through an ordeal, a trauma. You fought your entire life to make something out of it, so don't throw it away. I'm not saying it's going to be easy, but I'm here for you."

Josie tilted her head, and there was a flicker of emotion in her eyes. Was she considering what Hope said?

"My father felt guilty about what happened, and that's why he drank himself to death, leaving me responsible for my brother, who now lives in a group home. Every morning since I was nineteen, I wake up, and he's my first thought. And every night when I lay my head down on my pillow and close my eyes, he's my last thought. Do you know how exhausting that is?"

"I can't imagine."

"Day. After. Day. From the time I was nineteen. I should have been in college, joining a sorority, dating some hot frat boy, but *no*, I was working my butt off to pay my brother's medical bills and my father's debts. So believe me, Hope, it's never been easy being me."

"Was killing Birdie easy?"

"I barely blinked."

Hope held Josie's gaze. Whatever emotion had been in her eyes had vanished. Now they were soulless.

"Why did you frame me for Birdie's murder?"

"I'd like to say I hadn't intended to, that things just got out of control. I really hate to lie, though." Josie reached out and stroked Hope's hair. "Especially to someone who doesn't have a lot of time left."

The reminder that her life was on the line hit Hope like a ton of bricks. She needed a better plan than just a distraction.

"You seemed to enjoy solving murders. It's like a game to you."

"No, it's not."

"Don't lie to me!" Josie twisted the lock of hair and yanked. Hope cried out. "You turned my life, my pain, into a game of Clue." She let go of Hope's hair and snickered.

"No, I didn't."

"I watched you the whole time. Running around town asking questions, looking for motives, and eliminating people when you deemed them innocent. I know about your notebook where you jotted down your observations and made your suspect list."

"I had no choice. You framed me for murder! I didn't enjoy one minute of being suspected of murder. I was fighting for my life!"

"I spent my entire life fighting to survive. I needed to teach you a lesson. You should have been arrested!" Josie's gaze bore down on Hope. Her jaw tensed, and her neck corded. "Looks like being the police chief's girlfriend has its perks. I thought for sure Detective Reid would have slapped the cuffs on you. He didn't because of your relationship with Ethan. Anyone else, they wouldn't have hesitated to arrest."

"You're right."

"Of course I am. You want to know how I did it, don't you?" she asked in a dark, teasing tone.

Hope nodded.

"It was easy. I snuck onto her property and called her landline because she detested cell phones, so I knew she'd have to get up and go into the house, giving me enough time to poison the muffin she was eating. She never knew I was there." Josie sounded proud of her duplicity.

"Did you post the video of Birdie and me arguing outside the library?" Hope's insides quivered, and beads of sweat formed on her forehead and lip. Time was running out. She had to figure a way to get out of the basement, away from Josie. If she could get her hands out of the zip tie, then she'd be able to fend Josie off and make a run for the staircase. It didn't look like Josie had a weapon.

"You're curious right to the end. I wish I had but no, I didn't post the video. Since I don't have time for twenty questions and you know how much I like efficiency, let me tell you what I did." Josie squatted down. "Remember that power cube you lost?" She used air quotes around the word lost.

Hope nodded.

"I took it and replaced it with one that had an itty bitty camera in it so I could keep tabs on you and what you were planning to do."

Hope's eyes widened at realizing why it had always seemed like she was a step behind the killer.

"What about at the Donovan house? It was you who pushed me down the stairs at EH? And you were also the person I heard outside the day of Birdie's funeral?" Hope twisted her hands, but the zip tie wouldn't budge. It dug deeper into her skin.

Josie nodded again.

"That's how Detective Reid knew I was there. You called the police and told them. You were spying on me. How could—?" Hope stopped. She wouldn't get a rational explanation from a cold-blooded killer, which Josie was.

"You're outraged? How do you think I feel? Birdie destroyed my family, and what happened to her? She ended up marrying a successful man and moving to a beautiful town. There were no consequences for her. Even though I set up the perfect frame to teach *you* a lesson, you weren't arrested. Anyone else would have been. But not Hope Early, the police chief's girlfriend."

Anger mixed with bitterness and jealousy made a deadly combination, and Hope was the target. She gulped. A bout of drowsiness hit her, and she forced her eyes wide open. She had to stay alert. Stay alive.

"Come on, let's get this over with so I can pack and get out of this town."

"Where are you going?"

"Far away, once I get my brother. Come on, get up so I can finish what I started at Turkey Hill Road."

Josie leaned forward and yanked Hope up by the arms.

"You won't get away with this. Ethan will find you and arrest you."

Josie barked a laugh. "He'll be too busy grieving his girlfriend."

Hope needed to do something. Make a move to escape. But what? With her hands secured, she couldn't strike Josie.

"Too bad I won't be around for the funeral. It will devastate everyone that the perfect Hope Early cracked. The pressure of being suspected of murder and having her career turned upside down proved to be too much for you.

Your sister and your niece and nephew will grieve deeply. Hmm, maybe I should stay to lend a shoulder for them and for Ethan to lean on."

Her nephew! That was it. The video Logan watched about breaking free of zip ties. Hope searched her memory for how the guy in the video released his hands.

Think, Hope, think.

In her mind's eye, she could see him freeing himself in one swift, forceful movement.

Could she?

She had to try because she wouldn't get a second chance.

"No one will believe I killed myself."

"You'll be amazed at what people will believe. You know, I'm pretty convincing, don't you agree?"

Hope ignored the question. She put all her energy and concentration into what she hoped was the first step to escaping the psycho killer. She dragged in a deep breath and jerked her arm from Josie's grasp. Before Josie could react, Hope raised her arms above her head and yanked them down in one sweeping motion, pulling her elbows back past her waist as she snapped her wrists out to the side, breaking the zip tie.

I did it!

Josie's eyes bulged at the sight. Hope had only seconds to take advantage of her captor's surprise.

She rushed Josie, knocking her shoulder into her like a running back, and forcing her backward. The workbench stopped their momentum.

Josie grappled, her strength increased, and she shoved Hope off her.

Hope tumbled backward but remained standing. Her

heartbeat quickened at the sight of Josie grabbing a hammer off the workbench. She needed a weapon. Fast!

Josie raised the hammer over her head and came swinging at Hope.

"Josie, stop!"

Josie lunged toward Hope, who caught sight of a stack of two-by-fours propped up against a cabinet. She grabbed one and swung at Josie.

Josie's midsection arched and she dropped the hammer, but then grabbed for the piece of wood.

They struggled for control of the makeshift weapon. Hope's head started to buzz with a woozy feeling. Now wasn't the time to pass out. With a surge of adrenaline, she thrust the piece of wood upward to Josie's jaw.

Josie screamed as she let go of the two-by-four and crumpled to the floor.

The basement door opened, and quick, heavy footfalls followed.

"Hope!" Ethan called out as he jumped off the last riser and rushed to her.

"Ethan! She killed Birdie!" Hope dropped the two-by-four and swung her arms around Ethan's neck. "She kidnapped me! She tried to kill me!"

"You're okay now. Slow down. It's all okay. I've got you." Ethan pressed her closer to his chest.

Hope looked up from Ethan's solidness and saw two Jefferson Police officers hurry toward Josie. When they reached her, they helped her up and then handcuffed her.

"She had me in a zip tie and told me she killed Birdie and how she framed me. The charger cube she replaced has a camera in it. She said she didn't kill Avery. She was going to make my death look like a suicide. She's the one who hit me at the house." Hope was talking a mile a minute, but she couldn't stop herself.

"Shhh . . . slow down . . . breathe, Hope, breathe." Ethan's calm and steadying voice washed over her, and every muscle in her body eased.

"I'm feeling a little dizzy." Her hand gripped Ethan's shoulder. "Whoa . . . I think I need to sit."

"Okay, over there." Ethan led her to a stool at the corner of the workbench. "We'll get you an ambulance and have you checked out."

"I'd like to argue, but I think you're right." She watched the two police officers lead Josie up the stairs as they read her the Miranda warning.

"Well, that's a first." Ethan grinned.

"Ha ha." She rubbed her temples with her fingers. "How did you find me?"

"When you didn't show up at the library, Casey called me."

"She did?" A pang of guilt hit Hope for suspecting Casey of being the murderer. She was a nice person, and it looked like she'd saved Hope's life.

"I had Reid track your cell phone, and here I am." He reached out and took Hope's hand and squeezed.

"I'm so grateful you're here. I was scared there for a minute."

"Only a minute?"

Hope shrugged. "I've kind of lost track of time. Can we get out of here?"

"The ambulance isn't here yet."

"I can make it up the stairs with your help." She smiled, hoping to sway him.

"Okay, let's go."

"Really?" She didn't think it would be so easy. She stood, finding her balance, only to be swooped off her feet. "You don't have to carry me. I can walk."

"I'm not going to risk you falling down the stairs." He gave her a kiss on the cheek.

Hope didn't protest any further. She relaxed her body and rested her head against his chest.

"Besides, it's good practice." He grinned and headed for the stairs.

Chapter Twenty-Three

Hope walked down the veranda steps of Emily's House as the flitting breeze kissed her cheeks. It had been seven days since she woke with her hands tied in Josie's basement. Every day since, she'd been grateful that Casey had the wherewithal to contact Ethan when she was a no-show at the library. When she came off the last step, she turned around. Drew lagged behind.

He ended his call when he reached the railing.

"So cute your mom called to congratulate you." Hope smiled. Seeing Drew looking chipper and receiving the accolades he so rightly deserved made her heart swell.

His investigation into Emily's House and Visionary Media Consulting uncovered that Ted had embezzled over a hundred thousand dollars. His scheme fell apart when Birdie became wary of documents she was signing. She started researching. That's when he realized his fraud was about to be uncovered. He was preparing to leave the country when Birdie was murdered.

"She's a proud mama, what can I say?" Drew's grin grew wider as he slipped the phone into a pocket in his messenger bag. Having a front-page newspaper story picked up by several media outlets always boosted his mood. He jogged down the wooden steps. "My interview with Erin went well."

"I'm so thrilled the board appointed her interim director. She'll do a lot of wonderful work here." Hope glanced back at the Victorian house. She hated to imagine what would happen to all the clients the charity served if it had closed.

"Well, she's off to a good start since she reinstated you." He slung his arm around Hope's shoulders and together they walked toward the parking lot. "How was class?"

"Fun," she proclaimed. When Ted terminated her services the previous week, she had been heartbroken. The ladies in the class were more than students. They'd become her friends, and she cared about their futures. Now, being back at EH, she could finish what they'd started. "We have one more session to go and then the ladies are off to start their online empires. I spoke to Erin about doing another class."

"You think you'll have the time? You lost an assistant."

"I'll figure something out. I'm not in a rush to hire another assistant." When and if the time came, she'd definitely have more boundaries with the person. No handing out house keys or accepting their electronic devices. Hope rolled her eyes at her own naivety. She'd been far too trusting with someone she'd only known a few months.

Lesson learned. More boundaries. Less trust. And better background checks.

They walked to the parking lot and reached her Explorer. She aimed her fob at the driver's side door and the car beeped.

"Did you hear Gary's left Jefferson? Jane said he left yesterday afternoon and he intends to come back for the trial." Drew fished out his car key from his pants pocket.

"It won't be easy for him. What strikes me is that they hadn't spoken in twenty years because he disapproved of her behavior, yet in the past two decades, she'd become more like him."

"Judgmental, intolerant . . ."

"Exactly. Josie hadn't seen that the whole situation with her parents and her mother's death had taken a toll on Birdie. Anyway, onto more positive things. You're coming tomorrow for breakfast, right?" To celebrate her escape, her career rebound, and the clearing of her as a murder suspect, Hope was hosting a big pancake breakfast for her family and friends. She had a huge menu planned and was headed home to bake.

"Wouldn't miss it for anything." Drew gave Hope a peck on the cheek and then continued to his sports car parked a few spaces away.

Hope slid into her Explorer and started the ignition. Her gaze followed Drew on his way to his vehicle. To think, seven days ago she could have easily become another one of Josie's victims and missed Drew's big accomplishment. *Let it go*. It was over. Besides, she had more pressing things to think about—all the baking she had to do for tomorrow's get-together. Backing out of her space, she made a mental list of the recipes for tomorrow.

Her eyes widened with an idea. She'd include a include a pancake toppings bar. Now that sounded like fun for both the kids and the adults.

The next morning, Hope dashed down the staircase with Bigelow on her heels. Since adopting him, she'd done some reading on dogs and their behaviors. Despite their late-night baking session, both were feeling pretty spry.

Hope returned home from Emily's House yesterday expecting to tie on her apron and pull out her twenty-pound flour canister and start making the muffins and scones for her breakfast. What she hadn't planned on were the dozens of emails in her inbox from food brands who wanted to collab with her. She read every email. Some looked promising as she shifted her blog and brand back to what it was originally, way back in her New York City days—food, food, and more food. She happily forwarded all the requests to Laurel and then headed into the kitchen.

With a full house planned for her celebration party, she had a lot of food to prepare. Bigelow remained by her side during all the baking and when she made dinner. Princess, on the other hand, supervised from her new multilevel cat tree in the family room. From the top of the lookout tower, Princess had an eagle eye view of everything Hope did in the kitchen. It was also a good spot to leap from and scare the daylight out of Bigelow. Yeah, that happened within an hour of assembling the tree.

Entering the kitchen, Hope scanned for her cat and found the little diva curled in the tree's condo.

"You're safe," she said to Bigelow as she made a beeline for the coffee maker. She'd have one cup before heading out to the barn to collect eggs and then she'd return inside to whip up the dozens of pancakes she needed for her event. Sipping her coffee, she scanned the to-do list she'd printed out yesterday. This quick review reminded her everything was under control.

Bigelow woofed as he trotted to the back door. He wanted to go out. She grabbed her camera and led him out of the house through the mudroom. It had been a while since she'd photographed the chickens and their coop for her readers. It had been a long time since she did a lot of things on her blog, and now she was going to follow her heart and not worry so much about her checking account.

After returning from the barn with a basket of fresh eggs, Hope set to work making the pancake batter. Ethan arrived with his girls and settled them in the family room with a video to keep them occupied. Bigelow wasted no time in joining them on the sofa.

"Morning, babe." Ethan came up behind Hope at the island and wrapped his arms around her and nuzzled her neck.

She inhaled his woodsy scent and all but melted. Luckily, she found an ounce of willpower to keep her from flinging her arms around him and getting lost in his embrace because she had pancakes to cook. She untangled herself from his hold and turned to face him, waving the spatula in her hand.

"I can't be distracted. Everyone will be here soon, and I need to finish making these pancakes." She pointed to the griddle with the spatula. She was almost done cooking the buttermilk pancakes. Next up would be blueberry and then chocolate chip.

He saluted. "Yes, ma'am."

"Don't ma'am me." She laughed as she returned to the pancakes. She flipped the perfectly round, golden little cakes of fluffiness. "Could you start the coffee? The urn is already filled with water." Before going to bed last night, Hope set up a coffee station in the dining area complete with her 55-cup urn and her collection of mixed-match china cups found at flea markets.

Ethan nodded and pulled out the coffee canister from an upper cabinet. He scooped out the grounds and then switched the urn on.

"Hey, there's something that still isn't clear to me about Avery's death." Since her escape from Josie's basement, she hadn't been talking much about the murder or about Avery. She guessed she needed time to absorb all that had happened. She flipped over the pancakes to cook a few minutes longer. "What really happened to her?"

"The investigation turned up a witness who saw Avery walking alone on the trail. For whatever reason, the witness held back several days before coming forward. It appears it was an accident." Ethan returned the canister to the cabinet and then snatched a pancake off the rectangular platter Hope was arranging them on.

"Hey!" She flicked the spatula at his hand but missed.

"Sorry. I'm hungry. And now I'll get out of your way." He kissed her on the cheek as he walked to the family room.

Hope returned to her cooking and was putting a platter of pancakes into the oven to keep warm when her guests began to arrive.

Mitzi and Gilbert were the first and came through the mudroom with their golden retriever, Buddy. He was

Bigelow's best friend and they could play for hours together. Mitzi carried a potted plant and quickly suggested the best place to plant it. Gilbert waved and commented on how good the house smelled. He wasn't the only one who appreciated the scent of warming pancakes, freshly brewed coffee, and dozens of muffins, Buddy also seemed appreciative, with his snout high and sniffing rapidly. Gilbert unleased Buddy and the dog trotted into the family room to greet Bigelow and the girls.

Behind the Madisons were Casey and her kids. The littlest carried a bouquet of flowers and handed them to Hope with a big smile on her face. Hope gave the girl a hug and told her to go into the family room to play with Molly and Becca. Casey's other children ran off with her reminding them to behave. Hope directed Casey to the coffee station to help herself.

The front doorbell rang and Ethan raised a hand to let Hope know he'd answer it. A moment later, he returned with Matt and Drew. Both men looked famished and ready to eat.

"Wow look at that spread," Matt said pointing to the buffet table. "It looks amazing, and it smells incredible in here."

"I hit the gym already so I'm ready to eat. I even wore joggers with an elastic waistband. See." Drew patted his midsection and then lifted his shirt and tugged at the elastic band.

"Good thinking!" Hope flipped another batch of pancakes onto a platter and set it into the oven. "Help yourself to coffee."

"So is it true that Sally's bringing her new main squeeze?" Drew lifted an eyebrow.

"It is. But don't make a big fuss. You know how Sally is." Hope returned her attention to the pancakes. "Oh, Ethan! Can you get the champagne?"

"Champagne?" Matt returned to the island with a cup of coffee.

"For the mimosas." Hope flashed a smile as she poured pancake batter onto the griddle. "This is a celebration, after all."

"Did someone say celebration?" Jane entered through the mudroom with Sally and her plus-one following her. "Good morning, everyone."

"Good morning," everyone said at once.

"Where's my Bigelow?" Jane passed the island with her purse dangling from her arm. Her turquoise dress enhanced her sparkling blue eyes.

"Welcome, Jeffrey," Hope said. "You know everybody. Come on in, grab a cup of coffee. We'll be eating in a few minutes."

"Thank you, Hope." Jeffrey removed his plaid newsboy cap. "Beautiful home."

"Coffee's over here." Drew waved Jeffrey to the coffee station.

Sally ambled toward Hope. "Thank you for including Jeffrey."

"Of course. He's always welcome." Hope leaned closer to Sally. "I'd love to know why you were keeping your relationship a secret."

"To tell you the truth, I'm not sure." Sally shrugged. "Maybe because at my age saying I have a boyfriend sounds so . . . silly?"

"Nonsense. I think it's wonderful you're dating. Jeffrey is a good man. He has a solid job, and he's active in the community. You two make a cute couple."

Sally blushed.

"Talking about me, are you?" Jeffrey came up alongside of Sally and swung an arm around her shoulders. "I'm a lucky man."

"Oh, stop the fussing. And, yes, we were talking about you," Sally said.

"Dear, this chalkboard is adorable. What a wonderful idea." Jane stood at the buffet reading the chalkboard menu Hope designed last night before going to bed. She thought it would be a nice touch to list all the offerings her guests had to choose from—buttermilk, blueberry, and chocolate chip pancakes; lemon poundcake and blueberry muffins; yogurt parfaits; and assorted toppings.

The back door swung open again, and Claire entered with her children. Hannah and Logan each gave Hope a quick kiss and then made a beeline for the family room. Claire lingered a little longer with her sister.

"You certainly look in good spirits." Claire wrapped an arm around Hope's shoulder and squeezed. "I'm happy to see it."

"It's a beautiful day, and my home is filling up with the people I love." Hope dashed over to the microwave and removed the pitcher of maple syrup. It was almost time to eat. She carried the pitcher to the buffet table, which she'd decorated with table linens she found at an estate sale in Vermont.

"Is Zara here?" Claire followed, and she perused the table, nodding with approval. Most of the time she avoided carbs but she had little willpower against Hope's homemade pancakes. Hope returned to the stove and lifted the last platter of pancakes. She slid it into the oven.

After closing the oven door, Hope turned to her sister. "No. She didn't even reply to my email." She was about to head to the buffet table to give it a final check before bringing out the platters of pancakes and bacon when there was a knock at the back door. She diverted to the door and opened it.

"Good morning, Hope." Alfred entered with Maretta behind him. "It smells wonderful in here. You must have been cooking for hours."

"Welcome, Alfred, Maretta. You're both right on time. We're just about to start eating. Please, go help yourselves to coffee."

"Thank you for your invitation, Hope." Maretta offered the thinnest of smiles. "We're both glad things worked out for you and the chief," she said.

Hope wondered how much it hurt her to say it. Hope was cleared and Ethan was back at work, effective three days earlier.

"Well, no hard feelings. Especially today." Hope grabbed a kitchen towel from a drawer.

Maretta reached out and unexpectedly grabbed Hope's hand and squeezed. Hope wasn't sure what was going to happen next. This was so unlike Maretta.

"I want to express my gratitude for helping bring my friend's murderer to justice. Thank you."

Hope wasn't sure she heard Maretta correctly. She let Maretta's words repeat in her brain again. And again. Just to make sure. Honestly, she couldn't recall the last time Maretta complimented her or thanked her. This was new territory.

"You're welcome. I'm glad I was able to help."

"To be perfectly frank, Hope, if you would just stop finding dead bodies, life would be so much quieter in town for all of us." Maretta let go of Hope's hand and swept by her with her sights on the coffee urn.

"Glad you're not a murder suspect any longer. And very happy the chief is back at work." Alfred patted Hope's arm as he followed his wife.

"Hey, are we going to eat or what?" Drew called out from the family room.

Before Hope could answer, a loud pop startled them all. Ethan had uncorked the champagne bottle and everyone cheered.

Claire dashed back into the kitchen and removed the orange juice pitchers from the refrigerator while Hope pulled out the platters of pancakes and bacon from the oven. Casey hurried to grab the warmed plates and carried them to the table.

Everyone gathered around the buffet and by the time Hope arrived with the last two platters, her guests were filling their plates with towers of pancakes, generous helpings of toppings, and muffins. Ethan handed her a plate and she plucked two buttermilk pancakes and drizzled maple syrup over them and finished with a dollop of whipped cream.

The chatter that had filled the opened living space earlier had quieted down as everyone ate their breakfast. Lucky for her, no one was shy about seconds or thirds, so she'd have no leftovers.

Hope, who had been cozied up to Ethan while they ate on the sofa, stood. She padded over to the coffee station. More milk was needed. She continued to the refrigerator, with Bigelow underfoot. No doubt he was looking for the little extra something she saved for him. He knew her so well. After taking out a container of milk, she pulled out a neatly folded paper towel and unwrapped a small piece of bacon she'd stashed in the corner of the counter. Not the healthiest for her pup, but every now and again wasn't so bad, and he'd been good all morning. She held the bacon and guided him into a sitting position, and when he did, she set the tasty treat on the floor for him.

While he gobbled up his bacon, Hope refilled the milk pitcher at the coffee station. She also poured herself another coffee and carried her cup to the front porch. Outside, she moved to the railing and her gaze traveled along her front yard. Flowers were swaying in the soft spring breeze, the trees were filling out, and cheerful sounds were drifting from her house. She sipped her coffee.

Yes, life was good.

And life was good in her old farmhouse. After a serious discussion, the decision was made she'd be staying put right where she was with Ethan, his daughters, and her neighbors.

Please turn the page for recipes from Hope's kitchen!

Double Chocolate Chip Cookies

Posted by Hope Early

It's no secret, I'm a chocoholic. When the craving strikes, these extra chocolatey, soft-on-the-inside cookies hit the spot. They're easy to make, so when the farmhouse is filled with kids, I can whip up a batch and serve with a pitcher of milk. But be warned, once the chocoholics in your life try these cookies, they'll be wanting more. And don't worry about storing them because once they're out of the oven and cooled, they're going to disappear.

Ingredients:

½ cup melted butter
½ cup packed light brown sugar
¼ cup granulated sugar
1 large egg
2 teaspoons pure vanilla extract
¾ cup all-purpose flour
½ cup dark unsweetened cocoa powder
½ teaspoon baking powder
½ teaspoon salt
¾ cup chocolate chips
Flaky sea salt

Directions:

Preheat oven to 350 degrees. Line baking sheets with parchment paper or silicone mats.

Melt butter; set aside to cool. Meanwhile, in the bowl of an electric mixer, add brown and granulated sugars. When butter is cooled, add to sugar mixture. Beat on medium speed until well combined, 2–3 minutes.

Add in the egg and vanilla extract, and continue beating until well combined with sugar and butter mixture.

In a large mixing bowl, whisk together the flour, cocoa powder, baking soda, and salt. Add mixture to wet ingredients, mixing at slow speed until dough starts to form.

Add in chocolate chips. Mix well.

Using a large cookie scoop, place scoops of dough on prepared baking sheets, 2 inches apart. Sprinkle with flaky sea salt.

Bake for 9–11 minutes. The center of the cookies should be slightly underbaked. Let cookies cool on the baking sheet for 10 minutes before removing to wire rack to completely cool.

Enjoy!

Easy Stovetop Mac and Cheese

Posted by Hope Early

Quick and easy dinners are becoming more of a necessity here at the farmhouse. Between after-school activities for the girls, Ethan's erratic work schedule, and my never-ending to-do list, meals need to be whipped up in the blink of an eye most nights. This recipe is pretty close to being made that fast, and it's far better than anything you can get out of a box. It's also a perfect comfort food on wintry nights. Still, since it's made on the stovetop, when the craving for ooey-gooey cheese and macaroni hits in the middle of summer, you can make this without working up a sweat. Served in a pretty dish along with a side of sauteed string beans or steamed broccoli and a loaf of rustic bread, any last-minute dinner guest will never guess you didn't spend hours cooking.

Ingredients:

1 package (7 ounces) elbow macaroni
¼ cup butter, cubed
¼ cup all-purpose flour
½ teaspoon salt
Dash of pepper
2 cups whole milk
8 ounces sharp cheddar cheese, shredded
2 slices American cheese
Paprika, optional

Directions:

Follow the directions on the package to cook macaroni.

In another pot over medium heat, melt butter. Stir in flour, salt, and pepper until smooth. Gradually whisk in milk. Bring mixture to a boil, stirring constantly. Cook and stir 1–2 minutes longer or until thickened. Stir in cheddar cheese and American cheese until melted. Drain macaroni and then add to cheese sauce, stirring to coat.

If you want, you can sprinkle with paprika just before serving.

Gingerbread Chocolate Chip Cookies

Posted by Hope Early

Hold onto your Christmas stocking, because this soft gingerbread cookie packs a wallop of flavor and all the cozy holiday feels. The soft gingerbread is filled with chocolate chips, so every bite is a flavor combination like none other. According to the girls, this would be the perfect cookie to leave Santa. I think they're right. These are also perfect when you want a gingerbread cookie but don't want to deal with rolling and cutting out the dough. They're also ideal when you want a gingerbread cookie but also a chocolate chip cookie. Come on, you know you've been there. I know I have. Now you have the recipe that will take care of that craving. Ready to bake a new favorite cookie?

Ingredients:

10 tablespoons unsalted butter, softened
½ cup granulated sugar
½ cup light brown sugar
6 tablespoons molasses
1½ teaspoons pure vanilla extract
½ teaspoon salt
½ teaspoon cinnamon
¼ teaspoon nutmeg
¾ teaspoon ginger
Pinch of ground cloves
¾ teaspoon baking powder
½ teaspoon baking soda
2 cups all-purpose flour
1½ cups semisweet chocolate chips

Directions:

Preheat oven to 350 degrees. Line cookie sheets with parchment paper or silicone mats.

In a large bowl, beat together butter and sugars. With the mixer on slow speed, add in molasses and vanilla. Add in the dry ingredients, reserving the chocolate chips until later. Mix until the dough comes together and is smooth. Remove from mixer or set aside hand mixer and stir in chocolate chips by hand.

Cover bowl and refrigerate for at least one hour, making sure it's chilled through but not firm.

Using a medium cookie scoop, scoop out cookies and space 2 inches apart on baking sheets. Bake for 10–11 minutes.

Let cookies rest on baking sheet for 1 minute, then transfer them to a wire rack to cool completely.

Store in an airtight container.

Orange Creamsicle Cupcakes

Posted by Hope Early

When I was a kid, orange creamsicle pops were what I lived for in the summer. The combination of cream and orange flavor was refreshing and heavenly. Whenever I think about those frozen treats, I'm transported back to the summers of my youth, though it's been a long time since I've thought about them. Maybe it's because warm weather is coming and I'm spending more time with the girls, allowing me to revisit some of my favorite childhood treats. Whatever caused the thought to pop into my head when I was brainstorming recipe ideas, I'm ever so grateful. Now I can indulge in the tasty flavors of my youth by merely whipping up a batch of cupcakes and topping them with a swirl of cream cheese frosting.

Ingredients for Cupcakes:
1½ cups all-purpose flour
1½ teaspoons baking powder
¼ teaspoon salt
2 large eggs, at room temperature
⅔ cup sugar
1½ sticks unsalted butter, melted
2 teaspoons pure vanilla extract
2 tablespoons orange juice
2 teaspoons orange extract
1½ tablespoons orange zest
½ cup milk

Ingredients for Frosting:
6 tablespoons unsalted butter, softened
4 ounces cream cheese

½ teaspoon pure vanilla extract
Pinch of salt
1½ cups confectioners' sugar

Directions for Cupcakes:

Preheat oven to 350 degrees. Line a 12-cup muffin tin with cupcake liners.

In a medium bowl, whisk together flour, baking powder, and salt.

In a large bowl using a hand mixer or electric mixer, beat the eggs and sugar until light and foamy, about 2 minutes. Gradually pour in melted butter and then vanilla, orange juice, orange extract, and orange zest while continuing to beat the eggs and sugar. Add in half the flour mixture, beating on slow speed. Then add in milk, followed by rest of flour mixture. Be careful not to overmix.

Divide the batter evenly into prepared muffin tin.

Bake until a cake tester inserted in the center of the cupcakes comes out clean, 18–20 minutes. Cool cupcakes in the tin on a rack for 10 minutes, then remove cupcakes from the tin and cool completely on the rack. Then frost.

Directions for Cream Cheese Frosting:

Beat the butter on high speed until fluffy. Add in the cream cheese, vanilla extract, and salt. Beat until well combined.

Gradually beat in the confectioners' sugar on low until well combined. Frost the cooled cupcakes.

Refrigerate frosted cupcakes for up to 2 days. Let come to room temperature before serving.

Chocolate Chip Scones

Posted by Hope Early

This combination of scone and chocolate chips is a winner in my recipe book. When I crave chocolate (it's almost daily, if I'm honest) yet I want something more substantial than a cookie, these scones fit the bill. Slightly sweet and crunchy on the edges, they're soft and moist in the center. They're handy to have when I need a quick breakfast when I'm doing barn chores or looking for a snack midday with a cup of tea. I know, I know, scones can sadly be hard and dry, but not these. And that's why a fresh batch rarely lasts more than a day here at the farmhouse.

Ingredients:

2 cups all-purpose flour
2½ teaspoons baking powder
1 teaspoon ground cinnamon
¼ teaspoon nutmeg
½ teaspoon salt
½ cup unsalted butter, cold and cubed
½ cup heavy cream (plus 2 tablespoons for brushing and a little extra if dough is dry)
½ cup light brown sugar
1 large egg
1½ teaspoons pure vanilla extract
1¼ cups mini chocolate chips
Turbinado sugar for sprinkling on scones before baking
Confectioners' sugar for sifting on scones after baking and they are cooled

Directions:

Preheat oven to 400 degrees.

Line baking sheets with parchment paper and set aside.

In a large mixing bowl, whisk flour, baking powder, cinnamon, nutmeg, and salt together. Set aside.

Cut in butter, with pastry cutter, two forks, or your fingers, until the mixture resembles coarse meal but there are pieces of butter throughout. Set bowl in refrigerator while you are combining the wet ingredients.

In a small bowl, whisk together ½ cup heavy cream, brown sugar, egg, and vanilla extract.

Remove flour mixture from refrigerator. Drizzle wet mixture over flour mixture and add in the chocolate chips. Mix until everything appears moistened, but don't overmix.

Transfer dough onto a floured surface and work into a ball. Dough will be sticky. Add a little more flour to work more easily or add up to 2 tablespoons of heavy cream if the dough is too dry. Gently pat and shape dough into an 8-inch disc. With a sharp knife or bench scraper, cut into 8 wedges.

Transfer wedges onto prepared baking sheet. Set them 2–3 inches apart. Brush scones with the 2 tablespoons of heavy cream and then sprinkle with turbinado sugar.

Place scones in refrigerator for up to fifteen minutes before baking. If space is tight, you can place the scone wedges on plates and then transfer to prepared baking sheet just before putting them into the oven.

Bake for 22–25 minutes or until golden brown around the edges and lightly browned on top.

Remove from the oven and cool on a wire rack. Dust with confectioners' sugar and then serve.

These are best eaten the same day but will keep in an airtight container at room temperature for up to 2 days.